FIRE ANGELS

A Novel

ELIZABETH KERN

ACADEMY

CHICAGO

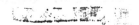

This is a work of fiction. Apart from the people, events, and locales that factor into the historical narrative, all other names, characters, and incidents are used fictitiously.

Copyright © 2017 by Elizabeth Kern
All rights reserved
Published by Academy Chicago Publishers
An imprint of Chicago Review Press Incorporated
814 North Franklin Street
Chicago, Illinois 60610

ISBN 978-1-61373-629-6

Library of Congress Cataloging-in-Publication Data
Is available from the Library of Congress.

Cover design: Sarah Olson
Cover image: Our Lady of the Angels class photo, Palomar Studios, Chicago, courtesy of Jane (Bondanza) Morrissey / www.olafire.com
Typesetting: Nord Compo

Printed in the United States of America
5 4 3 2 1

To the memory of those who perished
To the bravery of those who survived
To the heroism of those who fight Fire

"Labor to keep alive in your breast that little spark of celestial fire, called conscience."

—George Washington

CONTENTS

Part I
1953

1

There was this fat-faced kid who loved me. Not the normal attraction a kid has when he sees me in the flick of a match or in a candle on a birthday cake. This kid loved me too much. I saw worship in his watery blue eyes.

We met in church. (Isn't that where they say lovers often meet?) It was at Our Lady of the Angels, a modest redbrick church attached to a redbrick grade school and rectory in a tree-lined neighborhood on Chicago's northwest side.

The kid was five when I first spotted him among the many adoring faces from my place in a golden candelabrum on the altar. He was sitting on the edge of his pew in the fourth row center of the vast church, squeezed between his cutie-pie mother, Belinda, and his wrinkled great-grandma, Filippa. He was a chubby blond kid, his feet didn't even touch the kneeler, and he looked like a bear cub in his puffy quilted jacket with a scruffy fur collar.

You know how it is when someone's staring at you. You feel it, and eventually your eyes find them. That's how it was with the kid and me. For my part, I can't say it was love at first sight—I'm fickle when it comes to matters of the heart, because

3

my desire has been snuffed out too many times by buckets of water, blankets, and high-power hoses. But I was interested, and I pursued it.

That evening a procession was going on in church. Catholics had a lot of processions in those days—they paraded inside and around their churches like Shriners marching down State Street, with additional zealousness but without the camels. Catholics had processions for everything: feast days, holy days, holidays, novenas, baptisms, weddings, ordinations, canonizations, saints' days, Communions, confirmations, funerals. They just kept circling around with piety and circumstance, singing their songs, carrying their statues, hoisting their sparkly banners. I couldn't keep track of all their hoopla, still can't, even though I'm part of every one of their processions. I'm Fire, of course, and I'm essential to their rituals. I'm a showman, a trickster, a master of ambiance. I can make Saint Peter's in the Vatican glitter like heaven on its finest day. I can make the most humble chapel twinkle like the windows of Marshall Field's at Christmas. I can soften the hardest heart. I can make the most jaded soul feel passion, even compassion. I can make the guiltiest sinner feel as saintly as the pope.

———

It was a January evening when the kid and I met. It had been snowing since morning, but at sunset, right around rush hour, the snow stopped and the temperature plunged to below zero. Inside Our Lady of the Angels the parishioners sat pressed together, shoulder to shoulder, woolen sleeve to woolen sleeve, their shivers slowly abating, warmed by the moist steam of radiators and body heat. Ice crystals formed in the corners of the soaring stained glass windows. I remember these things because water in all of its permutations—snow, frost, steam, drizzle, rain—is my mortal enemy, and I keep an eye out for danger.

That evening I was in my element. If you counted all the candles glowing in the church that night—from the little votive lights that twinkled in ornate metal racks before painted statues of saints, to the tapers on the multitiered altar, to the thick two-foot-high beeswax candles in candlesticks held by pious acolytes with slicked-down hair and innocence—there were 478 of them, all ablaze with me. The showoff I am, I blinked and winked and twinkled shamelessly at the adoring crowds—gyrations I reserve for these kinds of church extravaganzas and fireworks displays.

Before the procession began, the great-grandma gripped the kid's hand. "Come, we light candle," she whispered loudly. On unsteady legs she rose, yanked down her skirt so the frayed hem of her slip wouldn't show, and led the boy past the rows of nuns in blocky headpieces occupying the first two pews. The kid ignored the nuns, because he knew his kindergarten teacher, Sister Remi, was among them, and he feared her almost as much as he did their pastor, Monsignor Cussen. He took small steps in his great-grandma's wobbly black shadow, following her to a metal rack of vigil lights that sat before a towering statue of Saint Joseph holding the Baby Jesus.

"Pray for a papa," the old woman told him. She snapped open the clip on her worn leather change purse, fingered the coins inside, squeezed out a dime, and slid it into the boy's fist, instructing him to slip it in the slot. The kid did as he was told. The coin clinked to the bottom and hit metal. With arthritic fingers she picked up a long, waxy wick from the metal trough, dipped it into the golden center of a lit candle, and placed it between the boy's chubby fingers.

"Now light candle, *bambino*, and say prayer."

The kid's small hand reached for the flaming wick. His round eyes scanned the rows and rows of opportunity. But rather than rushing into a decision and picking any old candle, he lifted the wick close to his eyes to get a better look at me. To him I was more fascinating than the cold, waxy plugs sitting before him in glass cups. He waved me and blew on me softly to make me dance, and I complied. It gave me the shivers, it did. In the puff of his boyish breath I blinked and swelled and did a little shimmy to let him know I enjoyed it. *I understand. I know who you are and I know what you will become.* It was as if he heard me. A sly smile crossed his lips.

His great-grandma yanked his sleeve. "Enough," she said. "*Flamma . . .* light the candle." The kid selected a candle in the middle, lit it, and then quickly, before the old lady could stop him, lit another one. The kid had spunk. Through the blood red votive glasses I sparkled at him like two jeweled eyes. Our eyes locked in communion.

"*Ragazzaccio. Andiamo,*" the great-grandma whispered firmly. Naughty boy. Let's go. He followed her back to the pew, but as I knew he would, he glanced over his shoulder, and his gaze hung on the glow of me for as long as it could. At that moment, I knew he was mine.

Although there were hundreds of people in the church, my attention remained fixed on him. The kid was mesmerized by the pageantry—the candles, the music, the chanting, the incense, the rhythmic bells: *kaklink, kaklink, kaklink.* The pastor, Monsignor Joseph Cussen, glided slowly down the aisle, hoisting with both hands a golden monstrance that held the Blessed Sacrament. His pale face was damp with sweat from the heat building inside the church. His pursed lips made him look like he was holding his breath, and his soulful Irish eyes stared straight ahead into the incense-laden air. He walked beneath a fringed canopy held by four of the parish's most respected men, silver-haired gents in double-breasted suits and diagonally striped ties from Sears, Roebuck and Company, tacked with identical Saint Vincent de Paul pins. Behind them strode acolytes in black cassocks and lacy white surplices, and behind them the fourth-grade girls in their Communion dresses and veils, followed by the fourth-grade boys, the images of their fathers in dark suits and white ties clipped to their shirts with pins of the Archangel Gabriel, gifts they'd received for their Communions a year ago.

The children held small vigil lights in their hands, with pin-points of me twinkling atop their melted wax centers. Bells pealed upon bells, the organ high above rumbled and seemed to shake the church, the men holding the canopy by tasseled poles paced down the center aisle in hypnotic steps, up a side aisle, around the back of the church, down the other side aisle, and back to the altar, then did it all again.

Baritones and sopranos, on key and off, sang one of my favorite church tunes, "Tantum Ergo Sacramentum," and every ten steps or so the pastor, dressed in gold and white, raised the monstrance above his head, then turned it to the right and the left, so everyone could get a good look at the starlike object with a hundred points of gold and the consecrated host encased inside. He smiled at the children, nodded at the adults. The lights in the church dimmed, a moment I especially enjoyed for the theatricality of it. As I said, I was at my best that evening.

The kid watched me and I watched him. His eyes were small and narrow warning lights of blue. He did not know it yet, but in two years they would be aided by eyeglasses, thick, round glasses with clear plastic frames, which explained part of his early fascination with me. He had astigmatism. If he cocked his head a certain way he could see double. *Double the pleasure*, they say.

2

B elinda lived with the kid and her grandmother not far from
Our Lady of the Angels in a tiny overheated cottage on
Springfield Avenue. When they returned from church, they
split up and headed in different directions.

Belinda lit a candle on the coffee table.

———

Pffft! And I sprang to life—smack dab in the middle of their
dreary little domestic scene. Without even taking her coat off,
Belinda flew to the telephone that sat on a small table between
the bedrooms.

Filippa scurried into her darkened room and lit a votive candle
at the base of a tiny altar she had created on her chipped
wooden nightstand. *Pffft!* Just in time to watch her prepare for
bed. She pulled her dress off over her head, peeled her girdle
and dark hose off her thin body, and sighed a breath of relief
from the constriction. She stepped into a fresh nightgown and
stood at the mirror brushing her sparse white hair with the
hairbrush her late husband, Victorio, had given her in 1887 as

a wedding gift. How do I know this? Let's just say I've been a guest in her boudoir many times before.

The kid dashed into his room, and in a wedge of candlelight I watched him devour, in a single bite, the mini Tootsie Roll he'd hidden under his pillow for later.

———

That evening Belinda had ideas other than sleep. She'd put in her time with her grandmother and son in church and now she wanted time for herself. She'd had a hard life, and she felt she deserved it.

At fifteen Belinda had gotten pregnant with the kid. Her mother and stepfather had taken off to *whoknowswhere*, leaving her to live with her grandma and a colicky infant she had no clue how to care for. She had no real friends, just the deepest feelings of emptiness and resentment. Those were the days of diaper pails, no social life, and evenings spent studying for her GED, which she never got.

Now she worked at Fonzi's Pizzeria, where she was on her feet serving ravenous customers twelve hours a day and taking crap from her boss, Franco Fonzi, a tub of lard who only wanted to get in her pants. Her home life was no treat either. Her grandma, generous but begrudging, had never adjusted to life in America and barely learned to speak English. Her cottage smelled of garlic, tomatoes, old age, and Catholicism—aromas that had worked their way into the walls. Often, Belinda felt, it was like living in a church. With crucifixes of the suffering Jesus and paintings of Italian popes on the wall, heavy drapery and venetian blinds, always shut, it wasn't the cheeriest place for a young woman and a little boy. But it was better than life on the streets.

Even so, Belinda thought, wasn't she entitled to some time of her own?

"Go to bed, buddy," she called to the boy. "Brush your teeth . . . kneel down and say your prayers and tell God you're sorry for your sins."

She sat down at the telephone table, lit a cigarette, pursed her lips, and took a comforting drag.

———

I'm never one to mince words. I'm an interrupter. I butt into people's business and I tell the truth. You'll learn that about me as we become better acquainted. Just preparing you.

Another thing you should know about me is that although I have amazing power, I'm ominous but not omnipresent, so I miss a lot that's going on in life. It's when I'm lit up—in the tip of a cigarette, the wick of a candle, the blaze inside a furnace, a pilot light, a campfire, a barbecue grill, or a burning building—that I burst into life and take a look, sometimes a long look, at the world around me.

When I'm contained, I'm quite harmless . . . until I get unleashed. Then I'm as unpredictable as hell—and that's an understatement. When I'm unleashed, I go berserk, crazy, ravenously mad, and there's no limit to the havoc I can wreak. I am evil. I have no self-control, and even if I did, there is nothing I can do about it. That's my nature.

OK, where were we? Oh yeah. We were in Belinda's living room, and I'll just say it: Belinda is one hot mama—ring-a-ding-ding. She has these full, pouty lips that get all cutesy crooked when she smiles. I love how her lipstick leaves red smudges on the cigarette paper, and how, puff after sultry puff, those damp smudges creep closer to the glowing tip of the cigarette where I wait for the supreme ecstasy of touch. That Belinda, she's a tease. When she gets close, she pulls away and crushes me into her ashtray. Snuffs me out. Just like a lot of gals do.

But then she lights up again, and I'm right back with her.

———

"Ya wanna come over, Vinnie?" Belinda purred into the receiver. She set her cigarette between the grooves in her Bakelite ashtray and waited for an answer. "Yeah. The old lady's asleep. She's snoring like a foghorn."

Belinda looked over her shoulder and spotted the kid in the kitchen in his pajamas. The kid was sliding open the junk drawer next to the stove, where they kept rubber bands, screwdrivers, bottle openers, paper clips, matches.

"*Get to bed.*" She formed the words soundlessly with her lips. "Yeah, he's down too. Out like a light, the kid," she said into the receiver.

Her eyes met the kid's and her face flushed. *It's for your own good*, she wanted to tell him. *Vinnie's got a good job and a car, a Chevy, don't you know? He treats me like a queen . . . and you're a handful, and you need a father, and I'm going to get you one.*

———

I may not be the most sensible flame around, and with many a disastrous misstep throughout the ages, who am I to give advice? But what I want to tell her is *Don't you remember? You said the same thing about Marco and Gino and Benny before Gino. You thought they'd marry you and take care of you and the kid, but what happened? Predictable! They skedaddled as fast as tomcats with their tails ablaze. They took what they wanted and moved on . . . and here you are.*

———

"I'll be waiting, Vinnie," she cooed into the phone, stretching out Vinnie's name like a piece of saltwater taffy worked smooth on her tongue. "See you in twenty minutes."

3

The kid couldn't get to sleep. He knew he'd be sorry the following morning when he'd have to get up at seven thirty for kindergarten. The nuns had no compassion. They made a big deal about being on time for morning prayers. It was part of their training as young Catholics, they said.

Phooey, he said.

But he couldn't close his eyes. Through a crack in the doorway he watched his mother with Vinnie. Music was playing softly on their Philco radio. "*It was just one of those things . . .*" The two of them were stretched out on the couch, his mother's bare feet with chipped red toenails entwined with Vinnie's feet in gray-white socks. He didn't like to see his mom like that, with a man all smoochy, but he watched them anyway—their bodies pressed together so tight you couldn't squeeze a dollar bill between them, their lips kissing. He could almost hear them kissing. It made him feel sick and lonely and weird, like he wanted something and needed something, but he wasn't getting it.

———

I'm glowing merrily on a small red candle on the coffee table. This is a treat for me—I love being close to romance, because doesn't love make the world go round? And being the lusty flame I am, I love being close to Belinda. I love watching her mold her body like electric putty into Vinnie's, seeing her smile at him, her eyes sparkly as a little girl's one minute, heavily lidded and seductive the next, how she moans with pleasure at precisely the right time.

———

When the kid was sure no one was watching, he slipped out of bed and tiptoed past his great-grandma's room into the kitchen. He opened the refrigerator door and helped himself to milk. Drank it right out of the bottle. Then in the darkness of the pantry he downed a couple spoonfuls of peanut butter and the six remaining Oreo cookies from the cellophane package on the shelf.

Back in the kitchen, quiet as a crook, he slid open the kitchen drawer and found the book of matches he had been thinking about—between thoughts of Vinnie and how he'd like to flatten the tires of his Chevy, beat him up, or worse, and about his pretty mother who he wished would love him. He struck a match—*pffft*—held it up and watched the yellow flame, watched the cardboard stem wiggle, shrivel, and turn black. He struck another—*pffft*—and another—*pffft*—and another, and one yellow flame joined another and another until the entire matchbook was empty.

———

Each time, just as I reach the kid's fingers, he blows me out, cutting me off before I can even think about putting on a show.

That's no way to treat a new friend. But my better self takes over. *He's just a kid learning the ropes. Give him time.*

Oh, how I long to brush my tongue against the tender pink flesh of his thumb and forefinger, to lick the residue of peanut butter and chocolate crumbs off his skin, to give him a tickle. I'm a passionate lover, but I'm patient, and I give the kid a break. Tonight is our beginning. All the signals are there. I know that in time we'll have a long and impulsive future together.

———

The kid buried the burned matches and empty matchbook beneath some newspapers in the bottom of the trash and, satisfied, went to bed.

Part II
1958

4

As usual, Jim Raymond awoke at 5 AM without an alarm clock. He opened his eyes to the familiar shadows of branches on the wallpaper, cast by the poplar tree he'd planted in the backyard years ago after Johnny was born. He marked the passage of time by the budding, blossoming, dropping, and decay of leaves on those branches. Now, three weeks before Christmas, the brittle branches were bare and stiff with frost.

Jim's wife, Ann, stirred beside him. "Time to get up," she said. Her comment was neither a question nor a command, just the same simple words she uttered every morning.

"Another day," he grumbled.

Jim slid out from under the comforter and set his feet on the cold floor. His body felt the shock of the frigid air. He slept in his underwear, didn't own a bathrobe, never had. Bathrobes were for rich people, the people they saw on TV who lounged around the house all day.

Even though his grumble suggested otherwise, mornings were Jim's favorite time of day. For the twenty minutes it took him to move from bedroom to bathroom to kitchen and out the front door, he had the house silently to himself, which was a rare occurrence in their household of nine. He patted the chenille-covered hump of Ann's behind. "Sleep, darlin'," he said in his deep voice, and she sighed as she did every morning. She reached for his hand, squeezed it, then rolled over to grab another hour of sleep before their five school-age kids would begin their treks to the bathroom, chattering and teasing each other so loudly they'd wake up the two little ones, who'd start rattling the slats of their cribs.

Jim dashed down the hall to the bathroom and ran cold water from the faucet so it would be lukewarm by the time he finished emptying his bladder. He'd heard older guys talk about how they had to get up and pee three, four times a night. At forty-three, he was glad he wasn't one of them. On the way to the sink he caught a glimpse of his scruffy face in the mirror, reached up, and stroked the stubble on his cheek. He'd shave for Ann when he got home. No need to look pretty on his job.

Back in the bedroom he slipped into the clean work clothes Ann had stacked for him on the straight-backed chair across from their bed. He pulled on woolen gray socks, then a worn pair of paint-stained pants and a denim shirt with frayed buttonholes and mismatched buttons. A wiry man whose body always seemed in motion, Jim moved quickly across the linoleum floor to the dresser, where he clipped a heavy ring of keys to his belt and cupped the change on his dresser into his pocket, followed by the Saint Christopher medal his daughter had given him the day before to commemorate the first Sunday of Advent. He remembered what ten-year-old Mary Kay had said, flashing him an angelic smile between two boxes of breakfast cereal. "Daddy, Saint Christopher is the patron saint of travelers, you know. He carries people safely over the river." She said it in the present tense, as if the brawny saint were still alive, carrying weary travelers back and forth across Lake Michigan. "Sister says if you keep the medal with you, you'll never faint or fall on that day." Jim rubbed his calloused finger over the embossed form of Saint Christopher and thanked God for small blessings. He'd had a good night's sleep. He woke up to a fine woman. His kids, "his little snappers," as he called them, were healthy and accounted for, and he had a shiny new Saint Christopher's medal in his pocket.

On his way to the kitchen he looked in on the kids. Mary Kay and the little ones shared the smallest bedroom, and the four boys, Robert, fourteen; Thomas, twelve; John, eleven; and Marty, six, slept next door, in a room barely large enough to hold two bunk beds and a dresser.

A night light in each room illuminated the compact mounds of their bodies, warm beneath boldly patterned comforters. The whatnots and doodads of childhood were piled on their dressers and on the floor: In the girls' room, board games, library books, Mary Kay's rag potholder—a stringy work in progress—and a fan of holy pictures. In the boys' room, dirty clothes, sports equipment, and leaning against the footboard of the bunk bed where John slept on the bottom, the red and white Sonic King bicycle his parents bought him from Sears for his confirmation a week earlier, a bike John would have slept with if he could. Johnny was itching to give that bike a spin through the neighborhood, to hear the *clickety-clack* of the playing cards—two aces—he'd pinned to the spokes, but his adventures would have to wait for a warmer day when the streets weren't blanketed with ice. It had been a stretch to buy him that bike, but it made Jim happy to know that its broad silver handlebars would be the first sight his son would see when he sat up in bed that morning. In passing he gently tapped each door as if he were tapping their backs for good luck.

Jim grabbed a turkey sandwich from the icebox, smiling at the stack of sandwiches, neatly wrapped in waxed paper, that Ann had made for all of them the night before. Each had a dollop of turkey dressing and a thin slice of cranberry gel, the kind that comes in cans. No one could stretch a twenty-three-pound turkey—a gift from the parish—as far as Ann could. The carcass, covered with waxed paper, was sitting on the middle shelf waiting to become soup. Jim's eyes jumped to the back, where he noted two bottles of Guinness that awaited him at the end of the day. His reward. He grabbed an orange from a glass bowl in the center of their kitchen table, which was covered with a well-scrubbed red oilcloth. At the door off the living room, from the first of seven hooks, he grabbed his worn gray parka and slid it on. The cold lining made him shiver. He pulled on his galoshes and donned the cap that had become his trademark—a flat cap the color of a burnt pork chop that he wore everywhere but in church. Gloves in hand, he dashed out the door and down an outside flight of concrete steps into the frigid morning.

He had more kids, more little snappers, to tend to now— 1,668 of them from among the 4,500 families at Our Lady of the Angels. He was the church's custodian, janitor, handyman, and keeper of church properties, which included the school, rectory, convent, and a parish center. His first job that day would be to stoke the furnace so the classrooms would be warm by the time the kids arrived. Having suffered through many Chicago winters, his body told him the temperature was in the twenties. Still reasonable; it could have been worse. Sometimes when the temperature plummeted to below zero

he'd be up and off in the middle of the night to feed the
school's ancient furnace.

Under the gray concrete sky he passed homes similar to
his own on Hamlin Avenue, yellow brick two-flats, inter-
spersed by a few brick apartment buildings, set off the sidewalk by rectangular patches of lawn and trees, now bare and
glittering with ice under the streetlamps. The windows in
most homes were dark, with shades pulled and porch lights
on. Lost in idle thought, or sometimes thinking nothing at
all, Jim headed south toward Augusta Boulevard, watching
the traffic lights turn from green to red and back again,
counting his steps between light changes, wondering where
the few cars out that time of morning were off to, being
entertained by the plumes of his own breath forming in front
of him. Jim Raymond wasn't a philosophical man given to
deep thought.

It had been twenty years since he moved into the Our
Lady of the Angels neighborhood from Holland, Michigan,
150 miles around the U shape of Lake Michigan. He was the
kid in the hardscrabble Raymond family who wanted to strike
out, who wanted to head to the big city, the toddlin' town
that Al Capone, speakeasies, and jazz had made famous; and
to the dismay and admiration of those who never thought
he'd do it, one day he hopped on a train and was gone. His
new neighborhood on Chicago's northwest side suited him
just fine. Five miles from the Loop, it was a compatible blend
of Italians, Irishmen, and Poles—first and second generation
immigrants from war-torn Europe, now owners of small busi-
nesses and blue collar workers like himself who were linked
by dreams of a better life for their children. Their families
attended Mass at Our Lady of the Angels on Sunday, and
their kids all went to school there. In the summertime the

parents sat on their stoops after supper, gossiping and telling jokes in broken English, Italian, Polish, while their kids
watched for the ice cream cart, played hide-and-seek, and
captured fireflies in jars. In winter the men bet on poker
games, the women played canasta, the priests stopped over
for Sunday dinner, and the kids, their wobbly ankles laced in
ice skates, hitched rides on the back of delivery trucks. It was
a neighborhood where everyone looked out for one another.

Jim Raymond never regretted the move, mainly because
that was where he met Ann, who was by then as tight as a
raisin in a muffin in her neighborhood. Ann had graduated
from Our Lady of the Angels in the 1930s, and she and Jim
met at a church carnival, the Ferris wheel lights flickering
above them, the popcorn-scented air charged with romance.
Together they created a good life with their seven kids, and
if he didn't compare it to the lives of wealthier people in fan-
cier neighborhoods, he considered himself luckier than most.

Today, December 1, marked the first weekday of Advent
and the beginning of the official rush toward Christmas. He'd
need to pull dozens of boxes of church and school decorations
out of storage. He'd have to touch up the paint on the largest
camel in the life-size Nativity scene he would assemble at the
side altar. Did he have enough paint? Did he have enough
heavy-gauge wire to fasten the thirty-five-foot evergreen trees
to the eyebolts he'd drilled into the plaster walls years ago?
Would those eyebolts hold another year? He had three weeks
to prepare, and he'd start tomorrow. Today, he expected,
would be a pretty typical Monday. There was the furnace to
stoke, the floor to mop in the rectory, and the annual clothing drive to wind up. The meeting hall in the building on
Hamlin was already filled with hundreds of bags of clothing
donated by the parishioners for the Catholic Salvage Bureau.

The truck would arrive at about two. He'd call Sister Florence, the principal, and she'd get some eighth-grade boys to help him load the truck.

He crossed Augusta and turned right on Iowa Street. The sky was a washed-out yellow, the same color as the lights that glimmered in the windows of the convent across the street from the church. The nuns were early risers. He could picture them quick-stepping down the hallway in their ankle-length black habits, boxy hoods, and fluted white collars, their arms folded and hands primly tucked inside the sleeves of the opposite arms, the only sound around them the swish of their skirts and the jingle of their rosary beads. They'd be walking single file from their chapel to the refectory, where at the communal dining table they'd break their bread and their nighttime silence.

Jim Raymond was the only man, other than a doctor or confessor, who had access to those rooms, where he was called upon to fix a broken chair or an embarrassing plumbing problem that even the most tenacious member of the Sisters of Charity of the Blessed Virgin Mary couldn't correct. Once he was called upon in the middle of the night to capture a bat that had swooped from the attic into the hallway leading to their private rooms. As he was stretching up to whack the creature with a broom, he'd caught a glimpse of young Sister Clare Therese in her nightgown, got a hint of her bosom and a look at her shorn auburn hair curled around her frightened face. *You dames are all alike, afraid of a little creature*, he wanted to tease as he would have in the daytime, but in the hallway of the sacrosanct convent, with paintings of saints and Jesus on the walls, he thought better of it. He imagined what his Old World mother would have said if she knew her Jimmy had been anywhere close to seeing a nun in her nightie. *Keep your Irish trap shut.* And he politely looked away. Like their confessors and physicians, the good sisters knew Mr. Raymond could be counted on for discretion.

He passed the church and turned right into an icy gangway between the rectory and the school. He made a mental note to spread salt on the walkways so the kids wouldn't break their necks. The kids would be friskier today after an extended Thanksgiving weekend of stuffing themselves with sugar and gallivanting around the neighborhood to movie theaters and frozen ponds for ice-skating. He unhooked the ring of twenty or so keys from his belt and entered his domain, the boiler room. An empty thirty-gallon cardboard drum sat in the shadows next to the door. Near the end of every school day, around two thirty, a parade of boys would come loping down the steps to fill the giant drum with papers from their classrooms. Tomorrow he'd burn the papers. He always burned paper on Tuesdays.

The boiler room was like a claustrophobic cave. One breath and the cold, concentrated smell of carbon filled his lungs. He waved his hand above his head and searched for the frayed light cord attached to a single overhead lightbulb. One click and a weak light illuminated his work space. It was a tight and dank room with sooty floors and grimy plaster walls. Lining those walls were shelves that held cardboard boxes of greasy gaskets and valves, and hooks that held shovels, pokers, and a calendar depicting the flaming Sacred Heart of Jesus. The last hung above a stained sink in the corner, where some kid had placed it because it seemed appropriate to the surroundings.

Against one wall was a mountain of gleaming black coal, heaped almost as high as the trapdoor in the ceiling where it came sluicing down a chute from the delivery truck. Clinging to the opposite wall was the huge black cast iron furnace that looked like some grotesque, hungry monster in a scary movie. Jim's job was to keep the fire inside the furnace burning. He shucked off his parka and tossed his street gloves on a table. He pulled on his leather work gloves, by now molded like claws to the curvature of his fingers, grabbed a shovel, and yanked open the furnace door. The hinges of the door creaked. The embers were red hot, but not yet hot enough. Already his eyes burned, his skin itched, and hot sweat dripped down his temples and cheeks. It was time to feed the monster.

———

If I've learned one thing over time, it's that life is full of surprises. I can't believe that this man who is as skinny as a pencil has become my keeper. What's it been? Thirteen years now? You'll never know how shocked I was when I got my first look at him through the frame of the furnace door. Not the burly guy with the dark and curly body hair I expected. Just a hick of a kid with eager gray eyes and a shovel that was as tall as he was. But he's done good by me. This guy who was barely able to lift a heaping scuttle full of coal has kept me going day after day, feeding me shiny nuggets of anthracite, tossing them into my mouth—*one, two, three . . . shovel, lift, toss . . . one, two, three . . . shovel, lift, toss.* They melt like black butter on my tongue, and the gritty taste of carbon hits all the right spots. I croak and sputter, spit and drool, belch and regurgitate. I whisper. I roar. The bigger I get, the noisier I am.

I may be a glutton, but I'm no ingrate, you can be sure of that. Outside the furnace, unfettered and left to my own devices, there's no telling what mischief I might make, but contained inside I'm a hundred percent reliable. Here at Our Lady of the Angels I boil the water that rises through pipes that twist and turn in hidden places that lead to husky iron radiators that grunt and whistle and heat the kiddies.

That's our deal, Jimmy's and mine. He feeds me. I keep the kids warm and toasty.

———

While the water in the boilers heated, Jim walked over to the hot plate next to the sink and made himself a cup of instant coffee. He checked the gauges on the furnace and the boilers. Everything was as it should be. Grabbing his parka and a ten-pound bag of salt, he headed outdoors.

At eight o'clock the patrol boys with white sashes over their jackets carried wooden sawhorses to mark off crossing zones. One of them, Kenny Zagorski, called out to Jim and waved: "Mr. Raymond!" A second grader with blonde pigtails and a rosy nose caught up to Jim and yanked on the hem of his jacket. "Mr. Raymond, when are the Christmas trees going up in church?" "Next week, little darlin'," he replied. "I can hardly wait," she said, hugging her catechism book with mittened hands, sequins sewn into the knitted fabric. He tipped his cap to the pastor, Monsignor Cussen, bundled up in an overcoat, moving the kids along with practiced swats of a gloved hand.

The diminutive Sister Geraldita, a cherub-faced bit of a nun who was barely five feet tall, rustled over from the convent across the street. She had to completely turn her head to see beyond the frame of her stiff fluted hood. "Don't want to bother you, Mr. Raymond, but I'm going to leave this French doughnut by your coffee. Frosted," she said, waving a domed napkin up to his nose. In the quickest of seconds, her face reddened and she smiled shyly. It occurred to Jim that the nun was second-guessing her use of the word *French*—for all of its saucy implications—but, of course, Jim hadn't taken it that way.

"It's no bother at all, Sister. It'll be my breakfast," he chuck-led. "Thanks."

At 8:30 the school bell rang, the deep buzzer sounding for three seconds. Within minutes the church and streets were cleared of kids, except for a clique of eighth-grade boys in tough-guy leather jackets who loitered outside the door, one of them hiding a lit cigarette behind his back.

"Get going, you guys!" Jim called to them. "No smoking on school property. Put out the smoke, Leroy, or I'll tell your dad and he'll let you have it."

Leroy dropped the cigarette and crushed it with his rub-ber overshoe. Jim watched the boys take their time trudging up the staircase.

He stood alone holding his empty bag of salt. He shook his head, breathed in the cool, crisp air, and hustled back to the boiler room. At Our Lady of the Angels, he felt at home and important, even though he was only the guy who pushed a mop around and stoked the furnace.

5

The day before, Sister Clare Therese had written in crayon on her roommate Sister Andrienne's medicine cabinet, "Today is Recollection Sunday. We can't celebrate, but tomorrow we'll make whoopee!"

In the Catholic tradition, the first Sunday of Advent, Recollection Sunday, was a day for silence and solitude, a time to detach from earthly things and allow one's soul to be with God. Sister Clare Therese had spent her Sunday alone in her fifth-grade classroom decorating the bulletin boards for Christmas—which, in addition to giving her quiet time to pray as she clipped and pinned sparkly angels and pointy stars into a corkboard, put her in a playful holiday mood. Without a moment of guilt she had allowed her mind to wander and found herself doing a modest little dance around her classroom to the melody of a new song, a religious one, that she'd heard on the radio. *Come they told me, pa rum pump um pum . . . Our new born King to see, pa rum pump um pum . . .* She hadn't been able to get that song out of her head.

The next day at breakfast, Sister Andrienne looked across the table at Sister Clare Therese and with raised eyebrows asked, "So today's the day we make whoopee?"

Sister Clare Therese chuckled. "The kids will see to it we have fun," she said in a slight Southern drawl, a remnant of her childhood days in New Orleans. "It'll take us half the day to settle them down after Thanksgiving." As she spoke she wondered how she could get a record of that *pa rum pump um* song to play for her fifth graders. She would use it as leverage . . . an end-of-the-day reward for good behavior. She made a mental note to ask Eva Adamski, the generous president of the OLA Mothers' Club, about finding her the record. Just a month ago, Eva had surprised her with a 78-speed record of "He's Got the Whole World in His Hands," another tune that stuck in her mind for days. She and her class had lots of fun singing that song, loudly, in three-part harmony:

He's got the sun and the rain in His hands,
He's got the tiny little baby in His hands,
He's got the whole world in His hands.

She found the lyrics to that old Southern spiritual so wholesome and inspiring that one morning she transformed her religion lesson into a raucous sing-along. With each round the kids sang the lyrics louder and louder, causing a vocal disturbance throughout the hallways and bringing her a stern reprimand from the principal, Sister Florence. "I suggest you reserve such frivolity for the last ten minutes of the school day, Sister."

At twenty-seven, Sister Clare Therese was in her third year of teaching at Our Lady of the Angels. She had decided to become a nun in her senior year of high school in San Francisco.

On her application to the order of the Sisters of Charity of the
Blessed Virgin Mary, she gave her reason: "To love God more."

Before she took her vows, Sister Clare Therese was known
as Eloise Champagne. She was the eldest child of Cajun Catholics, Louis and Carmelite Champagne. The convent was not
the life they'd wanted for their only daughter—she was too
lively, too beautiful, too fun-loving for a life of isolation from
the world. She played the piano and the accordion with the
zest of a dance-hall dolly. A typical bobby-soxer, she had
boyfriends and dates and an enormous crush on Frank Sinatra, a man her father ferociously disapproved of. "The guy's
a draft dodger," he'd tell her, and when she persisted, he'd
tell her the same thing again. But he knew there was nothing
that would stop his Eloise from waiting in line to see Frank
Sinatra perform in Hollywood—just as, eventually, nothing
would stop her from joining the convent. That would be like
trying to stop a star from shining.

After breakfast Sister Clare Therese wrapped her woolen
cloak over her shoulders, slid on her rubber overshoes, and
walked across the street to the school with Sister Andrienne,
a more experienced nun who taught seventh grade. Outside, cars were pulling up along the curb, ejecting kids at the
school's front door. A local undertaker who drove a long black
Cadillac limousine, by far the fanciest car in the neighborhood, unloaded his own two kids along with the eight others
he'd picked up along the way. The jolly driver, who looked
nothing like the mortician he was, hollered out the window,
"Be good to your nuns," and waved as the kids skittered up
the steps, some of them returning the wave. A few eighth-
grade boys were hanging around the steps, joshing with each
other, squeezing the last few minutes out of their Thanksgiving weekend. The bell rang. Mr. Raymond, shovel in hand,

tipped his hat at the nuns scurrying into the building, then sprinkled the last of the salt on the sidewalk. The nuns waved to Monsignor Cussen, who was moving the kids toward the door.

When they reached the second floor, Sister Clare Therese and Sister Andrienne parted ways with tight-lipped smiles, their signal to face their young charges with patience and discipline. Sister Andrienne, as petite as some of the girls in her class, headed toward room 201, just across from the stairwell in the south wing, while Sister Clare Therese hurried down the hall to the north wing. Outside her classroom a swarm of jabbering, high-energy kids were waiting. They buzzed around her: "Sister, please, will there be an arithmetic test today?" "Sister, did you have turkey on Thanksgiving?" "Sister, my aunt had a baby on Thanksgiving Day! It's a girl." "Sister . . ." "Sister . . ." "Sister . . ." Sister Clare Therese led her fifty-five kids into room 212.

———

Midmorning, Sister Clare Therese watched Antonia Fiorello set her arithmetic quiz on a pile of papers on the teacher's desk. She was the last in the class to turn her paper in.

Noticing Toni had left blank spaces everywhere, Sister asked, "You hadn't prepared for the test?"

"I studied," Toni said. "I knew it yesterday."

"I see you haven't worked most of the problems?" Sister said. She shifted in her chair and looked up into the child's serious face.

"I couldn't concentrate."

Sister Clare Therese had heard the Fiorello girl was having problems at home. There were rumors that her parents were getting a divorce, which was not the norm for families at Our Lady of the Angels. Sister Clare Therese could count on her fingers the number of divorces she knew about in their parish. Kids could be cruel in how they judged one another, as if a divorce were something they caused. Kids weren't responsible for the sins of their parents, Sister believed. She waited for an answer from Toni, but if Toni decided not to say anything, she'd understand.

The girl rubbed her forehead and ran her fingers down her nose and tapped her lips. "I had a dream last night and I can't stop thinking about it, Sister," she said.

If she hadn't known better, Sister might have considered it just another effort by a crafty fifth grader to explain her lack of preparation. But Toni wasn't that way. She was a conscientious student, overconscientious sometimes, a nervous child, a worrier, something Sister Clare Therese hated to see in one so young, because she knew those intense fears were hard to shake. She thought about some of the elderly babushka-headed women who filled the first few pews of the church at daily Mass, their lips moving in prayer, begging forgiveness for sins most people would have long ago put to rest. There would always be those women. Did they start that way as children? Would Toni become one of them? Not if Sister Clare Therese could help it.

"Dreams can be troubling," Sister acknowledged. "Do you want to tell me about it?"

Toni looked sideways at a girl in a front-row desk who was eavesdropping. She nodded apprehensively.

"Let's step out in the hallway and have a talk, Toni," Sister Clare Therese said.

There was a chair outside the classroom door, and Sister sat down to bring herself to eye-level with the girl. The child's

arms hung along the sides of her skirt, trembling. Her fingernails were chewed to the quick, and she was slightly pigeon-
toed in her black-and-white saddle shoes. Sister thought back
to her own days as a grade school student in New Orleans,
and the image of a baby sparrow came to mind, a trembling
fledgling afraid of falling, afraid of trying, afraid of flying.
*Lord, help me say the right thing. One so young should not be
so afraid.*

"I had a nightmare," Toni whispered, looking down at
her shoes.

Sister Clare Therese took hold of both her hands. "Look
at me, Toni, and tell me what's going on."

Toni's eyes swelled with tears. "I smelled smoke and it
was everywhere, Sister, and everything around me was black,
and I couldn't see through it. People were screaming. I woke
up screaming, and my mother said it was because I had a
fever and the fever was breaking. But, Sister, it was so real. I
couldn't tell where I was, but the smoke, I could smell it . . .
I could see it before my eyes. It was there."

"Your mother was right, Toni," she answered in her lilting voice. "Sometimes kids have fever dreams that are scary.
When I was a little girl we had this flowered drapery with all
these vines and huge red poppies in our living room and once
I fell asleep looking at it and I dreamed I got so twisted up
in the vines and so lost in the thickness of it that I couldn't
get out."

Toni smiled. "That's how my dream was, only smoke. My
mother smokes. She said maybe that's what caused it. She
said I shouldn't come to school today, but I wanted to come
because I didn't want to miss out, because I already missed
out on going to the movies on Friday 'cause I was sick. So
my mom said yeah, go."

Sister smiled and felt Toni's forehead. "How are you feeling now?"

"Better," she said, smiling.

"It doesn't feel like you have a fever. Looks like you're on the mend. Would it help if I let you take the test over tomorrow? Review the material tonight, get a good night's sleep, say a prayer, and tomorrow will be a brand new day. How's that?"

"It's good. Thank you, Sister."

———

I have my own name for Sister Clare Therese. I call her Sunshine, because that's how she looks when she bops around the room singing and dancing Christmas songs with her rosary beads clicking like dance-hall baubles along her skirt, and her gold cross swaying between her breasts. She knows she shouldn't be dancing and singing (how un-nunly!) but here's a little gossip: she does it anyway—*pa rum pump um pum*. I watch her from the vigil light she keeps lit in the corner of her classroom on a pedestal at the foot of a statue of the Virgin Mary, and the party boy I am, when she taps the toes of her sturdy nun shoes on the polished hardwood floor, I shimmy right along with her. And you should see her with the kids! She sings in a teenybopper voice and dips and sways like a showgirl on the stage of the Moulin Rouge. Sometimes she feeds them candy—suckers, Baby Ruths—sugaring up the little rascals before sending them home to their parents at three o'clock.

Sunshine, that's what she is.

6

The kid was a fifth grader in Miss Pearl Tristano's second-floor classroom, room 206. He didn't want to be there. He didn't want to be in any classroom at that dumb school his mother made him go to. He wanted to be roaming the streets, peeking in other people's windows watching other people's lives, or sprawled out on the couch reading comic books, watching *The Three Stooges* on TV, and eating Tootsie Rolls. Tootsie Rolls were his favorite candy because he could chew them for a long time and he liked the feel of the warm, chocolaty goo filling his mouth and sliding like liquid satin down his throat.

Miss Tristano's voice was hurting his eardrums. She kept yakking and yakking, something about carets and remainders in long division, and the more she yakked the more the kid squirmed in the confinement of his wooden desk. She could have been speaking in a foreign language—Puerto Rican, for all he knew. He looked at the clock: 1:45 on the button. The hands on the clock weren't clicking forward fast enough for him. He had to get out of the classroom.

The kid waved his hand vigorously, like a flag. "Miss Tristano, Miss Tristano, excuse me. Please may I go to the washroom?"

She nodded him out the door.

———

It was not the first time the kid had asked to leave the classroom that day. That morning after their religion lesson, he'd asked to be excused because he had to go, and Miss Tristano told him to be quick about it. As usual he had taken the long way to the washroom and back, playing the game he always played when alone in the hallways. He pretended he was a fugitive running from justice. He scurried past closed doors, darted around corners, checked over his shoulder to see if he was being followed. He loved those moments when all his senses were tuned like a shiny set of rabbit ears. He was a spy, an observer, an invisible voyeur. That morning in room 210 the fourth graders were reciting their multiplication tables: "Seven times eight is fifty-six, eight times eight is sixty-four." In room 212 Sister Clare Therese's chalk was *peck-peck-peck*ing on her blackboard. Downstairs, the third graders in room 101 were reciting the answers to questions from the Baltimore Catechism. The kid thought their singsongy voices sounded like robots:

TEACHER: *Who is God?*
ROBOTS: *God is the creator of heaven and earth, and of all things.*
TEACHER: *Why did God make you?*
ROBOTS: *God made me to know Him, to love Him, and to serve Him in this world, and to be happy with Him forever in the next.*

He was always on the lookout for a nun, some lay teacher, or a goody-goody girl who would turn him in. His thick glasses were magic glasses. If he saw movement, even a suspicious shadow, he'd quickly turn a corner or hide behind the curtain of coats hanging on hooks in the corridors. When the coast was clear, he'd slide along the slickly varnished hallway floor and, hugging the banister, slink down the stairs.

Sometimes he'd go into the washroom and sit on the toilet too long. Then he'd spend minutes waiting for the water to run hot, lather up his hands, and scrub them until they were white. Once he even lit some toilet paper on fire and dropped it in the wastebasket, but a kid reported it and someone else put it out. Sometimes he'd sneak into the chapel in the basement, and if the chapel was empty, he'd creep behind the altar into the sacristy and open the huge mahogany wardrobe next to the locked cabinet where they stored the chalices and he'd run his fingers down the priest's brocade vestments. He loved to be where he shouldn't be. He'd snoop in polished mahogany cabinets for wine, boxes of unconsecrated hosts, and matches that he'd help himself to. Mission accomplished, he'd return to his class, stopping on the way to jimmy the lock of the Candy Room with the hairpin he kept in his pocket just in case. There he'd cop a Tootsie Roll or two.

That morning he took so long that Miss Tristano sent two goody-goody girls out to look for him. They found him in the chapel standing in front of the altar. "Miss Tristano's looking for you. Come back immediately," they said in unison, one girly voice bouncing from wall to wall over the other in the vast, empty chapel. They spoiled his plan. He couldn't run because they'd just chase him and he didn't want to be chased and caught by girls. So he pretended he didn't see or hear them, but he followed them back to the classroom ten steps behind, humming the theme song from *Dragnet* softly to himself. *Dum da-dum-dum.*

There were times when their principal, Sister Florence, found him. But even that wasn't so bad. She'd grip his shoulder firmly and march him back to class, chewing him out as they moved forward, looking down at him with her beady eyes, always saying the same thing: "You keep this up, young man, and we are going to have to expel you." But the kid was too smart for that. He knew they'd never expel him—they needed his tuition money to keep the school going. Four dollars a month was a lot of cash. She'd yell at him and she'd pick up the telephone and dial his mother, which was no big deal either. His mother was a pushover. "But, Mommy, I had to go to the washroom . . . I couldn't hold it," he'd say to her when he got home, with his head cocked and an innocent twinkle in his eye. It was a look he had perfected over the years. She'd melt soft like vanilla ice cream and say, "Well, of course, but you must remember to mind the nuns." And that would be that. But when Manny, Mom's boyfriend, heard about it, which he was bound to because his mother told Manny everything, all hell would break loose.

———

Manny. First there was Vinnie with the Chevy; then Morrie, who ate leftovers out of their refrigerator, who snooped in their dresser drawers. Once the kid saw Morrie slide a quarter he found on the kitchen floor into his own pocket. *Do you know what you could buy for a quarter?*

Now her mother's new boyfriend was Manny. Manny with his greasy Vitalis hair and plaid flannel shirts that fit tight like sausage casings over his he-man chest and arms.

Last summer, when Manny wore short-sleeve shirts, the kid got a look at the tattoo of the hula dancer on his bicep. Her near-naked body shimmied when he flexed his muscles. He hated that hula dancer, with her ebony hair and pink hips, and he hated how Manny made himself at home in their flat like he paid the rent or something. He'd flick ashes from his Camels into the ashtrays that Belinda would set out on every flat surface—"for his convenience," she'd say. The kid knew when Manny was coming over because there'd be ashtrays everywhere.

Manny said the kid needed a good whipping so he'd know who was boss. And to let the kid know he meant business, once when Belinda wasn't looking, he gave him a wallop across the back of his head that knocked his glasses off and made him cry. "Gotta toughen you up, son, and make you a man, *ha ha ha*." He bought him a bat and a ball and a hockey stick, which the kid had no interest in.

Manny said he cared about him like a son, but that was bullshit. He wasn't his son, just like he wasn't Vinnie or Morrie's son. The truth was that the kid didn't know *whose* son he was. He'd never seen a picture of his father; he didn't even know his name. All he knew is that his grandma and step-grandpa on his mother's side took off before he was born (fine thing for grandparents to do!) and that he and his mother lived with his great-grandma until she died a couple years back fingering her rosary beads in her chair. The kid had been afraid of his great-grandma too, with her churchy Old World superstitions. She'd tell him stories, mostly about God and dreams and premonitions, because that's the stuff she believed in. Once she told him she knew how she was going to die. "*Bambino*, I'm going to die of a broken heart," she whispered, tapping her chest with her bony fist, and nodding tight-lipped, like it was a secret between the two of them and God. Then when she did die, the kid assumed that that was exactly what happened: his great-grandma's ancient heart cracked somewhere deep inside her chest, a little hairline crack first, then a larger crack like a fissure in the sidewalk, and then it stopped beating.

The kid hated when Manny called him *son*, and he also hated when he talked sexy to his mother. "*Hubba hubba*," he'd say to her. "Shake it, baby." And it was disgusting when his mother strutted around the kitchen, making meat loaf with mashed potatoes for Manny, giggling like a prom queen and shaking it for him.

Most of all, the kid hated when Manny stayed overnight. The closet in his bedroom was on the opposite wall from his mother's room, and it had a wooden sliding door that closed. Those nights he'd drag his pillow and blanket into the closet and sleep there. He'd take off his thick glasses and lay them on the floor, and with the door cracked just a little for air he was able to block out the sounds coming through their thin walls. Sometimes he'd sneak a candy bar to take to bed with him, one of those big fat five-cent Tootsie Rolls that came scored in five pieces. He'd warm it in his hands and mold it into a shape of a you-know-what, and eat it, bite by sticky bite.

———

It was 1:45 now and he headed for the washroom.

He followed his usual pattern. He dashed down the stairway, brushing past an older student heading the other way. The boy, tall and popular, was one of a group of guys who gave him a hard time. "Watch where you're going, brownnose," the boy snickered. "Same to you," the kid called back, then when the boy was out of earshot the kid whispered, "asshole." In the basement, he turned left and headed into the washroom. He sat on the toilet with his elbows on his knees and his head in his hands, staring at graffiti on the wooden door in front of him, glad to be away from the jackass and his like, listening to the silence. He wanted to be alone in a place where he could think.

Once, last year, Father Joe Ognibene, a popular young priest with a gentle manner and kind, dark eyes, had come to his classroom to pass out report cards. Afterward, he sent the girls out to the choir room to sing and stuck around to talk to the boys. Father Joe talked to them about taunting and bullying. The kid knew Sister Florence had put him up to it. He knew he was the reason for the talk, because he had complained to her that the kids teased him. "What did they say when they teased you?" Sister had asked. The kid looked down at his shoes. "They said, 'How can you see out of those Coke bottle glasses? They said, 'What'd you eat, a hippo last night for supper, or are you just a girl having a baby girl?' And other stuff."

Father Joe Ognibene's talk didn't help one bit. The boys knew he was the one who tattled, and that only made things worse. After that they called him other names: Snitch. Brownnose. Stoolie.

Five minutes later the kid got off the toilet and made his way to the chapel, where he sat in the same pew he'd sat in that morning before the goody-goody girls found him. He looked at the altar, a marble table covered with a long white cloth. On top of it sat a vase of wilting flowers and a thick missal bound in red. At the base of the altar his eyes followed a single slat of the polished hardwood floor down a step to the pew where he sat. Against the wall to his right was a wooden table covered by a cloth with embroidered edges. He followed a crease in the carefully pressed linen to the tabletop. In the center of the cloth were two matchbooks. He looked both ways to confirm that he was alone. He couldn't resist. He stepped over to the table and slipped one matchbook into his pocket, cozy and warm next to his thigh. He opened the other matchbook and struck a match, *pffft!*

———

I pop to attention. The kid's two blue eyes are staring at me from behind his thick plastic-rimmed glasses. The look on his face is the saddest I've ever seen on a ten-year-old face. The kid is dejected. You don't know how I want to wrap myself around him and tell him everything will be rosy, that I'll take care of him, and better than that, if he sticks with me, I'll give him the greatest rush he's ever known in his life, and I'm loyal. That's what I want to tell him.

Then the muscles in the kid's jaw tighten into a sinister smile that says he knows what I'm thinking. He lights another match . . . *pffft!* Then another . . . *pffft!* And he plays with me, toys with me, flicking and blowing me out and flicking again, and I can see my reflection dancing on the flat panes of his eyeglasses, which makes me feel like I'm his only friend in the world.

That's the moment I know I have him.

———

He blew the third match out, flipped all three burnt matches and the matchbook onto the floor, and walked away with a swagger in his step.

There were no sounds, no voices, nothing but the sadness of his thoughts as the kid left the chapel and ran toward the northeast staircase. It was a staircase that was seldom used and had become a storage place for newspapers, boxes, an old roll of tar paper, some bottles, and assorted junk. He reached into his pocket and pulled out the matchbook he'd copped from the chapel. He struck three matches with one swipe, watched the sulfur ignite and turn golden, and without a conscious thought or moment's hesitation flipped all three matches into a cardboard drum at the foot of the stairway, a can much like the one in the boiler room. Then he got the heck out of there.

———

I start out as a spark and before you know it, I'm a raring-to-go flame. I crackle and stretch out and devour whatever's near me in that trash can: edges of paper, pencil shavings, napkins, and crusts of bread from leftover lunches. But then . . . I sputter. *Psssh . . . Pssh . . . Psh . . .* There are lots of yummy snacks in this trash can, but I need air. Without it I'm a goner. All I need is a smidgen of air. Please. Just a smidgen.

There's a window with frosted glass nearby. I hang on. I smolder. Minutes go by and I'm in a stupor. More minutes pass and I'm struggling to stay alive. I smolder some more. I reach 120 degrees, 135 degrees, 150 degrees. My heat spreads and finally, VICTORY, the window cracks. The sight of it, a glittery glass mosaic, gives me hope. I reach 175 degrees and make the window shatter to the floor in a million sparkly pebbles. A gust of lifesaving air blasts in. *Ooosh* and I'm on my way. It's SHOWTIME.

It probably didn't seem like a big deal to the kid when he struck those matches. He's done it many times before and got me going pretty good. Once in a garage. Once in an alley. A few times in mailboxes. Usually the firefighters arrived lickety-split with their hoses and did me in, turned me into a sad, sopping puddle. But this time I know I have the advantage. There's plenty of fuel in this container—and as I stretch above the rim of the trash can I see more delicacies scattered about the stairway—more than I can count. Stacks of paper, rags, cardboard boxes with surprises inside. I like surprises, especially around Christmas. And no one's watching. Jimmy's out and about, nowhere to be seen.

My appetite is gluttonous. I have no choice, so I go for it.

You can't put Fire back into a match.

——

The kid rushed back to his classroom and slid into his desk. He looked at the clock: 2:05. *Maybe we'll get out early. Even if it is just forty-five minutes before the bell, it'll be worth it.* He tried to relax, to look nonchalant, cool. But he wasn't cool inside. His heart was hammering like bongo drums, his palms were sweaty, his throat was dirt dry. He folded his hands on his lap, dug his fingers into his skin, and feeling the fan of his bones knew he could break them if he pressed harder. Everything inside him felt sparked by electricity. He felt exhilarated, as if he were on the Bobs at Riverview, *click-click-click*ing up the roller coaster track. He liked to sit in the first car, where at the top of the track . . . *click, click, click* . . . there'd be a pause where all he could see was vast blue sky. He'd grab a shallow breath and get ready to scream. *Ahhhhh. Geeze. Holy shitballs!* Then in a rickety, wobbly *shoosh* he'd plunge to the bottom of the tracks. That was the kid's favorite part of the ride. The fall. Then things would slow down again. He'd feel empty and it would all be over and he'd want to do it again.

Now all he could do was wait. He glanced at the bright red hands on his Hopalong Cassidy wristwatch, the one Manny gave him for his tenth birthday. It was 2:06. *Best gift Manny ever gave me.*

Miss Tristano was erasing the blackboard, putting an end to an insufferable long division problem that had way too many numbers in it. "I hope you understand the concept," she said in the squeaky voice he had come to detest. "Tomorrow there will be a quiz."

A kid behind him groaned.

A car door slammed somewhere outside. A fat pigeon pecked his way along the ledge of their window, probably leaving more white shitballs on the frost. Piano music wafted in from the music room around the corner. He could feel the beat of *"Angels we have heard on high, sweetly singing o'er the plains . . ."* Some goody-goody girl was learning the song for their Christmas pageant. *She stinks. Her parents should save the money they spend on lessons for her.* Coming from the gangway below he heard the joshing voices of the eighth-grade boys picked to man the clothing drive. The popular ones who got chosen for everything. They were heading to the parish center on Hamlin Avenue. Kids were clapping erasers down there as well. *"Glo-ooo-ooo-ooria, in excelsis Deo! Glo-ooo-ooo-ooria, in excelsis Deo!"*

Miss Tristano was writing out a homework assignment on the blackboard. Long division problems, pages 75–76. *Peck. Peck. Scratch.* The sound of her chalk on the blackboard nearly made the kid leap out of his seat.

I know something you don't, he wanted to stand up and shout. *We're going to get out early and you can thank me for*

it. Don't say I never did anything for you. What would happen if he did that? If he stood on his seat and yelled with
the force of the great George Patton or Jack Webb, *I know
something you don't?*

The kid knew perfectly well what would happen. Some
smart-aleck boy would say, "You don't know anything, four-
eyes." Miss Tristano would say, "Sit down and pay attention,
and if you don't you'll be heading to the principal's office
again."

The kid poked the eraser of his chewed-up lead pencil into
his ear, and the goody-goody girl in back of him poked him
and said, "Cut it out, stupid."

"What? I didn't do anything," he turned and snapped.

"Turn around and behave," she said.

The kid turned and looked up to check the pointy black
minute hand on the clock above the door, waiting for something to happen, for the show to start. *Ten minutes past two.
Ten and a half minutes. Anytime now.*

He cracked his knuckles. Everything took on a heightened
color and meaning. The messy chalk erasures on the blackboard looked whiter, the girls' navy uniforms looked brighter,
Miss Tristano's pink polyester puffy-sleeve blouse looked
sharper. The thick black rings of her eyeglasses made her
look like a badger. She was about his mother's age—young—
but she looked as old as his great-grandmother. He shifted
his gaze to the frosted glass transom above the door, cracked
slightly to let in air. He wondered, "Where's the smoke?" He
jerked around in his seat and looked at the framed portrait of
George Washington on the back wall. George's sort-of smile
looked friendlier than usual. *He likes me.*

Miss Tristano looked up at the clock: 2:15. "Do I have vol-
unteers to take the trash downstairs today?" Along with most

of the other boys, the kid raised his hand. Miss Tristano's eyes passed over his flat blond crew cut like a foul breeze over the stockyards. The kid kept his hand up, stood halfway up in his seat and waved until his wrist hurt. Another trip downstairs would give him a chance to check on things. "Miss Tristano! Miss Tristano? *Pay attention to me!* She pointed to two other boys. "Grosso and Sprovieri."

Typical. Her favorites. That's what she always did.

The minutes ticked away. James Grosso and Paul Sprovieri returned from the basement and set the empty trash cans in the corner. *It's 2:26 and nothing is happening. When are things going to get going?*

And then they did.

Frank Grimaldi raised his hand to go to the john and Miss Tristano let him. But when he opened the door, a pillow of smoke stopped him.

Seeing it, Miss Tristano shouted, "Get back in here!"

Frank backed into the classroom, waving smoke away from his eyes. "Holy cow," he cried.

Miss Tristano hurried out of the room to check what was going on.

"I smell smoke," whispered one kid.

"*Pew-ee.*"

"I smell it too."

"Something's on fire."

I know something that you don't. We're going to get out early. There are going to be fire trucks.

It was like watching a movie, a movie he was a part of, where he had written the script, where only he knew what was going to happen. He was also the star of the movie and had to play his part. Although his heart was racing, he had to play it cool. Miss Tristano returned to the class.

"Is everything all right?" Linda Powell, the smallest girl in the class, asked in a thin voice. She sat in the first seat, first row, next to the kid. The kid smirked at her.

"Everybody rise," Miss Tristano shouted. "We're leaving the building." There was no nonsense about her. Poker-faced and moving at lightning speed, she had them marching row by row out of the classroom into the smoke, in fire-drill formation. The kid had to give her credit for that. She wasn't like some of the fussy nuns who would hem and haw and twist their fingers and dillydally.

The smoke was getting thicker. Hacking, holding their hands over their noses, the fifth graders hustled through it like little soldiers. The kid was surprised by how heavy the smoke had gotten so quickly. It was so oily and black that he could hardly see his hand in front of him. He was agitated and becoming afraid, but he also felt a surge of power. *I'm in charge, but they don't know it. I'm running the show now.* He stepped on the heels of the boy in front of him, once, twice, then again. "Hurry up, jackass, don't you know the school's on fire," he taunted. "It's gonna be your fault if we don't get out of here."

Almost immediately they were joined by more kids—Mrs. Coughlan's combined class of fifth and sixth graders in room 205 next door, and, close to the stairway, by Miss Rossi's sixth graders in room 203. Crowding, pushing, crying for their friends, their moms, their teachers, coughing, holding on to each other's sweaters and shirts, holding their noses, whimpering, losing their shoes, they rounded the corner, formed a bottleneck, and pushed each other down the steps leading to the school's front door on Iowa Street. On the way out the kid saw Miss Tristano's hand reach up and flick the fire alarm. It was one of those on/off light switch kinds of things.

Good move, he thought. *Tristano to the rescue*. But nothing happened. No alarm sounded. *It must be broken.*

It was only after he and his classmates were safely seated in the pews of the church, and only after he saw Miss Tristano leave the church, that he heard the alarm finally ring inside the school building. She or someone else must have gone back in and gotten it to work. He looked at his trusty Hopalong Cassidy wristwatch, its face covered with soot. He rubbed the soot off on his pants. It was 2:38.

7

Sister Clare Therese took her job seriously. She kept a schedule and stuck to it: Religion first, science and arithmetic before lunch, English and geography after lunch. Sometimes there was time left for fun, which she believed was important, because there were no recesses in which the students of Our Lady of the Angels could work out their energy. By two thirty they were usually squirming like fifty-five puppies stuffed inside a shoe box.

The sight of boys and girls seated in tight rows at the same wooden desks with defunct inkwells that many of their parents had once sat in—all of them dressed in regulation uniforms (dark trousers, ties, and white shirts for the boys; navy jumpers with OLA insignias in the upper right hand corner and white blouses for the girls)—reminded her of her sacred obligation to educate them. She was their daytime parent, responsible for their academic achievement, moral development, and safety, and the well-being of their eternal souls. And with it came the role of disciplinarian, which she, an inexperienced nun, was learning about. Though not always perfect, she strove to strike the right balance between giving her charges freedom and giving them rules. For all the innocence she saw in their young faces, they could be an unruly bunch full of excuses and tall stories. She knew the kids joked that OLA stood for Old Ladies Association, and she was aware of the rumor circulating that she was once a Mardi Gras queen, a rumor she neither confirmed nor denied. "We nuns must remain mysterious," she'd tell Sister Andrienne with a twirl of her rosary beads and a mischievous twinkle in her eye.

That afternoon she stayed on schedule until their English lesson, when she got carried away diagramming sentences on the blackboard, trying to explain the chutes and ladders of prepositions, modifying phrases, and independent clauses that confounded the kids. Today there wouldn't be time for fun. She glanced at the clock, pulled at the tall, stiff collar beneath her chin to let in some air—it seemed unusually hot in the classroom—and forged on. Sentence diagramming completed, Sister decided to cram a last-minute geography lesson into the day.

"Open your textbooks to page thirty-seven. Canada."

"Johnny, are you paying attention?"

"Yes, Sister," he fibbed.

"Then why are you watching the clock?"

It was two thirty, and she knew that Johnny Raymond had his mind on his new bicycle and spinning around the more interesting geography of his neighborhood. She'd overheard him telling his buddy that no matter how cold it was, today was the day he was going to take his bike out "come hell or high water."

"I, uh, I don't . . ."

"Johnny . . . Saskatchewan . . . Where is it?"

"I don't know, Sister."

Twenty-five or so hands shot up. "Sister! Sister! I know!"

"Maybe another Johnny can tell us the answer. Johnny Jajkowski?"

"Central Canada. It's a providence."

Just as Sister was about to correct him, Sebastian Rivan, known as Sebby, leaped out of his seat. "Sister, there's smoke coming in!" he cried, pointing to the space beneath the back door.

"What?"

"It's smoke. I'm not kiddin'."

"Go take a look," she said quickly.

Sebby was large for his age and stronger than most eleven-year-old boys. He shot up from his desk and pulled the back door open. Thick gray smoke rolled into the room from the corridor and he slammed the door shut.

Sister Clare Therese flew from the blackboard to the front door, dropping the chalk she held between her fingers. She grabbed the metal doorknob. It was hot and she let go quickly. With the apron of her skirt she grabbed it again and pulled. Stuck. She pulled harder, opened it a few inches, and thick smoke shot in from the corridor, socking her like a fist, stinging her eyes, nearly blinding her. She forced the door shut. *Jesus, Mary, and Joseph. There's no way out, and even if there were, the rule was to wait for the fire alarm.*

Sister looked back at her kids. Some were waving smoke away with their hands, rubbing their eyes. "What's going on?" they whispered, looking to Sister Clare Therese for reassurance.

"Quick," Sister said, "open the windows." Her eyes darted everywhere—to the four globe lights suspended from the ceiling, to the stern picture of Pope Pius XII on the wall, and then to the Christmas stars she had pinned on the bulletin board the day before. Finally, through a growing thicket of smoke, her gaze settled on the terrified face of Antonia Fiorello, who sat frozen at her desk.

Mother of God, make this a dream, Sister prayed.

———

Gregory Rafferty and the other boys in the row closest to the outer wall followed Sister's orders and ran to the windows. There were four vertical windows, two on either side of a bulletin board. The boys climbed up on the hot iron radiators to reach the locks, dumping stacks of books, a globe, a pencil sharpener, and a wooden crucifix off the radiator cover. Gregory's knee grazed a foot-tall ceramic statue of the Blessed Virgin Mary and it came crashing to the floor, momentarily distracting him from the windows. The statue, Sister Clare Therese's favorite, broke neatly in two, severing Mary's head at the neck from her blue-gowned body. "I'm sorry, Sister." *It could be glued back on . . . I'll take it home and my mom will glue it back on,* Gregory thought of apologizing, but didn't.

Gregory looked over his shoulder to see if Sister Clare Therese had noticed, but she hadn't. Her demeanor was different than it had been seconds ago when she was teaching geography. Her dark habit blended in with the heavy gray smoke.

———

"Stay calm. Say a Hail Mary," Sister told the fifty or so other kids who remained in their seats. "Stay put," she gently ordered them. "Let's recite three Hail Marys together."

In shaky voices they prayed: *"Hail Mary Full of Grace, the Lord is with thee, blessed art thou amongst women and blessed is the fruit of thy womb Jesus. Holy Mary Mother of God pray for us sinners now and at the hour of our death."*

The boys worked in teams trying to yank open the windows. With all their might they tried to pull them up, but as if a powerful force were at work against them, the windows wouldn't budge. They had been painted shut over the years. In the heat the layers of paint were bubbling, and finally with all the strength the boys could muster, one window opened, then another, and then the last two. But instead of cold air flowing in from outside, more smoke, blacker and thicker, tumbled in through the transoms above the doors. The oxygen was feeding the fire.

Trying to muffle a cough, Sister Clare Therese ran to the windows. *Don't panic*, she told herself. *Don't let the kids see you're afraid.* Across the sidewalk was an alley, and abutting the alley was the brick wall of Mrs. Glowacki's candy store. Through the window she saw navy-blue-and-white columns of first and second graders, running out of the school, coatless, many of them crying. Neighbors were dashing toward the school. Mrs. Glowacki in her gray jacket over a housedress was rushing toward the students carrying a stack of blankets and a brick of butter. These little ones on the first floor had been able to scurry right out. It was the older kids who were trapped on the second floor. *Surely someone has called the fire department. Help's on its way*, Sister thought. All they could do was wait at the windows, try to find air to breathe, and pray.

Even heavier smoke rolled into the classroom now. Finally, the fire alarm sounded.

"Stay still. Sit at your desks and pray," Sister told her students. "The firemen will come."

"I can't breathe." A small voice coughed out the words.

"We're going to die," someone else screamed.

When a huge globe light above them shattered and poured shards of glass on their heads, Sister lost control and it was pandemonium.

"Mommy, I want you," a girl with a black pigtail cried, covering her head with her hands. Others crawled under their desks and held on to the desks' curved iron sides, hot as oven racks, for support. That's what they did during an air raid. Same for a fire. "Stay close to the floor," a thin voice murmured.

Another globe light burst, and then another. More glass shards fell upon them.

"Sister, I can't breathe!"

"Let's get out of here," a boy cried.

"Mommy! Daddy!" others cried.

"Please, God, help us!"

"We're going to burn up!"

"Sister, help me," Toni screamed. "I was right about the smoke."

Pushing over each other, coughing and crying, kids stormed for the open windows. "Come on, move it," a boy yelled.

"Hold my hand," Johnna Uting called to her friend Rosemary Zagone.

Sister Clare Therese couldn't see two feet in front of her face. Her white wimple was black with soot. She rubbed her eyes and saw soot on her fingers. She began to stagger and cough and cry. Johnny Raymond handed her his handkerchief and she pressed it to her nose.

Kids pushed and crowded at the windows as even more smoke—twisting bundles of it, blacker and more opaque, pushed into the classroom through the transoms.

At the window Sister Clare Therese climbed onto the radiator and grabbed a breath of air. "One by one, get out on the ledge," she ordered the children bunched around her.

———

With help from the big kid—Sebby—Jimmy Erbstoesser, George Pomilia, Johnna Uting, and Rosemary Zagone climbed onto the narrow ledge outside the window. To them the people on the sidewalk looked like midgets. Their horror-stricken faces stared back up at them. Everyone seemed to be shouting at once. One mother twisted her handkerchief between her fingers and begged, "Get out of there. Leave the building!"

"We can't," Johnny Raymond yelled. "We're trapped. Help us!"

"Jump, I'll catch you," a father in a plaid lumberman jacket yelled. "Stay put, Rosemary, the firemen are coming," a mother with pink curlers darting out from her babushka shouted. Another mother pleaded, "Jesus Mary and Joseph, my Ronald's in that class . . . that's his classroom . . ." Parents prayed aloud in Polish, Italian, German. Some of the men had rushed to the school carrying ladders from their own garages, but few were long enough to reach the second-floor windows. The second floor at the school was considered a high second, because the basement was constructed half above the ground. It would take a fireman's ladder to reach them, but the firemen weren't in sight. Every second seemed like an hour.

"Sister, I gotta jump," Johnny Raymond cried from the ledge.

"Say a prayer and go," Sister Clare Therese said, gasping for air, making the sign of the cross.

There were sirens in the distance. "Stay here . . . Wait," she coughed the words out, changing her mind. People below were yelling, "Jump!" Johnny dove off the ledge. He fell clumsily through the air, legs akimbo, arms outstretched, batting the smoky air. As he plunged downward he thought that cold air had never felt so good. He took a breath and landed on his right hip. For a few seconds he lay motionless. Then, coming to awareness, he felt a stabbing pain in his side and started crawling away on the hard gravel.

Smoke engulfed the remaining children like a doubled-up army blanket. Small bodies clogged the window frame trying to get out. Once on the ledge more kids jumped. The big kid, Sebby, remained inside, helping Sister Clare Therese move kids onto the precarious ledge, holding their legs to brace them on the bubbling wood, telling them to be brave. Sebby grabbed the kid closest to him and helped him onto the ledge. Sister steadied the boy and pushed him off.

Kids hit the gravel screaming. Parents were trying to break their falls with their outstretched arms. Jimmy Erbstoesser jumped and hit ground on his hands and feet. George Pomilia heard something inside him snap when he crashed. He didn't feel pain, but when he tried to crawl away, he couldn't move and started screaming. A strong adult grabbed under George's arms and dragged him away.

Carlos Lozano jumped. Johnna Uting jumped. Disbelieving parents and neighbors began dragging the downed children across the alley, leaning them against the brick wall of Mrs. Glowacki's candy store. The skin on her arms bubbling, Rosemary Zagone jumped. Strong arms dragged her through pools of blood to the wall. Mrs. Glowacki, still in her house slippers, threw a stiff blanket on top of Rosemary and the child groaned from the weight of prickly wool on her raw skin. "Why is this happening?" she sobbed.

Sebby's lungs were filling up with poison smoke. Dizziness overcame him. He tried to think through his confusion. He knew he had to escape before he blacked out. Having done all he could, he climbed out onto the ledge and jumped.

Now they could hear the fire engines approaching. Sirens screeching, horns honking, their sounds fearsome but getting closer.

——

Sister turned around and looked into the classroom. Dark shadows of kids and overturned desks and electric wires hanging from the ceiling spun around in her head like fever dreams. The pretty gold paper stars she had so carefully pinned to the bulletin board were charred black.

Desperate, weakening voices were calling out for Jesus, their patron saints, moms and dads, firemen for help. Sister Clare Therese was their mother now, but there was nothing she could do. She pictured her own mother's comforting face and wanted to run into her arms. Thick, toxic smoke was filling her lungs. She was losing consciousness. She was tangled up in ropey vines and there was no way out. Where was Antonia Fiorello?

"Toni!"

"Here, Sister," a feeble voice cried out from the floor behind her.

Toni grabbed Sister's hand and struggled to her feet. The girl's chin barely met the top of the radiator. Sister reached over and with whatever remaining strength, breath, and will she had left, lifted Toni and pushed her out onto the ledge.

Toni stood like a fragile doll, her legs trembling, her body engulfed in smoke. She was too afraid to jump, too terrified to scream. All she could do was pray for the firemen to save her.

The firemen arrived with their tall ladders. A strong hand grabbed the child's waist and plucked her out of the roiling bale of smoke that engulfed the ledge. Other gloved hands grabbed Mary Brock, Frank Consiglio, Frances Panno, Maureen O'Brien, whose legs were on fire, Don Traynor, whose ears were burning, the girl with a long black pigtail tied with a bow, and another and another.

Trapped inside, the young nun lost consciousness and fell onto a heap of the lifeless boys and girls stacked like firewood at her feet.

8

Seventh grader Kathleen Adamski shoved her book inside her desk and with bowed head rolled her eyes so the nun wouldn't see. Sister Canice had just announced a surprise history test, and history was Kathleen's least favorite subject. Having to memorize boring events and dates had nothing to do with the kind of history she knew firsthand, the kind of history that separated families and blew up villages. The only dates imprinted on her mind were from stories her parents told of the war years in Poland from 1939 to 1945, and, of course, the jagged identification number—A1822—that had been tattoed into her father's forearm by the SS monsters at Auschwitz before she was born.

Kathleen was six when she and her baby sister Camille immigrated to Chicago in 1952 with their parents, Peter and Eva Adamski. She knew that her father had fought in the Polish army, the Home Army, during the war. He had been captured by the Germans and was deported by train to Auschwitz—along with two hundred thousand other non-Jews—and imprisoned there. Miraculously, he survived.

"Music saved me," he'd say, but he would say little else.

It was only by listening to the late-night conversations her parents would have with other war refugees in their cozy living room—in Polish, when they thought their children were asleep—that Kathleen was able to piece together parts of her father's story.

"The SS guards pulled us off the train like animals," he'd said. "They separated families. Thank God, I was young, without a wife and children then. The guards looked us over one by one. If we were strong, we went one way. They took our bags, shaved our heads, branded us with numbers like cattle, and marched us to barracks. The weak ones who couldn't work went into another line . . . directly to the gas chambers. Those with useful skills got a break."

"A guard asked me my occupation. 'Musician,' I said. 'Violin.' They pulled me off to the side and assigned me to a camp orchestra. And for two years, in addition to doing hard labor from sunrise to sunset, I was forced to make music for the SS—classical music on Sunday for the guards and the prisoners, jazz for SS parties, robust marches for leading teams to work and back. They demanded perfection. Our fingers were bloody from labor, our backs ached, and on demand we played perfect music to survive."

He played to survive. These were words Kathleen would never forget.

"The hardest times were when we had to play at the train depot during *Selektionen* when new prisoners arrived. They made us play rousing music then, Polish and German folk tunes. 'Smile,' they commanded. So we grinned like hypocrites as those monsters wrenched babies from mothers' arms, separated women from their men, selected the healthy to work, the frail to die—all while tears were running down our cheeks."

"They were beasts."

"I played in the orchestra for two years, and then when it was dissolved and we were no longer useful, I had to determine how to escape."

Kathleen never heard her father talk about his escape, so in the absence of information, she conjured up heroic stories about his bravery that could have been scenes from a movie. On the silver screen of her mind, she pictured a Gregory Peck version of her dark-haired father with gray-blue eyes making his way to the warehouse block of Auschwitz in the black of the night, climbing in through a window a fellow musician had left open for him, his stained, graceful fingers trembling as he rummaged through stacks of brown boxes, and finally dressing himself in an officer's uniform and cap. She imagined him jumping into an SS vehicle and courageously driving through the main gate, past a sleepy guard who saluted him and called out "Heil Hitler," a salute he returned, all the while thinking, *Burn in hell, Hitler.* In her mind's eye she saw him foraging alone in the woods, tattered, filthy, and half starved, and after months of surviving on his own, encountering a camp of partisans who fed him and kept him safe, and while he was in hiding—this part was true—fortuitously meeting Eva, a young Polish schoolteacher whose azure eyes, kindness, and graceful body that moved like a melody instantly captured his heart. Peter Adamski, who defied and outsmarted the SS guards but was too humble to talk about his feats, was young Kathleen's hero.

Europe was Europe—the Old Country. But here in America, in the safety of her neighborhood, Kathleen most often preferred to think about her friends, the movie playing at the Alamo, the boys she was starting to like, and, of course, Christmas coming in a few weeks. She looked forward to an American Christmas sprinkled with Polish traditions, and always there was music. Kathleen had started playing the piano at six, and now she was learning to play *Polonaise in G Minor*, a piece written by Chopin when he was seven years old. Her father would tell her stories of his own musical upbringing in pre–World War II Poland. Music had been as essential to his parents' lives as water, and with this as their priority, Peter was immersed in violin lessons, tutored by his father, who taught music at the University of Kraków.

"It was music that saved us and brought us to America," he'd tell her.

To her America meant the blending of two worlds—the consumerism of America with the cherished religious customs, food, and music of the Old Country.

Kathleen looked forward to Wigilia, a meatless meal on Christmas Eve featuring fruit and cheese *pierogi*, mushroom soup, fried potatoes, huge bowls of fresh shrimp, a Polish *babka*, and dainty *kołaczki* and *naleśniki*, words only her mother's silky voice could transform into music. Any day now her mom would begin many an afternoon of baking, filling their home with sweet, spicy aromas, storing the *kołaczki* in tins for the girls to nibble on and to present to guests on silver trays, covered with paper doilies, on Christmas Eve. Then there'd be gifts for the kids: Perhaps Clue—with Miss Scarlet, Colonel Mustard, and Professor Plum—a board game everyone was playing. And, perhaps, a flirty neckerchief, preferably hot pink, which all the girls were wearing knotted beneath their collars. She had dropped enough hints. Maybe she'd even get dollar bills she could spend at Woolworth's on nylon stockings and tubes of lipstick. She had already tested the colors when the saleslady wasn't looking, smearing the softer shades of Revlon on the palm of her hand. She decided "Prom Pink" would be her color, because it went well with her blonde hair and blue eyes, and because she had read in *Photoplay* magazine that Sandra Dee "adored" it.

On Christmas Day Kathleen looked forward to the sharing of *opłatki* with her family and their guests. Her father would begin the tradition by passing out crispy white squares—unconsecrated Communion wafers. Everyone would mingle in their small living room, cracking off chips of everyone else's wafer, wishing them good fortune—usually health and happiness for the adults, and good grades for the kids.

At Christmas, she knew she would see joy and sadness in her parents' eyes, sometimes switching in a moment, as if a cloud had slid before the sun and stayed there. She knew they'd be remembering the faces of family members and friends who perished in the war. She knew how her father especially longed for his homeland, now brutally carved into pieces as a result of Roosevelt's postwar compromise with Stalin. Kathleen had often seen the sadness in his gray-blue eyes as he mellifluously ran his bow over the strings of his violin in the living room, the music speaking to a depth of feeling words could never express. In church she could see his pain when he and his countrymen stood shoulder to shoulder, their hands pressed to their hearts, tears streaming down their cheeks, singing "God Bless America," followed by the rousing, marching, brave chorus of the Polish national anthem. Not everyone was as lucky as the Adamskis. Mindful of their war-torn homeland and the people still suffering there, Peter and Eva were people with one foot in America and the other in Europe.

Kathleen knew that what kept her parents hopeful was the joy of watching their daughters, bright and carefree girls of twelve and six, blossom and blend into the rich fabric of America. "We send you to a good Catholic school where you learn about God. We teach you piano. We keep you safe," her mother would say. What mattered most was that they were safe. "May you never know fear," her father would say to them at the end of their evening prayers.

———

At about the same time Sister Canice announced the history test, the door at the back of the classroom rattled.

"It must be ghosts," a boy sitting close to the back door called out.

"Room 208 is haunted," another boy shouted, and everyone laughed. Kathleen looked over her shoulder and smiled warily. *Maybe if we keep talking about ghosts, there won't be time for a history test.* "Yeah, it's probably a ghost," she said, joining in the fun.

Then the expression on the boy's face changed. He stopped laughing and his face turned white. He leaped from his seat and ran to the door at the front of the classroom, where Sister was standing. "Sister, lookit, smoke's coming in from under the doors, that one and this one!" He gestured to both doors.

Kathleen stopped laughing. She felt it getting hotter in the room.

Sister Canice turned swiftly toward the front door, her rosary beads clinking from her waist, and saw what they all saw now: thick smoke seeping into the classroom and rising to the level of the blackboard, and from above, smoke billowing in through the transom.

"Sit tight," she told the kids, gesturing with her hands in a movement that said, *Stay in your seats.* Kathleen struggled for a logical explanation for what was happening. No fire alarm had sounded. Surely it was something explainable, like Mr. Raymond overstoking the furnace. Sometimes he pumped up the heat when kids told him they were cold. Or maybe someone outside was burning leaves and the smoke had entered through a window. At the same time Sister Canice was going through her own checklist of possibilities. "Maybe the furnace backed up. Stay calm. Just sit tight," she told her students.

Kathleen bit the inside of her cheek and waited. A serious, scholarly nun of forty-four, Sister Canice always had the answers, especially about religion and the mysteries of heaven and hell. She'd taught them more than they ever wanted to know about her favorite subject, Dante's *Divine Comedy*, probably to instill fear in them. Each of her students knew about the nine circles of hell that Dante believed were where the gravest of sinners get sentenced: Cowards get stung by wasps. Lustful people are blown around by violent winds. Gluttons lie in vast pools of vile slush. Sister knew the nine circles of hell as well as she knew the decades of her rosary, and because Dante's allegory was so terrifying, Kathleen remembered Sister Canice's descriptions of the grit, violence, and permanence almost word for word.

The room seemed to be growing darker, and hotter still. The white paint on the walls was turning brown; Kathleen was having trouble seeing. She removed her plastic-framed glasses and rubbed her eyes. It was hard to breathe. Everyone was hacking. She dug into her uniform pocket, pulled out a handkerchief, and pressed it to her face.

"Get down on your knees and pray," Sister Canice told them.

Many kids, including Kathleen, fell to their knees. Kathleen pulled her rosary out of her other pocket and followed

Sister's lead in reciting prayer after prayer—Our Fathers, Hail Marys, and *"Glory Be to the Father, the Son, and the Holy Ghost"*—as thickening smoke enveloped them. As she recited the words, her mind was spinning. *Camille is downstairs and I can't get out to help her. What about Mom and Dad? If I die, what'll they do without me, especially with Christmas coming? They've already suffered so much.* She could see their faces: her mother's smile turning to despair; her father's chiseled features hardening into stone. She had to save herself and get Camille out. She looked around at her classmates. Helen Buziak was praying . . . no, pleading with God. "And I promise to go to Mass every day. Amen."

Prayer wasn't getting them anywhere. It wasn't bringing them the help they needed. One boy leaped from his seat: "I'm not staying here anymore." Following his lead, the kids stopped listening to Sister and suddenly there was bedlam. Boys were scaling desks to get to the windows. Girls were pushing each other, hoisting themselves onto windowsills to get air.

"Janice, we gotta get out of here!"

"Hold on to my shirt, Patty!"

"Help me!"

"Mama!"

"Sister, do something!"

Tears were streaming down their cheeks. Some kids had made it onto the window ledge and were working up the courage to jump.

Kathleen leaped to her feet and ran toward the window. She saw a flash in the corner of her eye. Flames were breaking in through the door, cutting through the seams in the blackboards, creeping along the walls, and with them came a putrid chemical smell that could have come right from

Dante's sixth circle, where sinners spent eternity in a flaming
tomb. Sister Canice, who had given up on rallying them to
prayer, was now urging them to jump. She gave one girl a
firm thrust out the window, then made the sign of the cross.

Kathleen pushed her way through the wall of kids, bur-
rowing between bodies, wedging her thin frame into any gap
she could feel, clawing her way toward the window and fresh
air. She could feel flames at her back. That day she had
worn her new shoes to school—black suede oxfords paired
with nylons and bobby socks. Her mother told her to wear
them to give her an extra layer of warmth. She could feel
her nylons melting on her calves, tongues of heat creeping up
her legs, licking her skin. She climbed on the back of another
girl who was lying facedown on the floor, to the top of an
iron radiator that was hotter than a frying pan, pulled herself
onto the windowsill, and, still clutching her rosary, crawled
out onto the ledge.

On the ground below she saw adults running toward the
windows, some of them carrying ladders, leaning them up
against the building, but most couldn't reach the second floor.
One man hooked two ladders together, but the top one broke
and a girl who had climbed onto that ladder plummeted to
the ground. Kids from another classroom were making a chain,
with one girl hanging onto the legs of the boy above her, and
grown-ups on the sidewalk were clustered together with open
arms to rescue them.

Time was running out. Kathleen swung her body over the
ledge. In turning she caught a glimpse of the trembling, tearful
faces of her classmates still inside. Edward Pikinski. Rosalie
Ciminello. Helen Buziak. Philip Tampone. For a brief second
Sister Canice's eyes met hers until, in a *whoosh* as loud as
a speeding freight train, fire flashed over the classroom and

in one hissing sweep turned Sister's body into a straw figure that posed grotesquely for a split second, then withered. In an instant Sister Canice and many of Kathleen's friends were gone.

What hideous horror show was she caught up in? Now hanging from the burning ledge by her fingertips, Kathleen shut her eyes and let go. She could feel her glasses falling off her nose. She could feel her legs on fire, then the scrape of hot bricks on her face as she slid down the building, and seconds later she heard the crunch of her pelvis smashing into gravel. Everything went black.

9

Sal Martinelli was one of sixty-two students in Sister Davidis's eighth-grade class, room 209. There were six rows of desks in their classroom with ten or eleven seats in each row. The rows were so close to one another that Sister Davidis in her wide habit over wide hips could hardly squeeze between them. Thus, she preferred to stay in the front of the class, which was fine with the kids—especially with the kids who sat in back, because they could get away with more.

Sister Davidis was a skilled teacher and she wasn't too strict, definitely not as strict as the other eighth-grade teacher, Sister Helaine, who was the most feared nun at Our Lady of the Angels. They called her Sister Hurricane Helaine. Sometimes you could hear her shouts through the walls, the cadence of her booming voice trying to keep her sixty adolescents under control. Steady streams of "Settle down!" "Get back into your seat," and "Do I have to call your parents?" marked the difference between Sal's classroom and the one next door.

Sal sat near the front, close to the windows overlooking the courtyard between the north and south wings of the U-shaped school. Because he was a smart kid who didn't need to review a math principle four times, which he considered excessive, he'd often stare out the window and daydream.

From across the courtyard he could hear the muted voice of a girl singing in the music room, "Angels We Have Heard on High." For some reason the song reminded him of Sister Seraphica, his teacher from fourth grade, when he was more gullible and took everything literally. He remembered that Sister Seraphica was named after a special angel called a seraphim, an angel with six wings who stood before the throne of God. Although he was wiser now as an eighth grader, the image of Sister Seraphica's habited body surrounded by six wings never left him. Back then he was frightened to death of her.

A chorus of boys and girls joined in. "*Glo-ooo-ooo-ooria, in excelsis Deo!*"

Sal was jolted from his daydream by the urgent voice of Richard Sacco, who sat across the room from him. Richard spoke quickly: "Excuse me, Sister, it's getting hot in here and I think I smell something burning."

It was nearly two thirty and the kids had their math books splayed open on their wooden desks. Chalk in hand, Sister Davidis was pecking an equation on the blackboard. She ignored him and continued her pecking.

"Sister, I know something's burning." This time he shouted to get her attention.

"Let's take a look," she said, turning to face the wide eyes of her sixty-two charges. With untypical speed, she moved her ample body toward the closest door, at the head of the classroom. She reached out and touched the brass knob, then quickly backed away. At the same time Richard, who had sped to the back door, cracked it open and a wave of black smoke billowed in. Sister looked down to see black smoke curling around her ankles.

Back-stepping into the classroom, she thought fast. "Richard, you, Danny, Eddie, and John . . . start stuffing thin books under the doors to keep the smoke out . . . pack 'em in tight . . . and you boys"—she called to Sal and the boys near the windows—"open the windows! The rest of you get over to the windows for air. Be orderly. Say the rosary. Don't push. One at a time."

What ensued was less than orderly.

"Gimme your catechism books . . . they're thin. The math workbooks . . . anything."

Just as Sal leaped from his desk, books in hand, the plate glass in the transoms above the doors shattered and smoke poured into the room in thick, ugly waves. Sister inhaled a mouthful and started to cough.

Usually a polite boy, Sal ran to help Sister Davidis, but Sister, shaken and unused to unusual disruptions, directed him with a pointed finger to the window. "Get those windows open, Sal!" At the radiator, Sal kicked over a stack of books and a cigar box full of colored pencils that sat on top. He considered picking them up, but aware of the ridiculousness of wasting time on something so trivial, he struggled with the window. Behind him there was chaos. Kids were pushing and shoving one another, elbows elbowing elbows.

"Move, you're in my way. You're crushing me!"

"Beverly, hold my hand."

"Rosemary, help me . . . please!"

With the aid of a few other boys, Sal forced that window and the others open. The boys stuck their heads out and gasped for air.

"Keep your heads out," Sister yelled at them.

After filling his lungs with cold air, Sal looked across the courtyard and noticed that the kids in the music room were oblivious to what was going on. "Those kids. They don't know the school's on fire," he cried over his shoulder at Sister. "We gotta do something."

"Throw stuff at them!"

Sal and the other kids hurled whatever was in arm's reach across the courtyard: Pencils. Books. Rulers. Keys. An Our Lady of Fatima planter, dirt and all. Sal flung his prized Saint Tarcisius medal out the window, the one he got for serving as an altar boy. It spun in the air and struck the windowpane. The kids shouted, "Fire!" "Get out of there!"

Finally they got the kids' attention. A bunch of girls ran to the window. For a minute they stood there wondering what those crazy eighth graders were up to, thinking they were going nuts. At last, realization came and the music teacher, waving her arms like a traffic cop, started directing kids to open their windows.

Sal hung out the window and kept praying help would come. The kids at the farthest window were already jumping out to safety—onto an awning that covered a small porch on the first floor. Father Joe Ognibene and Rose Tortorice's father, Sam, had made their way to the awning and were catching kids as they jumped. Eddie Maggerise was the first to jump. Then Rosemary Gudz. Rose Tortorice's arms were extended out the window. "Papa!" she called to the horror-stricken man below.

Sal thought of pushing his way to the rear of the classroom and jumping onto the canopy, but the smoke was too heavy and the crowds too thick. So he stayed where he had air and waited for help to come.

He heard sirens in the distance, but where were the firemen? The paint on the window frame under his arms was melting. The wood surrounding him, thick with paint and varnish, puckered and bubbled. With his head out the window, he held on to the burning wood with all his might, crying for help, watching kids jump from the other classroom windows, two, three at a time, their flailing bodies smashing into the pavement.

He saw parents and neighbors running toward the courtyard to help. Some were carrying their own ladders. *Hurry. Hurry. Holy cow, they're taking forever*, Sal thought. It was like a bad dream where he was waiting for his parents to help him find his way out of an impossible maze and the clock was ticking and it was getting dark and he was worried they wouldn't come. *Hurry. Help us. Should I jump? Should I wait?*

He looked back into the classroom, but shouldn't have. What he saw there would haunt him for the rest of his life. Fire was bursting in through the ceiling and shattering the globe lights, which exploded above the room. Glass, plaster, and lath were falling everywhere. With each blink of his eyes, the air was getting blacker. He yelled, "Sister!" just as a shard of glass struck Sister Davidis's broad, square headpiece, knocking her to the floor.

"Sister!" he shouted. "Get up and get out," he called to her.

"You kids go first out the windows!" she said, struggling to pick herself up.

Chunks of flaming ceiling were splayed across the desks. Clothes and books were burning. Flames flashed like spears of lightning, spreading eagerly from one object to another.

———

I'm crazy-mad, wild as a nightmare, evil, out of control. I'm darting, leaping, devouring paper, pencils, cloth, wood, hair, anything to feed my addiction. I'm hissing huffing and blowing spinning jumping and dancing blazing crackling gulping and gnawing. I'm evil electric menacing consuming, and even if I want to stop, there's no way I can. Everything is fuel to me.

———

Outside the window, the throng of people were getting closer. But then, suddenly, as if they hit a brick wall, they stopped. The black iron gate with treacherous spikes on top was blocking their path into the courtyard. The gate had been padlocked to protect trespassers from entering the school premises.

We're prisoners up here, Sal thought. He watched as desperate parents tried to toss household ladders over the fence, a few successful. But he knew they weren't tall enough to reach them on the second floor.

"Come get us, 'cause we're going to die," he cried to the crowds.

"Let's bust this damn thing down." A burly man with a wrench in his hand shouted up at him, "Hang on up there!"

Parents rattled the gate, ramming it with their bodies, fighting to break it open. The clang of metal reverberated in the panic-filled air, but the padlock on the gate held tight. Sal could see Monsignor Cussen pumping his arms running, his overcoat flying in the breeze, and firemen pushing themselves forward, waving their arms and shouting, "Out of the way." But to Sal everything seemed in slow motion.

Seeing the gate was padlocked, the firemen threw a thirty-six-foot extension ladder over the iron fence. At the same time another group of firemen, aided by the brawn of parents and neighbors, grabbed a twenty-six-foot ladder and used it as a battering ram, finally breaking the padlock on the gate after a few powerful blows. A throng of firemen ran into the courtyard with ladders and safety nets. Two firemen rushed toward Sal's window with the twenty-six-foot ladder.

"I gotcha down here," a fireman called from below. "Get on the ladder."

Sal turned and slid his feet down onto the top rung of the ladder. Just then the burning window frame came crashing down on his head, stunning him and grazing the fireman's helmet. Dizzy and disoriented, Sal stumbled, slipped, and slid down the ladder, gripping, releasing, grasping at the sides of the ladder with his burnt hands pressing into the wood and his elbows already seared to the bone. His ears were on fire. He felt his hair sizzling. He face felt hot, like he had a raging fever. The cold air was an immediate relief, but then came the pain as he hit the concrete. The fireman was already climbing back up to get other kids.

He blacked out, then regained consciousness. Beside him was a priest giving a kid last rites. He crawled a short distance and with burnt fingers pulled himself up into a standing position. It hurt to think, but he knew he had to think.

He thought about his eight-year-old sister. *Where's Alice? Did she get out?* He knew his mother was at their furniture store with his father. Vincent Martinelli owned Martinelli's Fine Furniture on Chicago Avenue. That's where they always were in the afternoons this time of the year—selling tables and chairs, sofas, and televisions to their neighbors. Just yesterday Sal had helped them to string garlands of fake greenery and twinkle lights over the entrance, and to set up a cozy family tableau of a velvet sofa, recliner, and coffee table in the small front window, complete with a giant Evergleam aluminum Christmas tree with a red, green, blue, and yellow color wheel beneath it. Sal remembered watching Alice crawl beneath the tree, fascinated by the dancing colors the wheel made on her Barbie doll's vinyl hair. *Where's Alice now? I'll run to the furniture store to look for her.* But he collapsed before he even got started. "Help me, please" he called, as he hit the ground. Then with all of his willpower, he pulled himself up again.

A fireman hoisting a thick black fire hose heard him. "See that ambulance there, kid? Get into it! You're going to the hospital."

10

Kindergarten, first-, and second-grade classrooms were in other buildings, Mary and Joseph Halls, on Hamlin Avenue a block away from the main school. It was about 2:20 on Jim Raymond's wristwatch when he hustled out the door of Mary Hall, where he had just finished checking an oil burner, and in his haste, he nearly collided with a mother who was skittering on the ice carrying a cardboard box.

"Sorry, ma'am."

"Pardon me, birthday cupcakes," she explained, moving gingerly along the icy street.

"You be careful with 'em, madam."

On Hamlin Avenue Jim passed a dark-haired girl in a red plaid coat with her head scarf knotted at her chin. He recognized her as a former student.

"Miss Peggy Finan, whaddaya doing here? I thought you were in high school. What'd they do, send you back here for more edumacation?"

Peggy giggled.

She was always one of Jim's favorites, so he stopped to talk. "Where do you go to school?"

"Holy Family Academy on Division. Just came to talk to the girls in Sister Helaine's eighth grade about going there next year."

"How's high school treating you, Miss Finan?"

"Pretty good. The nuns at Holy Family are pretty strict, though."

"Oh yeah?" he laughed. "I bet you didn't tell our eighth graders that."

Peggy giggled again.

Seeing she was in a hurry, he wrapped things up. "Well, I'm sure you did a fine job talking to them. Better be on, then, or you're going to get in trouble with your new nuns."

Peggy waved a red-gloved hand and rushed for the bus. Taking his time, Jim sidestepped past a gaggle of sixth-grade girls heading toward Mary Hall. Nearly teenagers, they were leaping over their words jabbering. How can girls have so much to say? He thought of his own little Mary Kay and how in a few years she'd be just like them, wearing their head scarves knotted at their chin, walking outdoors with their coats wide open without their boots, because snow boots were not cool when you were twelve. He wished he could freeze Mary Kay at ten years old and not have to deal with the mysteries of adolescent girls, expertise he did not possess, having grown up in a household of men.

He looked at his wristwatch again. It was 2:30, give or take ten minutes because his watch wasn't terribly accurate. In a couple hours he'd be home drinking a bottle of Guinness, catching up with his kids on what went on in their classrooms, and probably arguing with John, who he knew would want to ride his bike on the ice. He saw it coming.

As he walked through the narrow gangway between the rectory and the back of the school, a flash of red light in a frosted windowpane in the basement caught his attention. Thinking there might be a problem in the boiler room, or maybe some boys were smoking, he picked up his step to a sprint. Upon entering the boiler room from outdoors he saw two boys dumping trash into bins. The door leading to the stairwell was slightly open, and Jim ran to where he'd seen the flashes of red. A fire was raging in the stairwell. The noisy boiler masked the crackle of the fire, and the boys were oblivious to it.

"Can't you see there's a fire in there? Get out of here, you guys!" he shouted. The boys dropped their wastepaper baskets and took off running outside. "Call the fire department," Jim called to their backs. The fire was roaring and he knew immediately that it was uncontrollable, but he had to do something. In desperation he took off his hat and batted the flames, then tried his jacket. Useless. He reached for a shovel and struck at the fire, but the flames were too violent for him to extinguish. Grabbing a flashlight from the windowsill, for a reason he did not know, he ran out of the building toward the rectory next door.

Nora Maloney, the housekeeper, was the first person he saw. She was at the stove stirring a sauce in a huge metal pot. "Call the fire department!" he shouted. Ladle in hand, Mrs. Maloney ran to the window above the sink to take a look for herself, and when she saw smoke she scurried across the room, where a black telephone sat atop a desk in a nook. Jim watched her fumble with the phone and with nervous fingers dial 0. The *click, click, click* of the dial seemed to take forever. In her thick brogue, Mrs. Maloney yelled "Fire! Fire!" Jim ran off before she could say more; later he'd learn that in her confusion she gave the address of the rectory on Iowa Street where she worked, not the school on Avers Avenue.

Running back to fight the fire, Jim remembered that five of his children were inside that building, along with more than a thousand other kids. He squeezed the Saint Christopher's medal in his pocket, the one Mary Kay had given him, and with his ring of keys rattling on his belt he ran back into the burning school.

———

Everything after that happened so quickly that Jim would hardly remember the sequence of events. A dash up the stairs into thick, choking darkness. A screen of smoke stopping him, stinging his eyes. A fall to the floor, where he groped on hands and knees trying to remember where he was, flicking on the flashlight, a useless beam of gray, feeling his way along the wooden floorboards around a corner, his body slogging and weaving like a giant worm in a dark tunnel. Smoke filling his lungs. Scorching heat. A murky glow from a window above. His flashlight smashing the window. The crash of shattering glass. Cold air. A dagger-sharp shard slashing his arm. Blood thick as tar oozing from his wrist. A rush of black smoke. Dizziness. The sight of another face in the smoke. Confusion. Then a familiar voice.

It was Father Charles Hund, one of the younger priests in the parish. On his hands and knees, he was also crawling foot by foot along the second-floor hallway.

"The kids in 207 can't get out!" he screamed at Jim. "Where's the damn key to the door that leads out to the fire escape?"

Jim fumbled for the right key on his belt. "I've got it," he called to the smoky figure whose charred face was feet away from his own. Gasping and coughing, the men locked arms and helped each other to their feet. Blood was flowing down Jim's arm, dripping to the floor.

———

Inside room 207, tiny Sister Geraldita was trapped in the smoky darkness of the "cheesebox" with her fifth and sixth graders—forty of them. Her classroom was called the cheesebox because of its size; once it had housed the school's paltry collection of library books. Everyone teased her that the smallest nun got the smallest classroom, a joke she was used to hearing, along with so many others about shrimps, midgets, dwarfs, and peanuts. The jokes only became worse at Christmas, with diminutive elves joining the mix. Thank goodness, the five-foot nun was gifted with a ready smile and cheerful Irish disposition.

Sister Geraldita's classroom faced the stairwell where the fire had started. Thus she was the first to see the flames through the transom above her classroom door. There was no way out through the hallways.

Through a door at the back of her classroom that led into a cloakroom, Sister had access to a fire escape, an iron behemoth that hugged the outside of the redbrick wall on the school's east side. With a person's weight on it, the counterweighted stairway would swing down to the ground.

Thank God we have another way out, she thought. In a flurry she hustled her kids quickly into the cloakroom. *God is good. He did not desert us. We have a way out.*

Standing before the door that opened onto the fire escape, Sister felt for the ring of keys she always had clipped to the cincture at the waist of her habit. Her breath stopped. *The keys. Where are they? It is my responsibility to have them with me at all times.* Then she realized that in her haste that morning she had left them on her dresser in the convent. She could picture where she set them the night before: at the foot of a plastic statue of Our Lady of Fatima with three children kneeling at her feet. A deathly chill, a feeling of impending doom, washed through her. *We have no way out.*

"I don't have the keys," she told her charges.

"But, Sister . . . "

"You have to have them . . . check your pockets."

"What do we do now?"

"We're in trouble, but we will pray," Sister Geraldita told them. "That's all we can do now. We will pray to Our Lady for help," she said in as confident a voice as she could muster. "Get down on the floor where there is still air. Our Lady will hear your voices from down there as well as up here."

Obediently, most of the kids fell to their knees in this small space, overstuffed with winter coats, boots, and empty lunch buckets. They huddled around her like a litter of pups around its mother. *"Hail Mary, full of grace . . ."* she led them in prayer. But there were deviants.

One boy gave a rallying cry. "Come on, you guys. We can knock this door down." A handful of boys, gasping for air, stormed the door. They pushed and kicked at it, but their eleven-year-old bodies barely made a dent in the wood that separated them by an inch and a half from the fire escape.

"Holy Mary, Mother of God . . ." a girl in the huddle prayed.

"I can't breathe," another girl cried.

"My eyes are burning."

"We've got to do something."

"Tommy, are you still breathing?"

"Yeah," Tommy's small voice cried.

"Keep breathing. We're gonna get out of here, 'cause we gotta go skating at Riverview next week."

"Yeah, I know."

"We can't die." A boy leaped from the huddle to his feet and ran back into the classroom. With strong fists he started banging on the window. Nothing. Panicking, he grabbed a crucifix off the wall and flung it through the pane. Glass shattered. The crucifix spun through the air, struck the brick wall of the rectory, and broke into pieces—the body of Jesus flying in one direction, the cross in another. But in the dark walkway between the school and the rectory, and with chaos everywhere else, the pieces of the crucifix caught no one's attention. With both arms he flung a porcelain planter out of the window. It too hit the rectory wall and shattered. "Save us!" he cried, but no one heard. His voice was a like a whisper in a tempest.

Overcome by fear and helplessness, he ran back into the cloakroom. Sister was slumped to the floor. *"The Lord is with thee,"* she was praying. *"Blessed art thou amongst women . . ."*

As she prayed, Sister Geraldita thought of her own mother, who had died on her twelfth birthday. *Am I also destined to die young?* She had already survived the odds, suffering from tuberculosis and losing a lung at the age of twenty-eight. She was now thirty-seven. *Is today the day I die? What about the other nuns?*

"I can't breathe," a girl cried. "We're going to die."

"Hail Mary . . ." Sister continued.

"What are my parents going to do without me?" a boy asked. "Please, God, get us out of here."

"Help me, Mother Mary. I'll be a good girl from now on," another girl cried, curling into a ball against Sister's side.

"Say an Act of Contrition," Sister Geraldita told them, and started to pray the prayer that every Catholic is taught to say for absolution of their sins, a prayer that is especially important to recite at the moment of death. That was all she could do now. "*O my God, I am heartily sorry for having offended Thee, and I detest all my sins because I dread the loss of heaven and the pains of hell, but most of all because they offend Thee . . .*"

As the smoke got blacker and denser, one by one the kids in the huddle grew dizzy and sunk lower to the floor, coughing, gasping for breath. Smoke was engulfing them. Suffocating heat was stinging their throats and lungs. The fire was winning.

"*. . . and I detest all my sins,*" one whimpering voice persisted. Soon the coughs abated and everything was becoming quiet. Sister Geraldita wrapped her short arms around the children splayed out on the wooden floor closest to her. *How could this be happening? These are great kids who never did much wrong. They tried to be helpful. They said their prayers. I did my best too, God. I tried to be a faithful nun, but I failed today.* Sister felt her eyes losing focus, her brain losing consciousness, her spirit leaving her. She felt herself floating up off the floor to someplace higher, far away, very nice. She pictured her mother's face, her blue eyes full of compassion, her mother's strong arms reaching out for her. *So this is what dying is like,* she thought.

Suddenly her hallucinations were jarred by heavy footsteps from behind.

"Let's get you out of here," a voice cried. It was Mr. Raymond, followed by another figure whose face was hardly recognizable in the smoke. "Let's get going." It was Father Hund's voice.

Jim Raymond leaped over young bodies toward the locked back door and, paying no attention to his bloody wrist, twisted the key in the keyhole and pushed the door open. Moving quickly, he and Father Hund aroused the kids and led them out onto the fire escape.

Jim's weight on the iron stairway made it fall to the ground. One by one, Father Hund pulled the kids upright and gently pushed them toward the door. "Grab my hand. I've got you." He began ushering them toward Jim, who moved them down to the safe arms of a parent below. "Hang on, keep going, come on, move, keep going, fast . . . breathe . . ." With the cloak-room cleared of children, Father Hund took Sister Geraldita's trembling arm. "Sister, I've got you." He helped her down the fire escape. "Don't look back," he told her, guiding her around the corner into the outstretched arms of another nun.

Terrified and dazed, Sister Geraldita filled her lungs with cold air. It took her a minute to catch her breath and get her bearings in the haze of smoke and the chaos of crying kids, neighbors, hysterical parents, police attempting to hold back the crowds, and firemen doing their jobs. She had never seen so many fire trucks, police cars, and ambulances in one place. Against Father Hund's advice, she did look over her shoulder—at the exact time that her classroom, room 207, burst into flames.

———

"Kids are up there," cried Jim Raymond from the gangway where the fire escape dropped him. He staggered one way and then another, trying to close the gash on his arm, wiping the black mucus off his nose onto his shirt collar. He was groggy and glassy-eyed, bloody. Smoke was puffing out of his nose. "Where's my flashlight? I'm going up there." He ran toward the stairwell near the boiler room, the spot where he first saw the fire.

A gloved hand grabbed him. "You're not going back in there, buddy."

"Let go of me, there's kids in there."

"Not on my watch you're not going back," said the guy, in a black fire helmet.

"Who are you to tell me . . ." Jim pulled away from him.

Clutching his pike pole in one hand, the fireman grabbed Jim by the shoulders and started walking him away from the building.

Jim turned and swung at the firefighter. "Hands off me." But the fireman caught his arm before it came down on him. "Don't give me a fight, buddy. Look at you. You're bleeding. Ya need help."

Jim took another swing at the fireman and pushed his way back toward the burning building. He had no choice and couldn't waste time. He heard heavy footsteps behind him and then it was lights out—in desperation the fireman whacked him over the head with his pike pole and Jim fell to the ground unconscious. That was the last thing he knew for several hours.

11

I've feasted on some of the world's finest cities, but Chicago has always been my favorite. We're old friends, Chicago and me. Since the earliest days at Fort Dearborn, when the buildings were made of wood and folks used candles to light their homes, Chicago has welcomed me with open arms.

They don't call Chicago the Windy City for nothing. Oh yeah, they say it's because of the politicians—Mayor Richard J. Daley and Mayors Edward J. Kelly and Martin Kennelly before him. They sure got that right: those guys were all windbags. But the wind in this city works to my advantage. Wind's my partner, always was, always will be. The gusts off Lake Michigan that twist westward between the skyscrapers, gangways, streets, and avenues, give me the edge and the energy I need to get going—and keep going.

Take the Great Chicago Fire of 1871. I tore through rows and rows of wooden storefronts and homes, devouring three square miles near downtown, and in my rampage I took three hundred lives. One of the only things that remained was the brick Old Water Tower, which I benevolently left, plop in the middle of Michigan Avenue. Tourists gush over it now. They line their kiddies up on the steps at the doorway, the wee ones in the front, ask them to say "Cheese!" and snap photos of them to send back to their families in Minnesota, Barcelona, and Hong Kong. But do they ever consider that the Water Tower was a gift given straight from my heart? I should get some credit. I gave them a first-class photo op!

Anyway, over the years I did that town like a dandy—turning up everywhere from the gritty stockyards on the South Side to the rickety elevated tracks that spark and screech throughout the Loop, to a surprise appearance before forty thousand spectators at the World's Columbian Exposition in 1893, where I got going in—of all places—the cold storage building, and of course, to the crispy, dry straw in the O'Leary barn a few years earlier. While we're on the subject of the Great Chicago Fire and Mrs. Catherine O'Leary, let me clarify: The poor cow that got blamed for kicking over a lantern and starting it all had nothing to do with it. That was a story made up by a newsman looking for an angle. I was there. I know how the Great Chicago Fire really started . . . but I'm not telling.

Then, in December 1903, there was the Iroquois fire. The Iroquois was a garish million-dollar theater located downtown on Randolph Street between State and Dearborn. *Mr. Bluebeard* starring vaudevillian Eddie Foy was playing there, and schoolteachers from around the city had purchased rows of seats for their students as a Christmas treat. Everyone wanted to see the funny Eddie Foy perform his popular elephant act, featuring a live baby elephant. The famous architect Frank Lloyd Wright's sons, Lloyd, thirteen, and John, eleven, were sitting in the third row center enjoying the heck out of themselves, nudging each other and clapping up a storm.

Just as a double octet was singing "Let Us Swear by the Pale Moonlight," in a flash of mighty surprise, I appeared on the scene and put on a razzle-dazzle show of my own. The newspapers reported that an arc lamp had sparked and I ignited the gauzy underside of the plush velvet drapery. What made matters worse—not for me, but for the audience—was that stupid Eddie Foy ran on stage and told patrons to settle down and stay calm. "There's no danger. This theater is fireproof!" he bellowed into the audience in a commanding baritone that reached the very last row of the sixteen-hundred-person theater. Boy, did I prove him wrong, sending sparks and flames everywhere. At first, they sat in their seats and obeyed the guy, but then I whipped across the stage and they panicked. All at once they ran for the exits, most of which were locked to protect unticketed freeloaders from entering. Unleashed, I took the lives of about six hundred theater-lovers that day; the Wright boys somehow managed to escape, as did the baby elephant. The building was razed and became site of the equally garish Oriental movie theater. Some say I left ghosts in that theater. The floor may still feel warm when you walk on it. I'll let you be the judge.

As much as I enjoyed Chicago's theaters, I also relished its hotels. Most memorable was the LaSalle Hotel. It was a balmy June evening in 1946, a little after midnight, when I got started. Lovers were still dreamingly milling about downtown arm in arm, and fashionable guests were enjoying after-dinner drinks in the hotel's Silver Grill Cocktail Lounge.

When the LaSalle Hotel opened in 1909, it was known as the safest, largest, and most modern hotel west of New York City. With its stately wood paneling and its rooftop garden twenty-three stories above the twinkling lights of Chicago, it was *the* place to be seen. The socialite Bertha Palmer often lunched there with the ladies in the Blue Fountain Room, and President Taft had turned the third-floor Presidential Suite into his Midwestern White House.

Anyway, that languorous evening in the Silver Grill Cocktail Lounge someone smelled wood burning, and of course, it was me. I'd been simmering behind the wood paneling, nipping on some electrical wires. I had just popped up between two wood panels to assess my opportunities when a tipsy fellow downing his second shot of amaretto noticed me. After a considerable amount of hollering and a spell of dithering, the hotel staff tried to extinguish me with a bottle of seltzer water and a couple handfuls of sand. Goodness gracious, by then it was way too late for that! I'd had the advantage of time and enough of a breeze coming through the arched windows facing LaSalle Street that right before everyone's eyes I exploded in a blast of ghoulish crimson and sent patrons and staff running helter-skelter. I gobbled up everything in sight—walnut paneling, rugs, furniture. I blasted into the lobby, spread up into the mezzanine, up the elevator shaft, and into the residential floors, where a full house of about a thousand people slept peacefully in their beds. Before someone called the fire department about fifteen minutes later, I had my run of the place. All the ladders, hose lines, and firefighters—three hundred burly young guys—couldn't get me under control until I had taken sixty-one lives and nearly leveled the hotel. I took the switchboard operator who remained at her station alerting guests. I took the mayor of Quincy, Illinois, who had switched hotels at the last minute. Five of my victims were Iowa teenagers who were given a trip to Chicago by their parents as a graduation present.

It disgusts me to think of it now, but I make no apologies because I had no choice. I'm Fire.

———

After the Great Chicago Fire, engineers—those geniuses with fancy college degrees—got smart and started building everything with brick, but they didn't get smart enough. Yeah, the outer walls were brick, but inside they indulged me with a lot of wood.

Take Our Lady of the Angels, which they started building in 1903. Timber joist construction. Wood lath and plaster. Acoustic tile on the ceilings. Wood railings, newels, and balusters. Walls slapped with fourteen layers of paint, the top two composed of a yummy, gummy, rubberized paint that produces the blackest, foulest, stinkiest smoke you can imagine. The blend of oil, resin, and solvent slides down my tongue like aged cognac. The folks who maintained Our Lady of the Angels set up a royal banquet for me, a "disaster martini," as some word-wizard reporter called it after the blaze. I do read the papers.

The classrooms were heated by radiators fueled by Jim Raymond's boiler in the basement, and he and the nuns, hell-bent on making things sparkle, bless their tidy hearts and hands, would slap coat after coat of fresh varnish on the wood, and the priests hell-bent on stretching a penny would place a new asphalt roof upon an old one, again and again. Unwittingly they catered to my palate, even leaving a three-foot cockloft—a sort of attic—between the broad ceilings and roof, where I could sprawl out and do the wild thing.

OK, so now for a little more history. You know I remember everything I hear, so I'm just passing this on . . .

Way back in the 1890s—only twenty years after the Great Chicago Fire—the school at Our Lady of the Angels started in an old store building. That was when a lot of immigrants from Ireland, Italy, Germany, and Poland, straight off the boat, settled in this city. The good priests thought they needed to be educated, catechized, molded into upright Polish, German, Irish American Catholics, so they got the whole thing started.

They built the first church in 1900, followed by a small school in 1903. The immigrants kept pouring into the neighborhood by the trainload—and the school expanded like a balloon to hold them. A chapel on the second floor was converted into classrooms for the seventh and eighth graders. The convent came in 1906, and a combination church and school followed in 1910 on Avers Avenue. Glory hallelujah, they had eighteen classrooms! Then in 1939, with Monsignor Cussen in charge, they built a new church and rectory. If you're keen on architecture, the church is Italian Romanesque. Lots of marbled pink-and-white columns, pastel statues of saints, wooden pews and ornamental confessionals, and space for eleven hundred faithful.

The parishioners were breeders and the priests were builders, so they weren't done yet. In 1943 they built another school on Avers, and in 1951 they connected the two buildings with an annex, so the school building took on its U shape, with the annex connecting the two wings. Now they had twenty-four classrooms, with 569 students in the north wing and 329 in the classrooms on the second floor. Always the protectors of their kiddies, the priests installed that seven-foot iron fence to close off the courtyard between the buildings. No riffraff wanted there. Did it ever dawn on them that they were cutting off access by fire trucks?

Our Lady of the Angels is Cussen's masterpiece. He looks after it the way other guys look after their cars and their mistresses. He loves to stand at the school doors and greet the kids. He knows them by name and he knows their parents and their problems. He is privy to a lot of dirt in confession, but of course he keeps those secrets to himself. Still, he knows.

But Monsignor Cussen and his merry band of padres weren't the only ones puffing with pride for their church. For many of the families who lived in the neighborhood—some crowded with six kids and grandparents in a two-bedroom flat, many sharing bathrooms with their neighbors—who walk or ride buses everywhere because they don't have cars, who don't own more than a table, a chair, and a couple of beds . . . well, Jesus be glorified . . . to them the sight of their burgeoning parish with its towering steeple, pink marble pillars, glass chandeliers, fragrant incense, clanging bells . . . well, it's like they'd been launched into heaven. From their pews they look at the turn-of-the-century frescoes above their heads. They're awed by the eye-popping stained glass windows of midnight blue that hold larger-than-life images of saints and martyrs within handcrafted frames. They're transfixed by the beatific glory of the place.

Those days I had opportunity aplenty. There were thousands of schools like Our Lady of the Angels that were easy pickings. Catholic schools, public schools, every kind of school.

Sure, the 1949 Chicago fire code required buildings be constructed of noncombustible material with enclosed stairways and fire doors. But to my advantage, these rules did not apply to buildings built before that time. Hurray for loopholes! Schools like Our Lady of the Angels were grandfathered in under the old laws. *Grandfathered*. Such a paternal term. Makes me want to hug an old man. Thus Our Lady of the Angels had no sprinkler systems to drench me, no alarm connected to the fire department to slow me down. The in-building fire alarm was unreliable, the fire extinguishers too high to reach, and there was only one fire door on the first floor to block me from the little kids. The absence of another fire door gave me rocket-quick access to the forth, fifth, sixth, seventh, and eighth graders on the second floor. Also, the fire alarm boxes outside on the street were two blocks away from the school. And those orderly nuns who ran the school had their rules: only the principal could sound the fire alarm—faulty as it was—and it looked like an ordinary on/off switch placed high on the wall. Figure that?

———

Anyway, back to true confessions:

When the kid who loved me tossed those three matches into that trash can, I got off to a good enough start, but then I smoldered. It could have been twenty or thirty minutes. I don't know how long because I was too busy struggling to stay alive. Then the window broke and I finally got a whiff of air, and that fresh oxygen tickled my parts until I couldn't stand it anymore and I had to explode.

I consumed the papers and the fiber container first, leaving the tough metal straps behind. Then I spread out and dug into a stack of newspapers under the steps, a roll of old linoleum, a book of wallpaper samples, a case of booze bottles left over from some church shindig. They still had the tastes of whiskey on their smooth glass. Oh, those Catholics—they like their whiskey.

Then, just when I owned the stairwell, in rushed Jim Raymond. I hated to fight with a friend, but the poor guy started beating on me. "Dammit," he swore. His wool jacket wasn't enough to smother me, and his metal shovel was no match for the monster I'd become. Score one for me, zilch for Jimmy. In a couple minutes, I got the best of him and he took off.

Then, opportunist that I am, I saw the possibility of a two-pronged attack—a blazing stroke of strategy, if I do say so. I saw a ventilator grille on the wall, and like a skater doing a triple axel, I twirled toward it. *Whoosh!* Perfect. The vent became my chimney—a clear path upstairs into the cockloft and to the roof. Then I shot up the staircase, past the metal door on the first floor, and burst into the second-floor corridor, all gritty, stinky, and black. Having built up terrific pressure, I made an explosive entrance, like Mephistopheles onto the stage of La Scala.

I chased everything I could see. When the roof collapsed, I sent hot waves of superheated air everywhere. That was when most of the kids who were still trapped inside died from asphyxiation. I stole their air.

OK, so you think I'm a monster, but before you become my judge and jury, consider this. When I'm contained and controlled, I have no penchant for carnage. I am not a sadist. Sometimes I'm even pretty.

I don't have to remind you of all the good I do. Warmth. Heat. Campfires and toasted marshmallows. Freshly baked bread and apple pie. I bet you can smell them right now. Potatoes charred a bit inside the foil. Ears of sweet corn barbecued inside their husks. And then I give you a cozy home to return to, a hot shower, and your morning coffee. Civilization wouldn't exist without me. You couldn't live without me, could you?

Part of my nature is to remain docile. In fact, I would have been content in Jimmy Raymond's furnace, eating the anthracitic meals he tossed me. I would have stayed in control inside the tips of sulfur on the kid's matches. In retrospect, my rampage through the Iroquois Theatre was unnecessary. The disaster in the stockyards was gluttony, and chomping on the sumptuous walnut-paneled lobby of the LaSalle Hotel was pure decadence. But I couldn't have changed a thing that happened. Whether I result from an act of nature or man's carelessness or malice, the result is always the same. Devouring fuel is what I do, and I can't stop myself.

In my contained moments I take responsibility for it all, and after the devastation I do feel remorse. I'm like an alcoholic who promises to stay dry but can't do it, a gambler who repents the next morning but returns to the blackjack table that night, the fatty who eats a whole pie every evening. I have no self-control, no willpower. That's my nature.

Then I leave it to others to clean up my messes.

12

Lieutenant Stan Wojnicki was at his desk doing paperwork when the call from the main alarm office downtown blared over the loudspeaker. "Engine 85, Fire. Thirty-Eight-Oh-Eight Iowa." His station, five blocks from Our Lady of the Angels, received the first call. It was 2:42.

A familiar shot of adrenaline propelled him into action. He rang the house bells that resounded throughout every room of the narrow redbrick firehouse on Huron Street.

As always, Stan and his men were prepared. That day they'd already fought two minor rubbish fires in the neighborhood, and according to procedure, they'd rechecked their equipment when they returned to the firehouse and made sure the pumper's water tank was full. They were fully staffed— an engineer to drive and pump water, three firefighters, and Stan himself.

Stan prided himself in running a first-class operation. He pulled on his boots and jabbed his arms into his coat. The other guys were already running toward their rig. Iowa Street was right up Hamlin Avenue, and they could be there in a minute.

He knew the neighborhood well. The address on Iowa
Street was either the church or rectory at Our Lady of the
Angels. Although he no longer lived in the area, he'd grown
up there and had made his First Communion and confirmation
in the redbrick church. It was probably a kitchen fire. Mrs.
Maloney was still there cooking and cleaning for the priests,
but she was getting old and forgetful. Just the other day he'd
seen her pushing her metal grocery cart out of Kroger's, a
scowl set on her face until he called out to her, "Mrs. Maloney, a fair day it is!" He trilled his greeting in his best Irish
accent, which he thought might get her attention. *Well done
for a full-blooded Pole if I do say so myself.* She looked around,
startled—she wasn't used to catcalls—but then catching the
charming fireman's eye, she straightened her hat and smiled.

Definitely a kitchen fire, or maybe the furnace. Fires in the
heating system were typical in Chicago winters.

Forty-seven-year-old Stanley Wojnicki had been a firefighter for fifteen years. It wasn't his first choice of occupation. As a young man he had his heart set on being a cop,
but he missed the height requirement. Solid and muscular, he
stood only five feet eight, and the requirement was five nine.
"By one stinkin' inch I missed it," he'd complained nonstop
to his brother-in-law, a Chicago police officer, and to everyone else who would listen. Then after he somewhat calmed
down, he applied for a job as a firefighter, took the test, and
got an offer. But still smarting from his rejection from the
police force, he wasn't sure he wanted it. "Take it, Stan, or
I'll belt you one," his brother-in-law said. "It's a good gig and
you got a wife to support. You know how my sister likes to
spend money," he laughed.

It *was* a good gig, and Stan never looked back. Like all
the other firefighters in Chicago, he managed to support his

family on $5,400 a year. As a bonus, he really liked the guys on his crew. Unlike the stereotyped volunteer firemen of old, who were rowdy and untrained drunks and bullies, his was a professional group he could count on.

With Stan in the front of the cab that afternoon and his engineer Hank Holden at the wheel, they sped north on Hamlin. But the minute they crossed Chicago Avenue the sight of billowing black smoke rising above the church told Stan it wasn't a simple grease fire. Hundreds of people were crowding around the building, slowing their passage. Frantic parents, neighbors, priests, and nuns were rushing, carrying children down the streets. Horn blaring, Hank eased his engine through the manic crowd to the curb on Iowa Street, and Stan jumped out before the truck fully stopped. It was his job to get water on the fire, which meant hooking their pumper truck up to nearby fire hydrants to tap into a continuous supply of water, then stretching hose lines to the fire.

Instantly he knew the source of fire wasn't in the building on Iowa Street, but wherever it was, it was a *sonofabitch*. He grabbed the mike on the engine's radio and called the main office. "Send more help!" he shouted into the mouthpiece. It was 2:47.

He ran around the corner to the Avers side of the building, and in passing the gated courtyard closed off to street access between the two wings of the building saw a sight that would remain etched in his mind forever: kids hanging out of the second-floor windows—the eighth graders in rooms 211 and 209, he'd learn later—throwing shoes and books, anything to get attention. Smoke was billowing out of the windows. *That damn gate is blocking our access.* He shouted up at the kids, "Goddammit, stay up there, help is coming."

His job was water, but where was the fire? Smoke ballooned out of the windows, thick and toxic. He had to find the source.

At the northwest corner he turned right and ran along the back of the building, where three classrooms—212, 210, and 208—overlooked the alley. Black smoke, thick as bales of cotton, rolled out of the windows. Kids with their clothes on fire hung from the ledges. More kids, gray-faced and grimacing, clogged the windows. The too-short ladders that neighbors brought leaned uselessly against the walls below. Kids with their hair on fire were jumping or being pushed out. Kids' bodies fell through the black air, thudding onto the gravel, some landing on other kids. Parents and priests with outstretched arms were trying to catch them. Injured and lifeless bodies were splayed across the ground in pools of blood. Mothers, fathers, neighbors were scooping them up, dragging them away, leaning them against the wall of the candy store, calling their own children's names up into the windows, tending to those who jumped, wrenching them away to make way for other jumpers.

"Jesus Christ," Stan cried. *The source. I need to find the source of this monster.*

Suddenly he spotted flames rising out of the door at the far end of the alley. Pushing his way through the screaming crowds—past parents begging him to save their own children—he pulled a two-and-a-half inch hose line to the door to cut off the flames and push his way into the burning stairway beyond. A mother who didn't speak English waved a hastily written sign in his face that said, MARY, ROOM 208. He wanted to stop, to save those kids, to help the woman find Mary, but he had to get water on the fire.

Just then Hank Holden and a fireman from a hook and ladder unit came running into the alley with a twenty-four-foot ladder. Stan caught sight of a young boy perched on the ledge, his clothing on fire, flames searing his skinny arms. The kid looked stricken, afraid to jump. Instinctively Stan and another firefighter speedily turned their hose and fired water on the boy. Still another fireman climbed the ladder and pulled the kid onto it. The kid slid down, his burning hands clutching, releasing, clutching the sides of the ladder. The fireman moved on to yank out another boy, and a girl whose legs were aflame. More firefighters ran into the alley with canvas life nets and immediately the kids started jumping, some to safety, some missing the nets entirely and landing on gravel. Stan and his crew squatted behind the nozzle and blasted water on the flames, trying to move forward into the building and to the source of the fire. The blaze was out of control. The fire had too great an advantage. *If only someone had called earlier. Five minutes, four minutes. Even two minutes might have made all the difference.*

————

Lieutenant Charlie Kamin's Hook and Ladder 35 had come from the north. They were the guys with all kinds of ladders: twenty, twenty-six, thirty footers and more.

Driver Wally Romanczak honked through the crowds and pulled up to the Iowa Street address they'd been given. Charlie and his five-man company moved into action, pulling extension ladders from the back of the truck. Crowds were swelling around the building. Dazed kids were running from the front door of the school into the arms of their parents. Charlie thought they were in the right spot until he heard a man in a plaid jacket on the corner of Avers, shouting hysterically, "This way . . . the fire's over here."

Losing valuable time repositioning on Avers, he caught sight of the dire situation in the courtyard behind the gate. *That damn gate. What were they thinking?* Kids, their bodies black with soot, were hanging from upstairs windows, jumping, screaming for help. He knew his guys had to get inside that locked courtyard to ladder the windows. Men from the neighborhood—grandfathers in their slippers, fathers desperate to save their kids, neighborhood Good Samaritans—struggled to break through the gate. One man pounded the iron with a sledgehammer, but the padlock held. In desperation Charlie and his men hoisted a thirty-six-foot extension ladder over the gate, then with another ladder battered it.

"Give it all you got . . . ONE!"

"TWO . . ."

"One more time . . . THREE!"

With the help of civilians they were able to break through after four powerful rams. The crew moved in with their life nets. The kids jumped into the nets three or four at a time, bounced out, landed on one another, created loads too heavy for the nets to handle. In frustration the firemen dropped their nets and started catching the kids in their open arms.

Charlie Kamin had been a firefighter for more than ten years. At thirty-eight, he was built like Tarzan and had the strength of a mule. Charlie was six feet two and well over two hundred pounds, his upper body rippling with muscles.

He and his crew laddered the windows. Charlie climbed to a window in room 211, the room closest to the gate. With sixty eighth graders, it was one of the school's most crowded classes. At the top he got a look at what was going on inside. Frantic, crying kids were reaching out for him at the windows. They must have been screaming, but Charlie couldn't hear their voices. All his energy, all his senses, were focused on how he could get them out. They were pushing for space at the window, gulping air, pulling at each other, begging for help. He looked into the classroom. On the floor were layers of unconscious or dead kids looking like they were peacefully asleep. Behind them, still seated at some of the desks, were more kids—their lips moving in prayer, their eyes focused on their nun, Sister Helaine, her face blackened by soot, her eyeglasses smudged with grease, still standing at the front of the class.

A globe light shattered and rained shards of glass on them. *Shit, the ceiling is ready to go. The place is going to light up*, Charlie thought. He felt his own face burning from the heat. He didn't know how much more he'd be able to take.

One girl made eye contact with him, leaped from her desk, and propelled herself toward him. Breathing hot smoke, he grabbed her around the waist and swung her out the window. When he knew she'd found her footing on the ladder, he reached in and plucked more kids out, one by one. The window was so stuffed with kids that he had to push some of them back so he could grab them one at a time. *Another. Another. Another. A boy. A girl. Another boy. Gotta get them outta here before the room goes.* He had better luck with the boys, because he was able to pull them up by their belts. He worked like an automaton, reaching in, pulling kids out, not worrying about getting them onto the ladder, just dropping them to the ground and hoping someone was there to break their fall. If they were to live, he had to get them out of there.

The classroom was growing darker, as if a deathly shadow were rolling over it. Time was running out. Smoke like filthy black clouds was tumbling in, heading straight for the oxygen at the windows, toward him. Then he saw fire breaking through the ceiling. *Any second this place is going to flash.* He pulled another boy out. Then came the horrendous *whooooosh* that he knew was coming, followed by the soaring roar of hot wind that almost knocked him off his ladder.

While most people expect fire to be silent, Charlie understood the voice of fire: There was nothing silent about it. Flashing flames roared and screeched like a derailed subway train shooting toward the window. The hissing flames seared his face, burned his hands, and caused his ladder to wobble against the brick wall. His heart was hammering. He knew no one could be alive after that flashover. Balanced in the path of the racing fire, he turned his head away and held on to the window frame for dear life. When he stole a look back into the classroom, he saw a sight he'd never forget—one that would flash into his dreams and make him cry out in his sleep forever: dozens of young bodies buckling, wilting, and collapsing like stick figures in front of his eyes.

There was nothing more he could do for those eighth graders. With blistering hands, he carried the last boy down the ladder and handed the child off to another fireman. "My God, the *sonofabitch* won," he swore. His glassy-eyed partner flung the boy over his shoulder and headed for an ambulance. Charlie folded his spent body against the building. He pulled off his fire helmet and rubbed soot out of his burning eyes. Through blurred vision he watched another firefighter stumble down the ladder with the badly burned body of a nun, her form looking like a blackened rag doll.

Charlie Kamin shook his head. *Those kids. They had no chance. This sonofabitch sucked the life out of them.*

———

Joe Murray, a young firefighter with Irish good looks, lived in Our Lady of the Angels parish. He'd graduated from OLA in 1942. Sister Canice had been his third-grade teacher in 1936. Having served as an altar boy, he knew the priests, nuns, and neighborhood well. He was unloading groceries in the kitchen of his firehouse and talking to his engineer when the call came. His fire company, Squad 6, a rescue unit, was on the scene in five minutes.

They too pulled up in front of the church on Iowa.

"The fire's around the corner . . . give me a hand with this ladder," called a firefighter from Truck 36, parked ahead of them. When the two men reached the alley, the pavement was full of injured children lying on the ground and others jumping from the windows, so Joe moved in to help catch them. Two kids, a frail girl coming down headfirst and a fat boy, came flying down at him. *I can save the girl, but I don't know about the boy*, he told himself, so he instinctively reached for the girl—a decision that would haunt him the rest of his career, because he wanted to save them both.

Joe rushed up the ladder to one of the windows of room 210, Sister Seraphica's fourth-grade class. He could see that some of the kids were afraid to jump; others couldn't reach the windowsill, almost three feet above the floor. At the top, Joe began pulling the children out. Then, clearing enough space for his 175-pound body, he climbed into the classroom and, staying low, continued to lift children out onto the ladder.

By that time cloud within cloud of thick, greasy, black, superheated smoke was pouring out of the windows.

"Get your footing . . . crawl down . . . slide down . . . get out . . ." he told them, trying to be firm and forceful, to instill confidence in the kids. Having six children of his own, he

knew the importance of encouragement. "You can do it."
One by one he reached for them and shoved them out of
the window, working as quickly as possible, knowing time
was running out. His eyes were everywhere—on the kids, on
the ladder, on the scene in the classroom, on the progress
of the fire. Behind him, just paces away, flames were rolling
in through the transoms above the doors, and fire, like an
expanding crimson crown of thorns, was ringing the ceiling.
He watched the fire drop lower into the room. He knew the
room was going to flash over any second and he had to get
the heck out of there if he was going to survive. In one final
effort, he grabbed two children off the floor and threw them
out ahead of himself, knowing as harsh as it was, it was their
only chance to live. Then in a deafening *whoosh* the room
flashed over. It was a crematorium in there, upwards of a
thousand degrees. The whole side of the building was going.

"My son is in that room," a father yelled at him as he
moved down the ladder.

"How do you know?" Joe said.

"He's in that room," the father yelled back.

Feet on the ground, Joe tried to move the sobbing man
away from the building to keep him from witnessing the
inferno that was consuming his son.

Knowing there was nothing more he could do for the kids
left in room 210, Joe rushed into the courtyard, grabbed a
high-power hose, and started spraying water into room 211,
Sister Helaine's eighth-grade class. More greasy bales of smoke
were pouring out of that classroom and rising into the ragged
sky. He knew that most of the kids who were going to make
it had gotten out already.

———

Richard Scheidt, whom everyone called Dick, was a member of Squad 1, the "dizzy squad," so named because of their crazy schedule. His search and rescue squad was sometimes called out twenty times a day.

Monday, December 1, started out as any ordinary day for Dick. He had coffee with his pretty wife, Nancy, and kissed their four kids goodbye: Richard, eight; Nancy, six; and twins Thomas and Timothy, who would turn two the day after Christmas. The twins were side-eyeing each other and spinning the pastel beads on the bars of their identical wooden high chairs.

Dick drove from his home on the South Side to his firehouse on Dearborn Street to begin his twenty-four-hour shift—twenty-four hours on, forty-eight hours off. While Squad 1 could be called to emergencies anywhere in the city, it was mostly responsible for the high-rent districts: the swanky Michigan Avenue shopping area, the financial district on LaSalle Street, the posh mansions along Lake Shore Drive, and city hall.

Dick Scheidt would say he was a lucky man, other than the fact that at thirty he was balding, but he could blame that on his father. An ex-marine, he'd married the love of his life, had four great kids—twins to boot. He often thought of how fortunate he was to work with a great group of guys at a job that was challenging and respected. He wasn't a high roller or the best-paid guy in his neighborhood—never would be—but that was OK with him. He was managing fine on his firefighter's salary, and he was doing something that mattered.

A man of few complaints, Dick enjoyed what most of his buddies dreaded—a long commute. His twenty-mile drive to work in his 1953 Chevy—north on South Shore Drive and then Lake Shore Drive—took him through the most scenic part of Chicago, past world-famous landmarks that are printed on color postcards. It was a drive most Chicagoans, confined to the inner-city grid of brick and concrete, experienced only occasionally. His northbound commute took him past the sprawling Museum of Science and Industry, through Burnham Park, with its wide beaches and glittering boat docks, past Soldier Field, where he'd spent many a boyhood afternoon watching football games, and the Shedd Aquarium, the Field Museum, and the Adler Planetarium, which jutted out on its own little peninsula into Lake Michigan. His path bisected the well-tended parks, beaches, and yacht clubs bordering the lake in the east, and the sleek Mies van der Rohe skyscrapers nipping the sky in the west—the choice real estate where the wealthy people lived. A special attraction was Buckingham Fountain off Columbus Drive, on which his grandfather had worked as a stonemason, carving the sea horses in the fountain's lower basin. It was one of the largest, most spectacular fountains in the world. Sometimes on a balmy summer evening after work Dick would pull over into a parking lot in Grant Park and take a few minutes to unwind from his day and watch the water spray, sometimes in magical colors, to a height of 150 feet and then cascade smooth as liquid glass over the fountain's tiers.

"Water drowns fire—that's probably why I love it here so," he once told his son.

Today was an easy drive. After turning west on Jackson and south on Dearborn he parked his Chevy and quick-stepped into the firehouse in a very good mood. He was looking forward to his first cup of coffee with the guys—shooting the breeze about the most recent Bears game, about their families and their plans for Christmas. He knew that at any time anything could come up. His team thrived on excitement. They might work a fire, open roofs, pull hose lines, do search and rescue. Or they might work Special Duty—tending to a jumper balancing on the ledge of a skyscraper, a highway accident, or a heart attack victim. They went wherever they were needed.

By midafternoon the dizzy squad had fought a small fire on Hill Street, then sped to an inhalator call on Van Buren, and then returned to do the daily equipment maintenance at the station, checking gas masks and cutting torches, maintaining vehicles. Compared with most days this Monday was slow. After dinner the guys would probably watch *Peter Gunn* on Channel 5, or some of them would want to watch *The Danny Thomas Show* on Channel 4 and they'd bicker and call the *Danny Thomas* guys sissies, then they'd probably watch *Peter Gunn* and make wisecracks about that. That's if it was a slow night.

By this point in his career, Dick Scheidt had fought some of the big ones. He'd worked the Reliance Hotel fire, where five firemen were killed, and the Barton Hotel fire on skid row, where twenty-nine men had lost their lives. He'd been out at the gruesome "L" wreck on Wilson Avenue a couple years back, where they had to raise ladders from the street to the track level to rescue passengers from a crushed train.

It was 2:42 when they heard the first alarm through the loudspeaker in the station. At first Dick thought the nearest station would handle it—and anyway it was out of their territory. But at 3:09, the loudspeaker called Squad 1 into action. The fire had gone from one alarm to five alarms almost instantly. *It must be huge. Probably a factory or a warehouse,* he thought.

Dick leaped onto the truck with his men, took his post, and sped off into the bristling air. With the wind chilling his face, he slipped on his rubber fire coat and pulled on his boots. By the time they got to the fire at 3:18, traffic was so snarled with other fire engines, ambulances, police vehicles, and crowds of frantic parents crowding all points of access, that he and his men jumped out of their truck two blocks away, clutching their axes and pike poles and sprinting on foot to the school. There must have been two hundred firefighters there already—running hundreds of feet of hoses, climbing dozens of ladders—tall, short, metal, wood—propped every which way along the building, pulling bodies out of the windows. A fireman stood firmly atop an aerial platform—the department's mighty "snorkel"—blasting water into the building's high windows.

Police were controlling the crowds and directing the ambulances taking kids to the hospitals in the area. The WGN traffic helicopter was whirling noisily above them, reporting the fire on the radio and directing emergency vehicles through gridlocked traffic. The city pulsated with the sounds of fire engines screaming their approach, and with emergency vehicles slicing through traffic on most every major thoroughfare. The streets vibrated with the pressure of wheels speeding upon them. To Dick, it felt like every engine, high-pressure wagon, and ambulance in Chicagoland was out fighting this monster.

On the scene, running over a spaghetti platter of hoses, Dick Scheidt and his squad found Fire Commissioner Robert J. Quinn and his fire chiefs, who stood outside the main entrance sending men to where they were needed. You couldn't miss him in the battered white fire helmet he wore over his snow-white hair.

Fit at fifty-three, Quinn had been a navy commander during World War II, in charge of firefighting for the entire
Atlantic Fleet. A year ago Mayor Daley appointed him to
Chicago's top firefighting job, where he now commanded
4,278 men. Already that year they had responded to more
than sixty-five thousand fires. Quinn made it a point to show
up at extra-alarm fires.

The powerful snorkel, now shooting water into the school's
second floor, was Quinn's brainchild. He got the idea from
watching tree trimmers in Lincoln Park using a similar platform to do their jobs, and he adapted it to firefighting. Standing firmly on a platform gave a firefighter greater stability
than he would have had balancing precariously, heavy hose
in hand, on a ladder.

"Get up to the second floor, you guys," Quinn barked at
Dick and his men. Dick's was a search and rescue operation,
but from the looks of things Dick knew there would be little
rescue at this point. By now the fire was out and the place
would be drenched. There was zero chance of finding anyone
alive.

On the second-floor landing, Dick and his buddies discovered that there was no reasonable access into the classrooms
through the corridor. Firefighters were up there already hosing the space down, venting the heat and smoke through
the partially collapsed roof. The only way he and his guys
could enter the rooms would be through the walls. So with
sledgehammers, axes, and pike poles, they tore away layers of
charred plaster and wood. When they breached a hole large
enough to crawl through, Dick braced himself for what they
would find. He remembered what he had learned in training.
Don't get rattled. Keep your emotions in check. Just do your job.

With flashlights in hand they entered room 212 and saw the devastation the fire had wrought.

Sister Clare Therese's fifth-grade classroom was eerily quiet. There was no sign of life. In silence, Dick and his men carefully slogged through water shin deep, around overturned desks, Sister's scorched Christmas decorations of stars and angels, shards of broken glass, a felled globe, a twisted metal crucifix. At the front of the class beneath the window, dozens of children were piled on top of one another like cordwood, with the body of Sister Clare Therese lying over them, her arms extended—as if she were still trying to protect them. Her black nun's shoe, fragile and sodden, lay beside her. More kids were slumped at their desks, some clutching rosaries and tinny religious medals in their young hands, some looking like they were perusing the geography book—*Our American Neighbors*—still open in front of them. No one was burned. Felled by toxic gases, they all had suffocated. One by one, silently, wordlessly, the firemen lifted their lifeless bodies from their desks and carried them out, exiting through the back door to the alley whenever possible. There a long stream of ambulances were lined up, waiting to carry them to the Cook County morgue.

As he gently lowered bodies on stretchers, Dick thought of the kids he was carrying out and their parents downstairs waiting for word, hoping, praying, and bargaining with God that their children weren't the ones he'd bring out. He wept as he carried them, imagining himself on the other side of the line, a parent praying to see the face of his own child walking out that door. He would remove nineteen dead children from the school that day.

One of the bodies Dick carried out of room 212 was that of John Jajkowski. The ten-year-old had sung in the choir, taken accordion lessons, and wanted to become a priest. Just a few minutes ago Johnny had been confusing *province* with *providence* in their geography lesson.

The boy's face and clothes were blackened by smoke. He was shoeless. His chestnut hair was wet and matted to his head. Steam rose off his body, blasted by fire hoses. At the moment Dick exited the school with the boy in his arms, the white light of a flashbulb blinded his vision. A newspaper photographer—just another guy doing his job—had snapped a picture of him carrying the limp, lifeless body of the dark-haired Jajkowski boy out of the main entrance.

Joe Murray from Squad 6 had joined up with the dizzy squad to aid in their search and recovery efforts. Joe found the captain of Squad 1 and told him, "We're going into room 212 and breaching the walls between 212, 210, and 208. When you hit those rooms, there's going to be a dozen and a half or two dozen bodies in there."

Together they breached the wall where the blackboard was, broke the slate off, and entered room 210, Sister Seraphica's fourth-grade class. Piles of kids lay stacked beneath the four windows, kids that Joe couldn't get when time ran out. The firefighters pulled their bodies through into the next classroom.

An eerie feeling washed over Joe as he set foot in the very classroom he had once occupied as a fourth grader. Instinctively he remembered his way around, knew where everything was. The door to the hallway was open and he could see firemen there hosing the place down.

The kids in room 210 were the youngest and some of the smallest on the second floor. Among them was the body of nine-year-old Mark Stachura, who just minutes earlier had been waving a painted pastel statue of the Infant Jesus of Prague out of the window to get the attention of his father, whom he had spotted in the alley below. He had won that statue earlier that day for correctly answering a quiz question. His father, John, begged him to jump, but little Mark was too afraid to take the leap, or perhaps couldn't climb up to the window. He'd slipped back into the classroom.

Some children could hardly climb up to the windowsill, which was three feet off the floor. Dick Scheidt and his fellow rescuers found Sister Seraphica beneath one of these piles, her cloak outstretched over a mound of children.

Inside Sister Canice's seventh-grade classroom, 208, they poked their way among overturned desks, a fallen wall clock that had stopped at 2:47, heaps of metal, glass, sodden books, and charred bodies, some of them pinned beneath the ceiling that collapsed upon them. They found the body of Sister Canice, splayed over the bodies of the youngsters, some still clutching the hem of her gown.

———

Dick Scheidt, Stan Wojnicki, Charlie Kamin, Joe Murray, and hundreds of firefighters worked into the early evening to clear the school of victims. Other squads labored under the glare of searchlights well into the night. The harsh white beams made everything look ghostly and surreal as they dug, lifted, hauled, and sloshed through frigid water in a nightmare that seemed endless.

Numb and nearly in shock, Dick returned to his station on Dearborn Street at 6:32 PM, earlier than many of the others. At 7:50 Squad 1 was called out again to sweep water from a broken main in a store on State Street.

Dick would remember nothing about that call. As he drove home that night, his mind was fixed not on the brilliant city lights or the dusty glow of moonlight brushing the frozen shore of Lake Michigan, but on the faces of the schoolchildren he couldn't save.

The following afternoon—after reporting to City Hall for a debriefing with Fire Commissioner Quinn—Joe Murray walked into his own home, took one look at his kids sitting at the table eating after-school cookies, and broke down and cried.

13

The kid spit-rubbed the soot from the face of his Hopalong Cassidy wristwatch. It was 3:00 PM. He ran from the church into the crowds and stood gawking up at the blazing fire from a curb on Avers Avenue. He wasn't alone; hundreds of children, parents, priests, and nuns were crowded around him. He had cleaned the soot off his glasses with his shirttail and they were back on his nose, so he could see everything. He was fidgeting—rocking back and forth, his hands buried deep in his pockets.

Look at that fire. I did it. All these people are watching what I created, but they'll never know it. They'll never know, but I want them to know. I want to say, "Look at me, I did this!" but I can't tell them, because I'd end up in the electric chair. I don't want them to know. They can't know.

All those people were running around because of him; it was he who set it all in motion. He was standing still—his feet on the curb—yet he had made all this happen. He hated his school and everyone in it. The principal, the nuns, Miss Tristano, the priests, and the bully kids who made fun of him. They were getting what they deserved.

But then a new thought swamped the old one: Was it what they deserved? No. He didn't mean to *kill* them. He didn't mean for it to get this big. He just wanted to get out of school early.

A cold shiver of remorse enveloped him, and he started to cry. Black, dirty, sooty tears slid down his cheeks, and he wiped them on his gray shirtsleeve. His arms were shaking like branches buffeted by the wind. The woman standing beside him, a pregnant lady with a belly protruding from her coat, saw him trembling and threw an extra jacket that she was carrying for her own child over his shoulders. "Here, put this on, honey," she said.

"Thanks." His teeth were chattering. He wanted his own mother now, but a different kind of mother than the one he had. As he stared at the fire, he recalled a fight he'd had with her a week or so ago. She'd been in a rage about a telephone call she got from the principal, Sister Florence, about his grades, his deportment, some other bullshit, and their conversation turned to his mom's suspicions about other fires he'd been accused of setting.

"You set that fire in that garage around the corner."

"Mom, I was only five when I did it. I've grown up since then."

"Baloney. What about that fire near Springfield and Ohio? You used lighter fluid on that one . . . And the fires in the garbage cans and mailboxes. Always I covered for you. How could I be so stupid?"

She looked like a monster, her face all screwed up. "I'm sick and tired of having to answer to the priests and nuns and cops for you . . . I'm sick and tired of the trouble you cause between me and Manny. I'm sick and tired of you." When she turned her back ready to walk away, he heard her crying.

"Crybaby," he snickered.

"What did you say?"

That's when she ran toward him and grabbed him by the shoulders and shook him so hard his head trembled. And that's when she said it:

"I never wanted to have you, ya know. I was fifteen. I got raped by my stepfather, your grandfather, and that's how you were born. A bad seed. You were a bad seed from the start."

Now, in the smoky devastation of Our Lady of the Angels, the kid leaned against the stranger, the pregnant woman. She draped her arm around him and pulled him close to her and he liked it.

14

Jim Raymond awoke to the confusion of bright lights and clipped voices.

"Where am I?" the janitor slurred. His mouth was as dry as dust. It hurt to swallow. His head was pounding. It took him a few seconds to remember the fire. What was he doing alive? The last thing he remembered was firefighters carrying kids out and drivers loading them into the backs of ambulances, their arms and legs black, some covered with white sheets.

"You're at Garfield Park Hospital, Mr. Raymond. You've got some minor burns and you've taken in a lot of smoke. Your wife is at Franklin Boulevard Hospital with your son . . ." The voice was coming from a nurse with a white cap and large blue eyes. Her eyes were wet with tears, as if she was going to give him the worst news possible.

"My son? Which one?"

"I don't know."

"Aww, God!" Jim closed his eyes and turned away from her. *My boys. Robert. Tom. Johnny. Marty.* Quick images of each of their faces flashed through his mind, but he couldn't focus. His thoughts were a tangle of memories. He flung one leg over the bed and tried to raise himself up. "I gotta get out of here. I gotta find out about the kids."

"We'll find out for you, Mr. Raymond," the nurse said, firmly lifting his leg back onto the bed. "You've had stitches and you've taken in a lot of smoke and lost a lot of blood. You need to rest."

Jim's arm and head were bandaged. Sterile white against the redness of his arm. He was weak and it hurt to breathe in more than short gasps of air, but there was no way he could rest. His thoughts were like a pileup of frightening shadows, one upon the other. His kids. The other kids. So many were injured, dead. He didn't have to ask. He didn't have to know how many. He knew it was bad.

"How many dead?" he asked anyway.

She shook her head and turned away, a diversion that told him the numbers were staggering. "We have no way of knowing right now," she said softly, evasively. "I promise to check on your boys for you though."

"And Mary Kay. Mary Kay Raymond. She's only ten."

"I'll try to find out."

Jim thought of the religious medal Mary Kay had given him. Agitated, he started patting his sides with his aching unbandaged hand. "Where is it?" he asked.

"What?"

"My medal? Saint Christopher. Mary Kay g- . . . g- . . . gave it to me."

"I'll check your trousers, sir," she said, stepping over to the gunmetal locker near his bed. "It's here, Mr. Raymond," she said, setting it solidly in his palm.

Jim pressed the medal to his chest and closed his eyes. His nurse tiptoed away.

Noise and confusion surrounded him. Another nurse spoke behind a curtain that separated him from a young burn victim. "I'll do this quickly, I promise. Be a brave little soldier."

The child bawled, "Please don't hurt me!"

Bells sounded outside his room. The earnest voices of nurses, the hurried roll of carts on tile floors, the urgent opening and closing of doors, heavy footsteps, rushing footsteps, desperate footsteps, the hum of machinery, the pleas of parents for information, more bells dinging for emergency care, more metal supply carts speeding past, elevator bells *bing*-ing, more orders and tears and anguished cries. Jim heard, but didn't hear. He was stuck inside his head, reliving images of the day, trying to fit together the thousand-piece jigsaw puzzle of what happened, starting that morning when everything was normal . . . until it wasn't.

He remembered seeing flames in the window. Trying to beat them down. Yelling at some boys. Who were they? He couldn't remember. Had they been smoking? Was there a problem with the boilers? That morning the boilers were fine. He had checked them. Everything was fine that morning.

What if he'd gotten there sooner? What if he hadn't taken his time walking from one building to the other? What if he hadn't stopped to talk to the young girl hurrying to the bus stop? Every step, every word had mattered, but he hadn't known it then. What if he hadn't tried to put out the fire himself, thinking it was his responsibility, thinking it was his territory and he could handle it without anyone's help? What if he had gone for help sooner?

He remembered crawling on the floor, losing his cap somewhere in the dark. The putrid smell of the smoke. Unlike the odor of burning coal or wood, which he was used to, this smell—of burning tar paper, varnish, paint, human flesh and hair—was lodged in his lungs, kneaded into his pores, ingrained in his memory.

Later, the nurse with the white cap peeked in on him again. "I learned that your son Johnny injured his hip and back. He's at Franklin Hospital and he'll be fine. The rest of your kids are fine too."

Robert, Tommy, Marty, and Mary Kay are alive. "Thank you, nurse," he said.

But, my God, what about the hundreds of other kids?

15

Kathleen Adamski thought she had died and gone to hell. *Isn't this what hell is like? Isn't this how Sister Canice described Dante's Inferno? Surely hell is where I am, but I'm only thirteen and I haven't even committed the kind of sins that would send me there.*

"You're in Saint Anne's Hospital, dear. What's your name?" a gentle voice asked.

"Kathleen Adamski," she said.

"Your name, dear? One more time." She put her ear close to Kathleen's lips.

"Kathleen Adamski" she repeated, trying to enunciate every syllable, but knowing she was falling short. Her tongue was heavy and her lips felt like hot balloons pumped up to triple their size. She opened her eyes.

"Spell it, please," the nurse in white asked.

"A-D-A-M-S-K-I."

The nurse scribbled something on paper and bustled off to the next patient waiting for admittance in the emergency room.

The room was crowded with people moving everywhere. Everything reeked of smoke. "There will be more coming, many more," she heard a man say. Kathleen was on a gurney, covered loosely with a sheet. Someone was pushing it fast from behind. Her teeth were chattering. Her whole body was trembling, but inside she felt on fire. *Where are my parents? Mamusia . . . Tata.* She was flying past gurneys of other kids crying for their parents, hysterical parents peering into her face to see if she was their child, nurses rushing about carrying heaps of blankets, green oxygen tanks, sheets, boxes of syringes, and plastic tubing, pushing metal carts, pulling IV trolleys. Amid the chaos she was being rolled into an area enclosed by stiff white drapes. A light housed in a stainless steel fixture shone down on her from below an acoustic tile ceiling.

A soft, cool hand patted her shoulder. A kind voice assured her that they were there to help. She felt a tug, heard scissors snipping cloth. Someone was peeling her uniform off her body. She tried to tell them to stop for modesty's sake, but all that came out of her mouth was a pathetic scream that pained her burnt throat.

"This shot will help the pain, Kathleen," said a man's voice from beneath a white mask. *A doctor.* He named a painkiller, said something about cc's. A nurse in a scrub cap plunged a needle into her ankle. "We need to do some X-rays of your pelvic area," another nurse said. Carefully they repositioned her body, and she screamed from the pain. There were more injections that flowed into her ankle from a tube attached to bags of liquid hanging on a trolley. She felt colder than she had ever felt before. She couldn't stop trembling. *Mamusia, Tata, where are you? Do you know I'm here?*

As she waited, she overheard snippets of other conversations:

"We have eighty children already, with more coming in."

"Bring her over here. She's a bad one."

"Please make it stop hurting."

"Call housekeeping for more sheets."

"I think this is my child, but I'm not sure."

Then her gurney was moving speedily again, skirting people and wheelchairs, carts and cries, this time into an elevator that delivered her to the sixth floor, into a large operating pavilion where everything was white, stainless steel, and much quieter. A gleaming dome of light, bright as an August sun, hung above her. A hand placed a cold metal cup over her nose. *Anesthesia.* She looked into the face of a doctor, whose serious brown eyes examined her from above a white mask. "I'm Dr. Segraves, and we're going to fix your hips," he said gently. He had kind eyes and a high forehead like her father's. *Maybe he has kids,* was her last thought. "Relax, Kathy," a high-pitched woman's voice said, "and count to ten." She was watching her lips move. *Ten, nine, eight* . . . Then she was unconscious.

———

Kathleen's parents had been looking for her everywhere— the church at Our Lady of the Angels, Saint Anne's, other hospitals on the North Side, even the Cook County morgue, before they learned that she was indeed at Saint Anne's, the first hospital they had called. The operator at admissions had told them they had no record of a patient name Adamski. Kathleen's tongue and lips were swollen, and because of her garbled speech, the nurse had scribbled a very different name on Kathleen's intake form, which was clarified later.

Kathleen was out of surgery by the time they found her in the orthopedic unit on the second floor, in a wing of the

hospital the staff had cleared for the fire victims. Many exist-
ing hospital patients were being discharged early to make
room for the children who were being speedily rolled from
ambulances into the emergency room.

It took Eva and Peter Adamski a moment to realize it
was their Kathleen in the bed near the window. Her arms,
burnt black like meat seared on the grill, were loosely covered with a sheet, her torso was suspended from a canvas
sling resembling a hammock, attached by tension springs to a
bar overhead. Her face was the color of stewed strawberries,
blistered and swollen beyond recognition. It was her blonde
hair they recognized, and her red glass rosary, which sat on
a metal table beside her.

Eva felt her whole body collapsing in on itself. "My God,
our Kathleen," she gasped. Peter's face froze and turned gray
at the sight of her. Their eldest child, their perfect daughter,
now horribly damaged, lay in a drug-induced sleep.

———

A doctor in white scrubs entered the room and introduced
himself as Dr. Jim Segraves, an orthopedic surgeon.

Eva looked into his eyes and nodded. Peter reached out
and nervously shook his hand. "We're Kathleen's parents."

Peter wished he could be anywhere else but here right now,
which was a different feeling for him. He was a man who
tried to put grim memories behind, who lived in the present
and tried to anticipate a better future, but now he would
gladly set the clock back a day or a thousand days—even
if it meant returning to the years he spent at Auschwitz—if
he could undo what his daughter was going through. Now he
was looking into the face of a stranger who had his daughter's

life in his hands, a doctor who knew more about his child's future than he did.

"How is she?" he asked.

Dr. Segraves, an imposing man in his forties, pulled off his scrub cap to reveal a disheveled mass of graying hair that he passed a hand over to tame. "We expect your daughter to recover," he said, "but it will be a long road for her." He wiped the perspiration from his brow. "We put pins in her hips. She has third-degree burns on her lower legs and arms, and second-degree burns on her hands. Her bobby socks protected her ankles."

"Oh my God," Eva Adamski muttered. "And her face?"

"Her face will be fine. The scrapes and swelling and blistering you see will diminish, and eventually you'll have your beautiful girl back." He smiled faintly.

"There will be no scars on her face," Eva repeated to her husband, who stood at her side hearing the same words. She leaned into Peter's arm and wiped her tears on the sleeve of his jacket. He patted her cheek.

"Thank you, Doctor," Peter said. "And her fingers? She plays the piano."

"They will be fine."

"Is she in pain?"

"Not right now. She's sedated. But there will be pain later. She'll need skin grafts and reconstructive surgery on her arms and legs, but I promise you we'll give her the best care we can, and we'll try to control the pain," Dr. Segraves said, looking at Eva and then Peter with compassionate eyes.

"Do you have children, Doctor?"

"I do. Two daughters."

"Then you know," Peter said.

Later, the Adamskis would learn more than they ever wanted to know about burns. Burns are one of the most serious injuries a body can endure. The human body is an interconnected system that massive burns throw violently out of kilter. All the organs are affected: kidney function slows down, blood pressure drops, heart rate rises. In third-degree burns, the affected areas become open wounds, seeping vital bodily fluids from the bloodstream into the tissues around the burned areas. When the protective cover of skin is lost, there is no barrier to the entrance of lethal bacteria, so death from blood poisoning, or septicemia, is a constant concern until the body's open wounds are covered and protected with new or substitute skin. Pain may not be present at first, because the nerve endings are destroyed, but it becomes excruciating during recovery, when new nerve connections are being made, and in the process of harvesting skin from one part of the body to graft onto another.

———

Across the room, Kathleen lay asleep, captive to wild, non-sensical dreams that swirled about her. She was climbing a spiraling ring of light to get somewhere, and a force of some sort was prodding her upward. There was no turning back, nowhere else to go. Slowly, the rings transformed into a thin and spiky mountain that grew thicker the higher she traveled. At the top, when she could go no farther, she stopped and looked down. Below her was a smoky pit like a narrowing funnel that grew darker the deeper she could see. She knew that it was the inferno that Sister Canice had talked about—Dante's Inferno—with each layer of the descending rings presenting a punishment more terrifying than the last. Her heart was beating wildly. She felt her footing slip and suddenly she was falling—plunging headfirst down the narrowing shaft, getting blown about by violent winds. *Ten. Nine. Eight.* Everywhere creatures reached out to capture her: rabid dogs with bared teeth, clawing arms as gnarled as parched branches, striking snakes, wasps, reptiles with snapping tongues. They all wanted to grab her, capture her. She was falling. *Seven. Six.* Her limbs flailed out of control. Then a withered arm reached out and snatched her, yanking her into Dante's sixth circle, an inescapable tomb of fire, claiming her as one of the straw people, who this time would not crumble into dust—as she saw happen to Sister Canice and her classmates—but who would live on forever in agony.

16

Anita Martinelli was in their furniture store, Martinelli's Fine Furniture, demonstrating a TV set to their neighbor Joe Krazinski, who thought he might want to surprise his family with one for Christmas. *American Bandstand* was just coming on, so Anita turned the dial of the impressive Philco pedestal model with a twenty-one-inch screen to Channel 7 so Joe could imagine the TV in his living room. Anita was thinking of two things at once: how surprised Rose Krazinski would be to have the TV set she was wishing for, and her own son Sal, who just the other afternoon, after school, she had caught in their living room doing slow dance steps to music on *American Bandstand*. The song that was playing was "To Know Him Is to Love Him." At thirteen, Sal was just starting to become interested in girls.

"Anita!" her husband, Vince, called. She looked up to see him running across the store, weaving his stout body between pieces of furniture, rushing toward her. Her first thought was, *What am I doing wrong? Vince is going to take over with Joe. He wants me to be more aggressive, but I just can't do that.* To her, sales was a way of helping their neighbors better themselves.

To her husband, sales was their livelihood. *Can't argue that,* she knew, but she could only be herself.

"There's a fire . . . at the school!" Vince cried when she was within earshot. "Anita, we gotta get over there. Sal and Alice are there and we gotta get them out." Within seconds they agreed that Joe Krazinski would hurry the other customers out of the store and lock up for them. Vince gunned the motor of their Plymouth sedan and took off toward Our Lady of the Angels, in what should have been a five-minute drive had they been able to move in traffic. In frustration they left their car in a loading zone outside the A&P and ran toward the school.

They found Alice frightened but safe in the church along with hundreds of other kids, but there was no sign of Sal— not in the mobs gathered outside, not on the path he took home up Chicago Avenue. With their daughter in tow, they raced back to their car and sped home, frantically weaving between ambulances, fire trucks, buses, and automobiles as quickly as they could. At home they started calling hospitals. Sal was at Saint Anne's.

———

"I'm OK, Mom," was the first thing Sal said when he saw his parents at his bedside. But he wasn't OK. Sal was the kind of kid who never wanted to worry his folks. He figured that Alice, the wildcard of the family with her risk-taking nature, was enough for his parents to handle. As a big brother he saw it as his responsibility to stop her when she tried to leap a picket fence, to hold her back from eating a tub of margarine as if it were ice cream, to keep her from setting fire to the kitchen when she claimed she could pop TV Time popcorn on her own.

Now it was Sal who needed protection.

Earlier, he had caught a look at himself in the mirror facing his bed, and he cried in shock at what he saw—a swollen and blistered face that looked twice its size, nothing like the face he was used to, and ears like barbecued potato chips with bites taken out. He could see his blistered scalp showing through the few tufts of charred hair that remained on his head. He thought he looked like a monster in a horror movie, and he smelled even worse. "Oh, Jesus . . . No!" he'd screamed. "No!"

Seeing his reaction, the nurse lifted the mirror off the wall and slipped it behind a dresser. "It will get better, much better, Sal. I promise you."

He hadn't wanted his parents to see him that way.

It wasn't any ordinary bed they put him in. They carefully laid him in a Stryker unit, a canvas sling that hung between two six-foot-tall circular frames that looked like giant wheels. The wheels were set into a circular track, and another sling above him could be lowered onto his body, allowing them to rotate the wheels and carefully turn him onto his stomach like a pancake without painfully lifting and moving him.

He looked down at his burnt arms and hands, raw as uncooked meat. In the emergency room downstairs they had already cleaned his arms and legs of blackened skin and dead tissue. "Aren't you going to bandage me up?" he managed to ask through the pain. His nurse's nameplate said "Miss Wilson."

"No, honey. We treat burns with the exposure method," she explained. "We've found that if we dress the burns, the likelihood of infection is greater." (Sal would learn later from Dr. Louis Dvonch, a kindly surgeon he'd taken a liking to, that the exposure method was introduced about ten years earlier in Edinburgh, Scotland, and pioneered at the Brooke

Army Medical Center in Texas, probably the leading burn center in the country.)

"For now, young man, you're going to have to lie naked on a sterile sheet with these sheets covering you." Miss Wilson gestured to the tent of sheets spread over the frame's steel bars. If you get too chilly, we can toss an electric blanket over the frame. We've got to let nature take its course as the burns heal. Thick scabs will form, which will be a natural barrier to bacteria. We'll be turning you every two hours."

"Am I going to look like this forever?"

"No, Sal, no. In a while we'll do skin graft operations to replace the burned areas with fresh skin."

"Where are they gonna get the skin?" he struggled to ask.

"From other parts of your body, honey, but we'll talk about that later. For now you must rest. We've given you a sedative, and we've got you on a drip of antibiotics and plasma," she said, gesturing to an IV rack beside the Stryker frame. "I'll be in every few minutes to check your temperature and adjust your medications."

"How many operations will I need?"

"The doctors will determine that, Sal. Rest now."

"OK."

Now with his parents beside him—both masked and gowned—Sal had no choice but to let them see his burnt face and body. "Thirty-five percent burns," he'd heard a doctor down in the emergency room say. *I'm the son they're going to have to look at for a long time, so they better get used to it, and I better get used to it too*, he thought.

His mother gasped at the sight of him.

His father looked away and wiped his eyes.

"Alice. Where's Alice?" Sal asked groggily.

"She's with a nun downstairs who is taking care of a lot of children who've come with their parents," his mother said.

"They have a room where they're feeding them cookies, which should keep her happy," his dad said, having regained his composure. "They have Oreos and those chocolate graham cracker cookies she likes, and I think those windmills." Like always, Vince Martinelli tried to fill uncomfortable moments with a lot of extra conversation.

Sal tried to smile, but it hurt too much.

His mom was staring at his ears. "Oh my God, why? My baby," she said. "I want to hug you, but I can't touch you." She waved her arms helplessly. His eyes were like slits and he was struggling to keep them open. "Try to sleep now, Salvador." Her voice cracked.

"Thanks, Ma. I love you."

His father tapped the bed frame. "Whatever you need, son . . . soda, ice cream, books . . . we'll be sure you get it. I'm going to make sure you have a TV in your room tomorrow. We'll deliver a portable unit from the store and sets for the other kids as well . . . "

"Come on, Vince. Sal needs to rest."

Vince took a step toward the door, following Anita, but then turned back. "The nurse, that pretty one there," he said, pointing to the woman entering the room, "is going to take good care of you, and we'll be back to check on you after we see how Alice is doing downstairs . . . with the cookies . . . and with the nuns."

"Come on, Vince."

Sal couldn't turn his head toward the door to see them leave. His lids felt heavy and he closed his eyes. "Bye, Pa."

17

Three days after the fire, a conclave of shaken prelates—Archbishop Albert G. Meyer, head of the Archdiocese of Chicago; Monsignor William McManus, superintendent of the archdiocese's Catholic schools; and OLA's Monsignor Joseph Cussen—strode soberly into the archbishop's living room, a rather unadorned space considering the opulence of the archbishop's mansion, a fortresslike residence near Lake Michigan on Chicago's Gold Coast. Trailing at their heels was the most essential guest of the evening, the archdiocese's attorney, Cornelius J. Harrington Jr.

Archbishop Meyer had initiated the meeting, summoning Harrington into this esteemed group to advise them on the Church's liability regarding the fire. Although each man's instincts told him it was inappropriate and even callous to discuss their financial and legal obligations so soon after such a tragedy, his business sense forced him to face the fact that the Catholic Church could be held liable for the deaths of eighty-seven human beings, with the count likely to rise.

They took seats on a sofa and in upholstered chairs beneath four decorative wood carvings on the wall of the Four

Evangelists—Matthew, Mark, Luke, and John, the recorders of Jesus's message. Harrington caught the irony and hoped he could influence the priests to proceed with the good judgment exerted by their biblical forefathers. Across from their intimate seating area was a clean-swept fireplace (one of six in the mansion) that under normal circumstances would have cradled a blazing fire for warmth and ambiance. In a nook near the windows, which overlooked a sprawling lawn and fountain now encrusted with snow glittering under the moonlight, was a graceful Steinway grand piano finished in gleaming ebony. Tonight the fireplace stood cold, deliberately ignored by the men. Tonight there was no music.

The three priests Harrington faced were raw with emotion for the families who lost children, the kids who lost sisters and brothers, the nuns who lost peers, a neighborhood writhing in pain, and the people of Chicago, who were all in mourning. Already one Chicago newspaper had referred to December 1 as "The Day Chicago Wept."

"Thank you for agreeing to meet so soon," Harrington began, "and thank you, Archbishop Meyer, for opening your home to us. I am sure you all have many other tasks to tend to, all of them urgent and unpleasant." He looked at the priests' sorrowful faces in turn. "But this meeting is important, and I hope it shouldn't take too long."

Archbishop Albert Meyer appeared dazed. At fifty-five-years old, this tall, reserved scholar and teacher had just assumed his position in November, having come to Chicago from Milwaukee. He'd barely had time to learn his way around the archdiocese, much less around the eight-thousand-square-foot mansion that came with the job. His mind was still reeling with images from the night of the fire. At Saint Anne's Hospital he had moved from gurney to gurney facing children burned beyond recognition, blessing them; in the morgue he'd consoled parents nearly comatose with grief. Now he sat, knees crossed, in a chair across from Harrington; the other two priests sat adjacent to him on the sofa to talk business.

"Thank you for coming," the archbishop reiterated, turning to Monsignor Joseph Cussen. "Especially you, Joe, who have lost many in your flock." Ashen and weary, Monsignor Cussen drummed his fingers nervously on his knee and mumbled almost inaudibly, "I don't know what to do. There's nothing I can do." He fixed his eyes on a painting above the fireplace, a Crucifixion scene: Mary clutching her Son's feet at the base of the cross. His thoughts flashed back to the night of the fire at the Cook County morgue, where he, Father Joe Ognibene, and others had tried to comfort parents. That night, the morgue was their personal Calvary. As if he were a spirit hovering above the room, he saw himself trailing behind Cook County coroner Walter McCarron and a procession of stooped and dazed parents, stepping between rows of small bodies covered with white sheets, helping them locate their children.

He felt himself shiver as McCarron pulled a sheet back to reveal a badly burnt young girl. "My God, no, it's Mary," sobbed the eighth grader's mother. "That's her crucifix around her neck." He watched himself lead the sobbing woman out of the room, sit with her, hold her icy hands until she was joined by her husband. The right words did not come to him.

In the anteroom, he saw himself watching other parents, broken and slumped over one another for support, as they identified their children by numbered objects laid on a long table: a necklace, a red ruby ring, a Cinderella wristwatch, a stocking, a saddle shoe.

"This is Sister Canice's medal, I know it is," said a bereft Sister Andrienne, pressing the oval Miraculous Medal to her heart. "I know because I gave it to her." The monsignor saw himself stop and wrap his arms around the small, grief-shaken nun. Her bones felt like a bundle of broken sticks in his arms. In a feeble voice she whispered the inscription on the medal, a common Catholic prayer: "*O Mary conceived without sin, pray for us who have recourse to thee.*"

Like all priests, Monsignor Cussen had studied eschatology in the seminary, that branch of theology concerned with death, judgment, and the final destiny of the soul. But that was theory, and although on an individual basis he could apply it in consoling the bereaved, this tragedy was different. These were classrooms full of innocent children. Why would God want them all at once? He knew he would never find the words, or the rationale behind the words, to explain God's intentions to the parents scraped raw with grief.

He saw himself rejoin the grisly procession in the morgue. "Yes, that's our Nancy," sobbed the brother-in-law of parishioner Tony Pilas, a firefighter who had fought the fire and was still searching the hospitals for his daughter. "Nancy laced her shoes backwards. She always looped the bows near her toes," sobbed the girl's uncle.

"Joe!" the archbishop said forcefully, kindly, bringing Monsignor Cussen back into the moment.

He looked up and nodded respectfully.

Cussen had barely eaten or slept since the fire. Those around him were concerned for his well-being. That first night after returning from the morgue he was so agitated that he couldn't calm down. In desperation, his fellow priests opened a bottle of Jim Beam and poured him several drinks that had little effect, until finally he fell into a drunken, nightmarish sleep, tormented by the sights and memory-stench of burnt, screaming children, and the stricken faces of his parishioners.

Every day thereafter, at the risk of his own health, he had been working to comfort parents, kids, his fellow priests, and the nuns, and second-guessing himself over what he could have done to prevent such a disaster.

Archbishop Meyer looked away from Monsignor Cussen. "So Cornelius, what advice do you have to give us?"

Six eyes focused on their attorney, a bright young man with the prestigious law firm of Kirkland, Ellis, Hodson, Chaffetz & Masters.

"First of all," Harrington began, "let's review what we know. We know that the fire most likely started in the northeast stairwell, outside the boiler room. I've been in touch with Sergeant Drew Brown of the police arson squad, who tried to interview the janitor, Jim Raymond, at Garfield Hospital. Brown didn't get very far with him. The poor fellow vomited and they had to leave him alone. Couldn't sign a statement. Brown also spoke to the boys who were dumping wastepaper baskets in the boiler room when Raymond discovered the fire. The boys said Raymond shouted for them to get out and call the fire department. They didn't see him leave the hallway. They thought he stayed back to fight the fire."

Harrington adjusted a small stack of papers on his lap.

"The police department's youth bureau is now reviewing written questionnaires from the students on the second floor who survived, supplemented by a number of face-to-face interviews. With the consent of their parents, kids were questioned about who saw smokers in that hallway prior to the fire, which children were out of their classrooms at that time, which boys were assigned responsibility for carrying the trash to the boiler room, and which children might be most likely to have started the blaze."

"Do they think it was arson?" Monsignor McManus asked.

"We don't know yet."

The men nodded.

"Jim Raymond had nothing to do with it. I can vouch for him. He has five kids in our school," Monsignor Cussen said emphatically.

"If he's responsible, it could have been an accident," McManus chimed in.

Monsignor Cussen closed his eyes as if to shut out that possibility.

"Here is a written report of what we know." Harrington passed out a thin report to each of the priests. Of course, this is preliminary, and it's being fleshed out as we speak."

"Let me remind you that this information is confidential. On page five you'll see that twenty-one boys have acknowledged smoking in the school at some time. None admitted smoking at the time of the fire. Their interviews are printed verbatim."

"Jim Raymond has seen smokers in the stairwells and always shooed them off," Monsignor Cussen added.

"What is of concern is that when Sergeant Brown asked for names of children who may have started the fire, one young boy's name came up repeatedly. You'll see his name at the bottom of the page along with his most recent school photo."

Monsignor Cussen squinted at the black-and-white photograph of the chubby boy with blond hair, crooked teeth, and eyeglasses. It was taken just a month ago, when the kids had lined up in the corridor by class to have their individual photos taken. "The little bastard. If he did it, I'll kill him."

Archbishop Meyer and Monsignor McManus looked up over their eyeglasses, surprised at their cohort's outburst.

"That's my point," Harrington interjected. "There are a lot of people who might want to kill him."

"What I meant to say," said Monsignor Cussen, trying to be more tactful, "is that this is a troubled lad. He comes from a broken home. He's been a handful to the nuns."

"That may be so. But here's my concern, one which I am sure you'll share," Harrington continued. "If that child's name gets out, and stories of his deeds become public knowledge, you could be accused of negligence in supervising one of your students—allowing him to walk freely in the hallways, getting into mischief with matches. According to one boy interviewed, this particular child has the reputation of being the neighborhood firebug, setting fires in mailboxes and so forth. That's covered on page six of your report."

The priests nervously flipped pages and nodded in agreement.

"There may be more deaths given the poor condition of the ninety more children in the hospitals. There may be lawsuits—wrongful death and personal injury. The parents could contend that they paid tuition to have their children cared for—intellectually, spiritually, and physically—and that this obligation was not met."

"Those parents trusted us," Monsignor Cussen said. "I can't imagine any of our families suing us." He rubbed his bloodshot eyes. "They won't blame us."

"You can't count on it," Harrington said firmly. "Today I warned the chancery office about the possible lawsuits stemming from the fire, and now it is my obligation to warn you personally. It is important to say as little as possible. Yes, of course, offer your condolences and your prayers, your tears. Be examples by your own courage, but please, no mention of names, no mention of trash accumulating in the stairways or overcrowding, or fire code deficiencies, which is a factor in many Catholic schools. It is correct that you were grandfathered in under the 1905 fire code, which didn't demand enclosed staircases, fire doors, a direct line to the fire department, and so on, so you are legally safe. You just passed a fire inspection on October 7 with no apparent violations. But I think you will agree that many of your classrooms are overcrowded. The 1949 fire code says that classrooms that have movable furniture, such as kindergartens, must allow twenty square feet per child, but that classrooms that have desks and seats attached to the floor can have as many students as you want, as long as you can fit the desks in the rooms. You're aware that many of your classrooms had up to sixty-five students, plus the teacher. Although you're legally clear on this one, you have to ask yourselves if your classrooms were actually safe. Parents will be asking you these questions."

"It was just a matter of time before something like this happened, if not to us, somewhere else," Monsignor Cussen stated glumly.

"You know I've been a stickler for safety in our schools," chimed in Monsignor McManus, his Irish brogue lilting defensively. McManus was in charge of Chicago's Catholic school system, with 270,299 elementary and high school students. He had only been on the job a year and was already scrambling to correct many of the safety issues he'd identified as problems, urging pastors to pay attention to matters overlooked by his predecessors. *I could get fired for having this happen under my tenure*, he thought. *They could transfer me to some godforsaken parish in God knows where.*

"I know, Monsignor, but somehow that doesn't count, now that the worst has happened," Harrington said.

"I say we want this to be seen as an accident, not arson, if it gets to that, and that we encourage our families, with the grace of God, to move on." Monsignor McManus said.

"Exactly," Harrington agreed. "It won't serve you well to point fingers and pass blame."

Archbishop Meyer closed the report and set it on the coffee table in front of him. "I don't want that young boy or any one of our kids to bear the stain of being responsible for all those deaths. Let's keep it under wraps, for his sake and for ours. There's going to be an inquest next week, a blue ribbon panel appointed by Mayor Daley, and I'll make my concerns known to the coroner's office. I'll also be in personal contact with folks at the mayor's office. Mayor Daley is pretty shaken up over all this, as you can imagine. We saw him break down in the morgue. It was all over TV."

"All this doesn't look good for him politically either," Harrington interjected. "Dick Daley has only been in office three years and he likes being mayor. If a scandal should erupt over the condition of Chicago schools, he's in deep political trouble. But I'll let *his* attorneys handle that."

Archbishop Meyer raised his hand. "Also, get the word out to our Catholic attorneys that none of them should accept any lawsuits that arise from this."

"I agree," Monsignor McManus said. "Will do."

Monsignor Cussen sat silently, looking distracted.

"Joe?" McManus asked, moving to the edge of the sofa and looking at him, "Are you OK?"

"Oh yes, of course. I'll support you as well," he said.

"Joe, you have a big job to do in your community, with your people, and closer to home with your nuns. You never know what's going to come out of the mouths of those women," Monsignor McManus said. "They've been traumatized, some of the nuns are hysterical, Sister Florence is being medicated, and they're capable of saying anything, those women, so talk to them, won't you? This was an accident and we've got to move on."

"I know," Monsignor Cussen replied.

———

What Monsignor McManus didn't know then was that a gaggle of reporters would gather at the convent for an impromptu press conference the following week, and even though the nuns, by then, had been instructed to remain silent, they welcomed the newsmen inside and cordially answered their questions, with Sister Davidis being their spokeswoman.

A reporter asked her, "Sister, do you have any idea of how the fire started?"

"I have no idea whatsoever," she said.

Another asked, "I understand there was a pile of wastepaper stored in the stairwell, and—"

She stopped him midquestion and responded with authority: "No, our principal, Sister Florence, kept the school immaculate. I know of no case where wastepaper was stored under the stairwell."

Monsignor McManus would have a fit upon hearing about the press conference, blaming it on Monsignor Cussen, but he'd later calm down when he's learn that "those women" defended the party line perfectly and with grace.

———

Just before his guests left the mansion that evening, Archbishop Meyer also brought up another issue the prelates would have to address soon enough: reparation and compensation. "I know we've agreed to pay all funeral expenses and hospital bills over the amount insurance covers, and I know that we may be getting ahead of ourselves with this, but I think we should also be prepared to settle any suits that are filed, and in addition, we should compensate every family whose child has died or was injured, regardless if they file a suit or not. Donations are coming in to Catholic Charities from all over the world . . . already we have a bushel of money. We'll have to establish a procedure for dispensing the funds."

"I understand. We'll work with you on that soon," Harrington replied.

In conclusion, the men bowed their heads in a prayer led by the archbishop, and then dispersed through the grand mahogany foyer they had entered ninety minutes earlier, somberly filing past oil paintings of former archbishops and one of the new pope, John XXIII. As they passed by a fragrant pine tree decorated with red and green bubble lights and handmade children's ornaments—stars, snowflakes, brightly-colored holy pictures of the Baby Jesus—Monsignor Cussen couldn't help but notice the crèche beneath the tree's lowest branches and the placid smiles on the faces of Joseph and Mary, so unlike the agonized countenances of his parishioners.

Outdoors, in the chilling press of the wind blasting in from Lake Michigan, they hung on to their coats and hats and folded themselves into their freezing cars.

18

Today they're saying a Mass for twenty-seven of the dead children at the cavernous Illinois National Guard Armory. They're not calling it a Requiem Mass. They're calling it a White Mass, a Mass usually reserved for popes and cardinals. Seven thousand people, sitting on the main level and in bleachers, are attending.

I watch the service trembling sheepishly from six candles set upon a makeshift altar on a stage, three on either side of a giant crucifix. I've been at countless funerals, but none as grim as this one. As a reminder of my rampage just four days ago, I am forced to look down at twenty-seven closed caskets lined up before me, each draped with white linen, each a reminder of the hell I inflicted on so many.

Not an eye is dry. Archbishop Meyer, Monsignor Cussen, and Cardinal Francis Spellman from New York step about the altar reciting the Latin words of the Mass like three men in a trance. I desperately want to be snuffed out, extinguished, doused, but I am forced to flicker high above the throngs and witness their despondence, the defeat and the despair that permeates every speck of air, every breath, every tear, every word. Bishop

Raymond Hillinger from Rockford preaches to the people about me: *"The fire was ghastly. It was hideous. It was horrendous. But God is not mocked. He does not allow disasters to happen without reason. The heavenly Father in His providence governs all things . . . He will draw untold good from the purgatory of this week. From the ashes love, phoenixlike, has risen . . ."*

A choir sings the haunting "Dies Irae," a chant I'd heard millions of times about the good guys rising up to heaven at the Last Judgment, the sinners banished to hell to burn forever. I am forced to look at each tearful, blotched, numb face present in the vast armory. Belinda isn't there, and neither is the kid.

After the service, from the tips of countless cigarettes, I catch many a good look at the front page of the *Chicago American*, the four-star final edition published that afternoon. It's flying off the newsstands by the hundreds of thousands. Everyone's reading it—on buses, in bars, after family dinners. The one-inch headline reads, CHICAGO MOURNS. Then below, filling the entire front page, are the photos of seventy of my young victims—some are wearing their school uniforms smiling into the camera; some are wearing their Communion dresses, veils, and suits. Chilling, even to me. The text beneath the headline reads, "The kids aren't dead . . . They've graduated to a state of perfect joy that never ends. That's the thought their faith teaches, the thought that consoles their relatives and friends . . ."

Contained and docile, I am humbled by the unwavering faith of these good people, from whom, by my gluttony, I have snatched away everything.

The rest of the children I took are being buried in private services.

I will attend them all.

———

Let me also mention another service, that of the three nuns whose lives I took. It was held at Our Lady of the Angels Church before a crowd of so many nuns and parishioners, police officers and firemen, that loudspeakers had to be set up outside the church for everyone to hear the eulogy. Monsignor McManus, the superintendent of schools, gave the sermon at that Requiem Mass.

"Our three sisters died a magnificent death," he said solemnly. "They knew what to do—pray and save the children—and they did this until their deaths." He said that they "taught, and believed, that all that matters is a happy death . . . and that no lesson was so ever so well taught as their last lesson."

Those poor women had names—family names and religious names—but oddly enough he never mentioned them—because, he said, "they never would have wanted it," which may or may not be true.

But I faced them as they took their last breaths. I saw the horror in their eyes as I sucked their lives and dreams away. The least I can do now is acknowledge that they were human beings—daughters, sisters, granddaughters—who dedicated their lives to educating other people's children. They are:

Sister Mary Clare Therese, BVM (Eloise Carmelite Champagne), whom I called Sunshine. She was twenty-seven.

Sister Mary St. Canice, BVM (Mary Ellen Lyng), who was forty-four. I remember her telling the children about Dante's Inferno and the nine circles of hell, a topic that resonated with me.

And Sister Mary Seraphica, BVM (Anne Virginia Kelley), who was forty-three. She tried to keep her children calm as I raged.

19

On December 10, Jim Raymond, accompanied by his attorney, John Hogan, and a bevy of press photographers, walked briskly into the auditorium in the Prudential Building. Built three years earlier on prime property overlooking Lake Michigan, the fifty-floor skyscraper was the shining star in a city revered for its magnificent architecture. The management of the imposing building donated use of the first-floor auditorium, off the sprawling, fluorescently lit lobby, for the coroner's inquest into the fire—an inquest that would last six days.

With his arm wrapped in bandages and his head patched where the firefighter hit him, Jim, dressed in his church clothes, a neat dark suit, and a slim dark tie, was nowhere near physically or emotionally healed from the fire. He was scheduled to be a key witness, but he was unsure when he would be put on the witness stand. No matter; he was bent on attending every session and cooperating fully to help identify the cause of the fire.

He was not alone in this objective. When he arrived, the huge auditorium was filled to capacity with hundreds of journalists, cameramen, parents, firefighters, nuns in their stiff black habits, police officers, clergy, and members of the blue-ribbon panel of businessmen, engineers, insurance executives, and architects handpicked by the coroner's office to question witnesses. There was no shortage of attorneys present to represent every interest: the Church, firefighters, witnesses, police. The room was charged with anticipation, the looks on people's faces businesslike and severe.

Jim, a bundle of nerves, and his attorney took seats on metal folding chairs near the front.

Coroner Walter McCarron opened the first session by stating that the purpose of the inquest was to determine the cause of the deaths and the origin of the fire, and to explore possible culpability. A gentleman in his fifties, with sparse, slicked-back dark hair and a penchant for wearing bow ties, McCarron had been elected Cook County coroner in 1952. He had been present at the denouement of many disasters, but this was by far the worst. It had been his responsibility, along with his examiners, to preside at the Cook County morgue the night of the fire, walking through row after row of small bodies covered with white sheets, examining their remains and identifying the dead.

Now this pallid-complexioned man, with eyeglasses pressing into his fleshy cheeks, looked every bit as shaken as he did in the morgue.

"This is a dark page in Chicago's history. I hope that something may come out of this to save lives in the future, not only in Chicago but throughout the country, because I think the eyes of the nation are watching . . ."

As Jim sat clutching his hands, McCarron called several parents to the microphone to establish that deaths had indeed occurred:

After verifying the name and age of her ten-year-old son, Joseph, Della Maffiola opened her heart to the jury. "We should just hope and pray that it would never, never, never happen again. It happened, but let us hope it won't happen again."

"Thank you, madam," McCarron said.

Olga Wisz, the mother of ten-year-old Wayne, looked at the audience with tears rolling down her cheeks onto the narrow collar of her cloth coat and pleaded, "Please, God, make the schools safe."

Jim looked around the auditorium. If he could have captured the anguish etched into the faces of the parents and relatives in the audience, he could have carved a trail of pain to hell and back. It hurt to think of the kind of week these good people had endured—full of wakes, funerals, eulogies, news stories, TV coverage, phone calls from reporters—to keep them dazed and numbed with grief.

It had been a hellish week for Jim as well. In absence of complete information, the news media, eager for answers, repeated what they knew about the fire in an unending barrage of grisly stories and photographs. Chicago's four largest newspapers—the *Chicago Tribune*, the *Chicago Daily News*, the *Chicago Sun-Times*, and the *Chicago American*—tried to fit together a thousand-piece jigsaw puzzle that still had half its pieces missing. And as happens in such a vacuum, gossip and speculation often overtook fact. Ten days ago Jim was a simple neighborhood guy just doing his job. Now, because of the proximity of his boiler room to the place the fire started and the fact that he was the one to discover it, he was held suspect.

But most damaging to Jim was an accusation made by a fire captain from the Austin neighborhood, who determined that Jim was guilty of "sloppy housekeeping." In a statement the firefighter made to a newsman, which was printed in thousands of newspapers around the world, Jim was accused of shirking his responsibility to keep the school tidy. Hundreds of thousands of people had read this story, and the words "sloppy housekeeping" stuck to Jim's psyche like barnacles to the bottom of a boat.

Looking for a quick scapegoat, people—even some of his most loyal neighbors—began pointing fingers at Jim, so that he was afraid to leave the house, hesitant to take a phone call. In a week's time he had received three death threats, which necessitated police protection for him and his family.

The memory of one of these calls in particular made Jim shudder so audibly that John Hogan leaned into him and whispered, "Are you fit to testify?"

"Yeah," he whispered back, but he couldn't shake the memory.

He had been in his kitchen, downing a beer. Ann was stirring a pot of split pea soup—a healthy meal for the nine of them, especially for Jim and their son, John, who had just been released from Franklin Boulevard Hospital and was recovering from the hip and back injuries he sustained after jumping from the window of his classroom. Any other time the aroma of steaming split peas and ham would have had Jim salivating, but that afternoon any thought of food nauseated him . . .

————

I watched this family scene from the ring of light around the burner of Ann's gas stove. Poor Jim looked like hell. His face was unshaven and he was wearing the same plaid flannel shirt he'd worn for the past week. It hung loosely on his shrink-ing frame. He was a far cry from the cheerful man who used to feed me—stumbling around, repeating himself, reliving that afternoon over and over in his mind. Poor Ann. She was stirring the steaming soup. She listened to him, nodded, commiserated. All day she'd been trying to keep the kids busy so they wouldn't overhear their conversations and take on their dad's pain. Yet it was getting to her. She closed her eyes and breathed deeply. She was exhausted.

———

The phone rang and Mary Kay answered it.

"For you, Pop," she sang out. Jim lifted himself from his chair and stumbled out to the nook in the hallway where the black telephone sat, its receiver off the cradle waiting for him next to an ashtray.

"Hello."

A man's voice barked, "Jim Raymond, you murderer! Almost a hundred kids are dead because of you and your sloppy housekeeping. Watch your back, buster. If me and my guys don't plug a hole in you first, someone else will."

Then the line went dead. And something died in Jim as well.

Jim would remember every word of that call, and the buzz-ing of the phone line that followed. The threatening voice, the caller's venom, and the buzz that ensued reverberated in his mind for the rest of his life.

God, don't they know I saved some lives. I had nothing to do with it. Ya think I'd set fire to a school five of my own kids went to? I tried to keep the place clean, God knows I tried. But I'm one guy. They had me running from floor to floor, convent to chapel, chapel to church, down the block to the little kids' annex, and then to the rectory:

"Mr. Raymond, there's a lightbulb out . . . would you please . . ."

"Jim, don't forget to salt the crosswalks."

"Mr. Raymond, make sure the clothes for the clothing drive are ready for pickup . . ."

"Check the oil burners in the annex, please."

"Feed the boiler . . ."

"Put up the Christmas decorations . . ."

"Burn the papers in the incinerator and shovel out the ashes . . ."

"Mop the floors . . ."

"Clean the toilets . . ."

"A kid vomited in church. Jim, if you wouldn't mind . . ."

"Make sure the boys aren't smoking in the basement . . ."

"Dump those whiskey bottles from the Thanksgiving Knights of Columbus party . . . No, save them. We can make candleholders out of them for the next party . . ."

"Mr. Raymond, when you have time, do you think you could cover this little table with this pretty tile? I could use it in the classroom."

"Put this on your list, Mr. Raymond. In June, let's remember to varnish the banisters."

Who do they think I am? Superman?

At Ann's suggestion, Jim telephoned his old friend John Hogan, an attorney. Not that they felt he needed a lawyer, but they wanted John's advice on taking a lie detector test to clear his name. John thought it was a fine idea and announced it to the media—and, of course, the media glommed onto the news and it made it a headline in all four top Chicago papers. Then upon talking to Jim further and observing his

fragile emotional condition, Hogan reversed his recommenda-
tion, stating that Jim was too traumatized by the fire and too
injured from a serious head wound and blood loss to take a
polygraph test now, a move that resulted in more accusations
lobbed his way:

"The guy's hiding something..."

"He knows more than he's saying... "

"If he wants to cooperate, why is he suddenly so reticent?"

"He was probably drunk. The guy likes his beer, ya know."

Now Jim sat waiting to tell his story to a panel of professional men who intimidated him, parents raw with grief trying
to process the nightmare, and a throng of journalists and press
photographers who had the power to portray him as they
chose to through well-crafted words and muddy gray photographs that would surely capture him as he saw himself—a
gaunt, nervous, and uneducated janitor who might not have
done enough.

Next, Coroner McCarron called firefighter Stanley Wojnicki
of Engine Company 85 to the microphone. Stan clutched his
notes with trembling hands.

"Just relax and tell us what happened," McCarron said.

Nervously eyeing the panel, Stan recounted his company's
role in attacking the fire—being the first to arrive at the scene,
calling the main office for more help, getting water on the
fire, later hooking hoses up to the snorkel. Then Stan set his
notes aside, looked deep into the audience, and in a voice
cracking with emotion, addressed the parents with words that
had run through his mind for the past week. "I want to say
this. There would have been more deaths if we hadn't acted
as fast as we did with the help of civilians and nuns and
parents... We did the best we could."

The jury's next questions were directed to Sergeant Drew Brown of the Chicago Police bomb and arson unit. A tenacious arson detective, rated by the fire insurance underwriters as one of the best in the nation, Brown had been probing the wreckage nonstop, searching for clues. A balding detective with deep-set eyes and direct manner, Brown had already interviewed hundreds of students about their whereabouts that day, what and whom they saw, what they'd heard. Now, facing the panel and the audience, he confirmed that the fire had started somewhere at the base of the northeast stairwell, but he was unable to report its cause. "As of now we have no evidence that the fire was set, but we have not ruled out the possibility of arson."

Jim sat stiffly in his chair listening to Brown. A few days ago he had learned that Brown tried to interview him at Garfield Hospital the night of the fire. But now Jim had no recollection of it. With this determined man sitting so close to him, eyeing him as if he were keeping a dark secret, Jim felt threatened, but mostly he felt embarrassed for his inability to be of any help when Brown visited him in the hospital. Now he felt even more inadequate.

Coroner McCarron called Sister Florence to the microphone next. On the day of the fire Sister Florence was not in the principal's office. She was substituting for a sick third-grade teacher on the first floor.

"I understand Sister Florence is under medication and sick," McCarron told the panel in introducing her. "We will have to bear with her."

Dressed in her severe black habit and looking as gaunt as many of the mothers in the audience, Sister Florence made her way to the microphone.

"Will you tell us what you know about the fire?"

"Yes, sir." Her voice cracked.

"Will you talk just a little bit louder, please, Sister?"

Sister nodded and moved forward a few inches. "The day was normal and then sometime between two thirty and a quarter of three the fire bell rang. The children ran out normally from my room and from the rooms on the first floor. They went outside normally."

"Then what did you do, Sister?"

"I . . . went back . . ." Her voice faded.

"Speak into the microphone, Sister."

"I retraced my steps back into the school and up to the second floor. Smoke and flames were at my feet. There were kids in the hallway . . . their faces were black with smoke and I told them to get out. Then I ran into the street and the firefighters were there with their hoses and ladders."

"Thank you, Sister."

"Are there any other questions for Sister Florence?"

In deference to the nun and her fragility, none of the panel members had further inquiries.

———

It was not until midafternoon of the second day that Jim Raymond heard Coroner McCarron call his name.

With trepidation Jim walked up to the microphone. McCarron, flanked by his jury of interrogators, faced him, studying him suspiciously over his large eyeglasses. He lifted a half-smoked Philip Morris from his ashtray, took a quick drag, and returned it to a glass ashtray already heaped with butts.

In answer to the first question, Jim said he'd been at the school for thirteen years, and he explained his duties. He said it was about 2:30 or so when he was returning to the boiler room after checking an oil burner in another building and he saw fire and smoke coming from the basement window outside the boiler room. He said he ran into the rectory and yelled to the housekeeper to call the fire department.

"Did you see her make the call?" McCarron asked.

"No, sir. I ran back to the boiler room, where I saw two kids who had just emptied baskets there. I told them to drop their baskets and get out of there."

"Speak up, please sir," McCarron said.

"Yes, sir," Jim said.

"Then what did you do? Did you try to extinguish it yourself?"

"I may have, I don't remember. It all happened so quickly and I may be confused on exactly what I said or did when. The fire was getting so big there was nothing I could do. I didn't have nothing with me. Only my two hands. I was worried mostly about getting the kids out of the school."

"So what did you do then?"

"I ran upstairs and smashed a window with a flashlight. That's when I cut my wrist." Jim rubbed the bandages on his wrist, partially covered by the cuff of his shirt. "I led the kids and the nun from room 207 down the fire escape. I had the keys to the door and got it open. By that time I was full of smoke and losing a lot of blood. I came down the stairs, tried to go back into the school, and I got conked on the head and ended up in the hospital."

Another juror, a no-nonsense representative of the National Fire Protection Association, took over: "As far as you know, Mr. Raymond, where did the fire start?"

"As far as I know, it started in the back stairway. That's where I saw the red window. Nothing touched the boiler room at all."

"Was there any material stored in the stairwell?"

"An empty drum of calcium chloride to melt the ice on our streets and sidewalks. I didn't see newspapers there, but I wasn't in that stairway that day until I saw the fire."

———

I'm listening to Jim's testimony from an ashtray and I want to remind Jim that there was a whole lot more stored in that space. But I give him a break. He's not thinking right and he's choosing his words, at Hogan's advice, to protect himself and the Church. He's also loosey-goosey on the timing—which is understandable, 'cause he was such a wreck with me in his face. Now he's fighting for his life, fighting the vultures looking for a scapegoat. Those guys are all too willing to pin it on him.

———

"Are kids typically in that stairway?

"No. The children use the other doors. The door leading outside in that stairway is seldom used because it leads into the alley and it's too dangerous for the kids to leave the building that way, with cars and garbage trucks speeding down the alley, so that door is kept locked. The kids use the other doors."

"Do kids ever loiter in that stairway? Did boys ever go down there to smoke?

"Once I found cigarette butts there."

"Did you report it?"

"No."

———

Jim is fibbing now . . . telling a white lie . . . definitely minimiz-
ing the situation. I've seen at least twenty boys smoking down
there in the past couple of months, and I'm sure, because the
area is his domain, he saw more than one. These are twelve-
and thirteen-year-old boys, for heaven's sake, and it's 1958
and these guys smoke because *everyone* smokes. They're mostly
seventh and eighth graders, boys trying to be men, imitating
their fathers, baby-faced kids talking like hard guys.

"I need a smoke before English class. It helps me think."

"Where'd you get those? Steal them from your old man?"

"Yeah. He doesn't count 'em."

"Is anyone coming?"

Also, here's a gossipy tidbit. On the day of the fire I saw
two of these guys smoking in that stairway right before the
afternoon bell rang. I don't know their names because, frankly,
all these guys look alike with their uniform dark pants, white
shirts, and ties. But they're innocent of any wrongdoing. At the
sound of the bell, they extinguished their smokes and stomped
them out on the floor.

————

Sergeant Drew Brown stepped in with more questions for Jim.
He opened his worn briefcase, took out a stack of papers, and
thumbed to the page he was looking for.

"Mr. Raymond, it says here you agreed to take a lie detector test, but then you backed out. If you said you wanted to
cooperate, why are you so reluctant now?"

Raymond's attorney John Hogan answered for him. "My
client will cooperate at the proper time. He isn't ready now.
He suffered a major laceration to his head and was in shock.
He is still having difficulty remembering."

Jim felt a roomful of eyes staring at him, wide eyed, expecting a revelation. He tried to swallow, but his throat was dust dry and he coughed into his handkerchief. Someone slid a glass of water in front of him, and he gulped down the whole thing.

Another juror, Dale Auck, a spindly engineer with glasses and a receding hairline, asked, "Mr. Raymond, do you have an opinion of how the fire started?" Auck was director of the fire protection division of the Federation of Mutual Fire Insurance Companies and had a vested interest in getting answers to this question.

"Well, if you want my opinion," Jim answered, "I think it was started by human hands."

"What do you mean by that?" he asked, brushing the sparse mustache skirting his upper lip.

"There are no electrical devices or heating devices in that stairwell."

"Do you believe someone started this fire?"

"That's my opinion."

"When you say by human hands, does that mean by matches? By cigarettes? What?"

"Well, replied Jim, "whatever a human hand would start a fire with."

———

Over the next four days, Jim sat beside his steadfast attorney listening to more testimony.

Deputy Fire Chief Robert O'Brien of Chicago's Fire Prevention Bureau, who had been a boyhood friend of Mayor Daley, said he didn't know the school was overcrowded and that all he had to go on was the report of the last fire inspection conducted there on October 7, less than two months before the fire. He passed the inspection report out to the jury members. Condition of the premises was marked "Good." "No apparent violations," the inspector had written.

When pressured by juror Dale Auck, O'Brien stated that while the school was not "actually safe" in that it did not comply with the fire ordinance of 1949, it was "legally safe" because, having been built in 1910 and expanded in 1943, it needed only to comply with the code of 1905.

Auck pointed out that after the fire, four electrical defects were found in the boiler room. "Why weren't they reported in the October 7 fire inspection report?"

"That was a job for the city's electrical department," O'Brien replied.

"And what about the overcrowding of the classrooms? Why wasn't that noted in the report?"

"That was the job of the building department. If the inspector believed the building was overcrowded, he would have referred the problem to the building commissioner, George Ramsey."

Until then Jim had never thought too much about the inner workings of the city. But now he saw its bureaucracy in action. Do your job and only your job. Blame the blamer. Sign off on a report you don't believe in and give the school a free pass. Protect the Catholic Church. Protect Mayor Daley and the city he runs at all cost. If your job is a patronage job, don't step out of line or you can lose it.

Damn right that school was overcrowded, he thought. *I could have told you that. I was there every day trying to keep things safe in spite of the overcrowding.*

When Fire Commissioner Robert J. Quinn came to the microphone, a pall of silence spread across the room. Everyone looked to the imposing white-haired man, all spruced up in his naval-style dress uniform—a uniform the firefighters called a "sailor suit"—to provide some inside information into the cause of the fire.

Quinn was already a legend in Chicago, and a hero. During his service in the navy in World War II, he'd been decorated for battling a fire on a tanker loaded with aviation fuel. Applying his naval training to his work as a firefighter, he believed the fire department should be run like a military organization. A tough taskmaster, he subjected his fire recruits to the same physical fitness training he practiced himself. Once, as a young firefighter, he had tossed a two-hundred-pound woman with her clothes on fire over his shoulders and leaped four feet to a neighboring building. This was a feat he expected each of his men to be capable of.

A stickler for regimen and detail, Quinn made a major issue over the time gap between when Raymond said he first discovered the fire around 2:30 and when the fire department was notified at 2:42. What happened during that time period was significant. In a deep, admonishing tone that could be heard without a microphone, he bellowed, "It was a delayed alarm!" He paused long enough to allow his declaration to settle in the minds of the jurors and the audience. "My firemen saved 160 kids in fifteen minutes before the fire flashed over. We could have saved most of the kids if we had just a few extra minutes."

Aware of the accusing eyes of hundreds of parents in the auditorium, Quinn stood to his full height and roared, "We cannot respond until we know there is a fire, and my friends, if you even entertain the thought that my firefighters lollygag in the firehouse after they receive a call, then you don't know a thing about what we do. My men are on call twenty-four hours a day, waiting to jump into their trucks on a fifteen-second notice."

Then he used his time at the microphone to enumerate a number of other problems:

"We were given the wrong location of the fire."

"The iron gate blocked our access."

"The school was grossly overcrowded."

He praised his men for doing a heroic job under the circumstances. "Once we got the alarm, it took us two minutes to get there."

When asked about some of the ladders being too short to reach the second-story windows, Quinn explained that by procedure the fire trucks closest to the fire come out first. Engine 85, under the direction of Lieutenant Wojnicki, arrived in two minutes. His priority was to get water on the fire. Hook and Ladder Truck 35 arrived three minutes later with an arsenal of twenty- to fifty-foot ladders. They were blocked from accessing some of the classrooms by the gate that closed off the courtyard. "My guys threw a thirty-six-foot extension ladder over that damn gate and used another ladder as a battery ram to tear it down."

Almost without taking a breath, he continued. "Let me sum it up. Our main office at city hall is responsible for dispatching all fire equipment. At 2:42, the time we were notified, we sent out five units; by 2:44, eight more; by 2:47, eleven more plus an ambulance and snorkel; by 2:57, eight more—by 2:57, when the roof collapsed and we called it a five-alarm fire, skipping the steps in between. In less than fifteen minutes we rescued 160 kids and nuns," he repeated. "A record for any single fire in Chicago. If we just had a few more minutes . . ." Then, wiping his forehead with his handkerchief, he sat down.

Jim saw Commissioner Quinn's testimony as a personal attack. He felt his face flush when Quinn said the words

"If we just had a few extra minutes . . ." He looked into his lap, couldn't make eye contact with the many parents in the audience whom he had once spoken to every working day of his life, whom he'd teased and slugged beers with in the neighborhood bar and at church events. *If I'd moved faster, run faster, yelled louder, maybe I could have saved their kids.* Those few minutes started with him.

———

After the last hour of the last day of the inquest, as fatigued crowds exited the auditorium, some gathered in the lobby in small groups to button their coats, pull on their galoshes, tighten their scarves around their necks, and dissect the information presented over the past week. Jim wove his way through under the arm of his attorney, overhearing their conversations:

"Sounds like a lot of passing the buck."

"The Church, the city, they're trying to protect themselves rather than find the truth. I heard that one father of a child who died handed a list of his own questions to that foreman of the jury, Roy Tuchbreiter, and you know what Tuchbreiter said to him? He gave him the brush-off and said, 'You don't want to ask anything that will embarrass the archdiocese.' What do you think of that?"

"The janitor wouldn't take a lie detector test. What does that tell you?"

Then slowly and in lugubrious procession, they stepped out into the frigid Lake Michigan air to scurry home. Some would ride rattling subway cars through concrete tunnels. Others would bump away from the glitz of Michigan Avenue in overheated buses with swooshing hydraulic doors, jolting through the lavishly decorated Loop crowded with holiday shoppers, carolers, and Salvation Army bell ringers. On the way they'd pass through the city's gritty industrial ring, its grittier skid row streets, and middle-class ethnic neighborhoods where the soaring steeples of Saint John Cantius, Holy Trinity, and Saint Stanislaus Kostka stood as reminders of the biblical promise that the next world would be better than this one.

That day Jim was fortunate. His attorney, John Hogan, gave him a lift home in his long, black, heavily chromed Oldsmobile Super 88. Riding next to him in the leather front seat, Jim, oblivious to John's chatter that he did a good job answering questions, saw rebuke even in the church steeples that pointed toward the murky sky. *What am I being punished for? I didn't start that damn fire. I saved lives!*

———

Jim, along with millions of other people, read about the findings of the coroner's inquest in the newspaper in early January: "From the testimony presented, we, the jury, are unable to determine whether this occurrence was accidental or otherwise." Foreman Roy Tuchbreiter elaborated on these findings: "Judging from the evidence presented, the fire originated in the stairwell at the northeast corner of the school and had been burning for some time before it had been discovered. However, the exact point of origin cannot be established and we therefore have reached the conclusion that the cause of the fire is undetermined."

———

The word "undetermined" left a black cloud of doubt over Jim's head. In fact, the accusations that preceded the inquest became more intense afterward—and, in Jim's mind, crueler. Every innuendo, every suspicious glance was another layer of shame on Jim's psyche that neither Ann nor the kids nor his loyal friends could help him shake. In addition to his own guilt over not being able to do more, Jim was deeply scarred by the disloyalty of the priests at Our Lady of the Angels and the powers that be within the Catholic Church, who did nothing to help clear his name. *None of these guys publicly stood up for me. It's almost as if they want me to take the rap. Every dagger thrown at me helps deflect blame from them for letting the school become such a firetrap.*

———

Everyone told Jim not to think about me, not to talk about me. The nuns told the kids the same thing—that their brush with me was over and done with, that it was the will of God, that God had handpicked the little kids he wanted and the rest should just forget it and go on. They didn't understand that a person never, ever—in five years or fifty—forgets my touch.

———

Over the months Jim would fall into a deeper depression and become a near recluse. He'd stop making his usual visits to the fruit stand and barbershop, stop going to church, stop engaging with his kids and teasing Ann in his lighthearted manner.

His evening beer became not enough and he turned to hard liquor. Hard liquor would become his salvation, and his seat at the corner tavern would become his sanctuary. There, with a glass in his hand he would ruminate over the sequence of events. In his own bed in the dark of night, he would lie still as a corpse and relive that afternoon. *Was it 2:25, 2:30, or 2:35 when I discovered the fire? What if I hadn't spent so much time checking that damn oil burner? How much time did I spend beating the fire down? How long did it take Mrs. Maloney to call the fire department? If I'd waited, I could have made sure she gave them the right address.* What would haunt him for the rest of his life was the belief that had he returned to the boiler room sooner from the Hamlin building—just a few minutes sooner—he might have been able to save many more kids.

Part III
1959

20

Two days after the fire, the Firemen's Fund Insurance Company hired John Kennedy, the founder of John A. Kennedy & Associates—the most prestigious fire investigation company in the world—to investigate the blaze. On the afternoon of April 15, 1959, an unseasonably warm day in Chicago, he presented his report in a conference room at the insurance company's downtown Chicago offices, in a private meeting with Monsignor Cussen, Monsignor McManus, and attorney Cornelius Harrington.

Kennedy's report was the culmination of a four-month investigation in which he spared no expense in order to trace the fire back to its origins.

Kennedy was not a man who took shortcuts. "When I hit a fire scene," he would tell potential clients, "I look for clues even most firemen don't know about. Every fire leaves fingerprints . . . you just have to know enough about chemistry to read them."

What he didn't mention is that the job took extraordinary patience and attention to detail. He spent countless days at Our Lady of the Angels, combing through debris on his hands and knees and shooting countless high-quality photos, employing the photographic skills he had learned as a young man. He also spent time at the police crime lab testing, among other things, whether any accelerant was used to start the fire.

Even though the group was a small one, Kennedy stood to present his report. He was a tall man with a domineering personality, which he used to his advantage in gaining instant command over his audience. In a booming voice, louder than necessary, he reported that in the basement chapel, accessible from the northeast stairwell, he found a matchbook from which several matches had been torn from the book and lit. "The person who lit those matches then tossed them haphazardly about the area," he said, flipping his wrist to demonstrate the perpetrator's possible action. "I have concluded that from the location of the soot—the cover of the matchbook and the top of the matches were sooty; the surfaces beneath them were clean—that these matches had been lit and extinguished prior to the fire in the stairwell."

―――

I'm starting to feel squeamish in this guy's presence, like you might feel when a doctor is about to read you the results of your full-body scan, or a psychic is about to reveal that you were reincarnated from a slug. I have the feeling this guy knows more about my behavior that day than I remember. He's a showman like me, strutting his six-foot-four frame about, balancing his stogie shrewdly between two fingers, and passing out his smarty-pants report, two inches thick. As the priests thumb through their numbered personal copies, I see zillions of charts and graphs, and photos of myself, taken both close up and from the helicopters that hovered above.

―――

Stroking his slicked-back hair, Kennedy strode up to the black-board. He took chalk in hand and drew a diagram of the northeast stairwell, marking it with a giant white X. "This is where the fire started," he said confidently, tapping the chalk against the slate. He passed around a photograph taken in the stairwell to show exactly what he found: a telltale ring on the floor where the trash can once stood, and a charred V near the baseboard, the origin of the fire.

———

Exactly. Just as I remember it.

———

"The manner in which the fire spread was most unusual," he continued. "The fire was smoldering for a long time . . . a half-hour, or as long as forty-five minutes, before it was discovered."

———

Right again. After a lot of smoldering I leaped out of the trash can, broke the window—*CRASH*—and gulped the air I needed to rage throughout the stairwell and skyrocket up the open ven-tilation shaft into the cockloft.

———

"The superheated gases and smoke which vented into the cock-loft were forced to the west and accumulated over the second-floor corridor at almost the exact center of the roof. This superheated air later caused a second ignition when oxygen blew into this area beneath the roof.

"In addition, hot air, smoke, and fire mushroomed up the open back stairwell to the roof area."

———

I'm reliving it. In the attic-like cockloft with its low two-foot ceiling, I had time all to myself. It's where I was superheating and burning—right over the classrooms—before the kiddies on the second floor had any idea. And that open staircase. No fire door. It was like a chimney, drawing me upward. Like an express elevator. I couldn't have asked for a better situation.

———

Kennedy looked at Monsignor Cussen, who was nodding in agreement. Kennedy reminded him that the surviving kids from room 208 had complained that their classroom was getting hot.

———

I hadn't known this.

———

Kennedy found evidence that a lot of items had been stored in the stairwell: two metal containers, a roll of linoleum, a platform-type brass scale, a metal bookcase, felt cloth, a snow-plow, as much as thirty pounds of newspapers, textbooks, a wallpaper sample book, test papers, remains of a cardboard box, and a roll of metal screening.

———

This guy knows his stuff.

———

"I made no less than ten visits to the police crime lab doing various tests. No accelerant was used. Those tests proved negative. There was no electrical equipment or machinery in the stairwell that could have sparked a fire, which leads me to the conclusion that the fire was set by a human being, either accidentally or intentionally."

At the end of the presentation, Monsignor Cussen closed his copy of the findings and sighed. "Well," he said, "that's the only thing that makes sense of all the stories I've heard."

Outside the building, the clerics planted themselves on the sidewalk to discuss the outcome of the meeting, as passersby politely skirted about them.

"It supports my worst suspicions," said Monsignor Cussen. "It could have been one of our own who set that damn fire."

"Enlightening," said Monsignor McManus, "but we must keep it to ourselves. As far as we know, it was an accident."

Because Kennedy was a private investigator, his full report was never disclosed by the Archdiocese of Chicago to parents or to the general public. The cause of the fire would remain "undetermined."

21

As Kathleen Adamski recovered from the surgery to repair her fractured hips, her body remained suspended from the hammock-like sling, her pelvis hanging uncomfortably just inches above her hospital bed. To add to her misery, the third-degree burns that transformed most of the skin on her hands, arms, and legs into open wounds lay exposed on the mattress. She would have many other surgeries and remain in the orthopedic unit of Saint Anne's for six months.

While the sling immobilized her and caused great discomfort, it was the burns that turned her life into a living horror show. The process of removing charred skin and tissue from the burn areas was excruciating; the process of replacing that skin was arduous, painful, and seemingly never ending. Doctors identified donor sites on healthy parts of her body, then shaved parchment-thin layers of skin from these sites with an instrument called an electric dermatome and carefully stitched them onto the burn areas. The hope was that the transplanted skin would begin to grow there in place of the removed tissue. Sometimes it did, and sometimes it didn't. Nevertheless the result was that two areas of Kathleen's body would throb with pain at the same time. The healing process also brought with it itches Kathleen couldn't scratch, or even touch, at risk of destroying the transplant or introducing infection. It was important that she lie as still as possible during this healing time.

Once the donor site healed, the doctors would shave more skin from it for another transplant. They would repeat this process every ten days or so. They tried to keep donor sites to a minimum, because these sites would forever be lighter in color than the rest of the skin, leaving the patient with a splotchy appearance. And transplanted skin posed its own problems: it would never be as pliant as original skin, so Kathleen faced the prospect of lifelong discomfort when stretching the burned parts of her body, especially in the joint areas.

Kathleen had been taught by the nuns to "offer up" any pain, disappointment, or inconvenience in life as restitution for the pain Jesus suffered on the cross for her sins. In the early days of her hospital confinement, this is what she practiced: gritting her teeth, letting the pain pulse through her body without complaint. She learned to hold her breath until painful probing with an instrument was completed, until an itch subsided. She tried to keep her requests to hospital staff to an absolute minimum, knowing how overwhelmed they were in caring for forty-five other fire victims. Kathleen would later learn that many of the doctors lived at the hospital for the first four days or so, with their wives bringing them changes of clothing. A number of them had temporarily suspended their private practices to care for the OLA patients, often without charge, turning their paychecks over to funds created for the victims. They refused to make any money from this tragedy. Nurses worked overtime to ensure that every burn victim was checked at least once every three hours. Some kids had to be turned every two hours, and each turn required many hands.

These people became Kathleen's heroes. Dr. Segraves, Kathleen's orthopedic surgeon, would later say about the kids, "These children whimpered, but they didn't cry. They didn't complain. They were abnormally polite, pitifully grateful."

As Kathleen progressed through multiple skin grafts and surgeries, she coupled the "offering it up" practice with a less noble coping strategy: appreciating the morphine administered after every surgery. It was the only thing that released her from the moment and gave her a good night's sleep.

In desperation she soon added another technique to help her manage her pain: black humor. "I smell like an outhouse," she'd joke with the nurses over the putrid smell of the burns and weeping wounds, which they could not cleanse with a good shower.

Eventually she got them joking about it as well: "Not an outhouse, a sewer maybe . . ."

"A rotting carcass," she'd say.

"The Chicago subway."

Then the nurses began bringing her sweet-smelling objects to make her smile: a cinnamon bun; a hankie sprayed with Estée Lauder's Youth Dew, her favorite perfume; a fragrant rose. Alone at night, in the dimness of an ever-present night light, she'd try to remember the aroma of chocolate chip cookies and her mother's yeasty *kołaczki*, the smell of new textbooks, the comforting scent of her father's Old Spice, hot buttered popcorn in a colorful paper cone at the church carnival, the sweet smell of a baby's head.

"How can you stand me? Even a kielbasa fart smells better than I do," she once told her mother.

"Kathleen!" Eva scolded, looking over her shoulder to see if a nurse overheard.

But in her dreams, where humor was not an option, she'd
be assaulted with memories of the gagging stench of smoke,
the rancid smell of burning skin, and the haunting screams
of her classmates echoing throughout the building in grisly
chorus, and she'd awaken to the sound of her own cries. "Help
me. Get me out of here!" The night nurse would rush in and
soothe her. "It's OK, sweetie. You're safe now, Kathleen."
Then she was left alone, fully awake, swamped by memories
of the friends she had lost: Helen Buziak, Patricia Drzymala,
Lorraine Nieri . . . and many others.

She thought, too, of Susan Smaldone, a petite fourth grader
who had a beautiful singing voice, and how, when she walked
past the music room, she'd sometimes stop to listen to Susie
practicing her scales.

Then, for no particular reason, she pictured Susie's classmate Victor Jacobellis, with his wide smile and big ears. Then
she'd hear the clank and slide of roller skate wheels on the
sidewalk on her block and see her friend Mary Virgilio pumping her arms as they raced toward the drug store on the
corner. Mary's favorite flavor of ice cream was Neapolitan,
because "it's really three very perfect flavors in one," she
used to say.

Kathleen remembered how the girls laughed when Mar-
garet Kucan told them she wanted to become a zookeeper,
and how they didn't laugh when John Jajkowski announced
he wanted to become a priest.

She recalled how all the boys were in love with eighth
grader Beverly Burda, who was sweet and shy and didn't have
any idea how cute she was.

Then, in the semidarkness of her hospital room, the frightening reality would hit her: *Those kids once laughed and roller-
skated and ate ice cream with me. Now they're dead and nothing*

can bring them back. Dead? She closed her eyes and tried to block out the ambient sounds of radiator noises and patient call bells outside her door. *Death is quiet, for sure. But death is something else. If the nuns are right, it's a place where all secrets are revealed. If they are right, my friends are now privy to the biggest secret of all: what happens to us after we die. Is it true—are they now in a state of eternal bliss with God in heaven? Do they know what's happening on earth, or are they having so much fun in heaven that they couldn't be bothered? Do they know I'm thinking of them at this very moment? Or is it all a big lie like Santa Claus, and are they just dead?*

"Sleep," she'd tell herself. "This is doing you no good." And sometimes sleep would come, but often she'd get lost in yet another troubling circle of memories and questions.

———

During those early months, while the media reports were ubiquitous and everyone was still in the Christmas spirit, it seemed the world was uniting to cheer up the kids.

There appeared to be no end to the cards and gifts that poured in—radios, portable TV sets, flowers, stuffed animals, candy, books, records—plus a string of celebrity visits: Ed Sullivan, Bozo the Clown, Jack Benny, sports figures, all of whom were more than willing to sign their casts, offer encouraging words (muffled behind protective surgical masks), or bring the children thoughtful gifts of their own. Choral groups sang in the hallways. Music was everywhere. Priests were in and out of rooms giving blessings.

Well intentioned? Yes, but their visits posed additional problems for the staff, challenged with balancing the need to maintain a germ-free environment with the importance of keeping up their patients' morale. Suspended rather early in the healing process was the hospital's "hands-off" policy, which had prohibited even parents from touching their children. The staff at Saint Anne's tried to balance the kids' need for human touch and hugs from their parents with their constant concern about controlling infection. To Kathleen, the cool touch of her mother's hand on her forehead meant everything.

———

In the middle of March, Kathleen celebrated her thirteenth birthday. To commemorate the milestone, her regular daytime nurse marched in after lunch ceremonially carrying a wedge of chocolate cake, with a lit candle set into its raspberry center. She entered the room singing "Happy Birthday" and put the cake under Kathleen's nose.

Kathleen's eyes widened and she screamed, "Get that out of here!" She flailed her hands—once slim and graceful, now swollen and crusty—as if she were fighting the flame. "I hate you!" she cried.

That was the first manifestation of a phobia that would last well into Kathleen's adulthood. A burning candle on a restaurant table, a sparkler on the Fourth of July, a cozy fire in the hearth, a movie about fire—every sight of flame would cause her panic.

The poor nurse hurried out of the room, embarrassed. She warned the others nurses and aides not to make the same mistake, not to light candles or allow fire of any sort in their patients' rooms. She thought carefully of how she could make it up to Kathleen. But as it turned out, she had little to worry about, because that evening Kathleen would have a special visitor who would make everything right.

———

"How's my girl?"

"Papa!"

"How are you, sweetheart?" Kathleen's father said, his eyes focusing on her flushed face, trying to avoid staring at the patches of new skin on her arms, covered with the flimsiest strips of sterile gauze.

She smiled stoically. "I'm OK."

Her mother was right behind, her eyes smiling above her white surgical mask. "Honey," she said, "your papa has brought you a birthday present."

"You brought me my piano?" she joked.

"No, but I brought you this."

Kathleen noticed he was carrying his violin case. *Oh no,* she thought. *He's going to play classical music right here in the hospital.* Although their home was filled with Mozart and Stravinsky, it wasn't the kind of music most of her classmates enjoyed. They preferred Elvis Presley and the Everly Brothers. The violin was fine inside their home, but on the outside, in front of her friends, Kathleen wished her father played the drums or guitar, or at least the dreamy saxophone.

But then this man—her sweet father—his mouth and nose masked in white, his stunning gray-blue eyes aglow above the crisp linen, lifted his violin and bow from its worn leather case, raised it to his chin, and played a few tuning notes. It was a 1940s Czech violin that had rapidly become his pride and joy after he inherited it from a fellow musician, an octogenarian, who stopped playing because of severe arthritis in his fingers.

Sliding the bow lovingly across the strings, he fixed his eyes upon his daughter. He winked, and dove into a jolly rendition of "Happy Birthday."

Her mother clapped enthusiastically.

Kathleen clapped gently and smiled up at him. "Thank you, Papa."

"Honey, let me get these knots out of your pretty hair." Eva picked up Kathleen's pink plastic hairbrush and started to gently brush her blonde hair. It was a feeling Kathleen enjoyed—bristles against scalp—one of the few pleasures of being incapacitated. As her mother gently lifted her daughter's head off the pillow and ran the brush through her knotted hair, untangling the strands with the lightest of touches, her father produced a roll of sheet music from his jacket pocket.

"And that's not all, my dear. As your mother makes you beautiful, recline and experience the remainder of the concert." His eyes spoke the gentlest, most loving smile she had ever seen. It made her grin to hear her father, a formal, Old World gentleman, say words like *recline* instead of *sit back* and *experience* rather than *enjoy*.

"Would you like some cold milk to go with the music, sweetie?" her mother asked. "And a *kołaczki* filled with apricot? I baked them today for your birthday."

"Thanks, Mom."

Eva retrieved a colorful metal tin from her oversized handbag and wiggled off the lid, unlocking the aroma of freshly baked pastry. She helped her take a bite of a flaky envelope of goodness, followed by a long sip of milk from a carton that remained on ice from her dinner. "Just like home," she whispered in Kathleen ear.

"I wish, Mama. Maybe soon."

Her father propped his sheet music up against a plastic pitcher on her bedside tray. Eva stepped over to assist him in turning the pages. "Your papa has been practicing all week," she whispered, her hand cupping her mouth.

"Pardon me, sweetheart, if I do not get every note right. This genre is new to me," he apologized.

"You are too modest, Papa, you never play a sour note."

With a European flourish, Peter Adamski lifted the violin to his chin, held the bow gracefully above the strings, and glided into a jazzy rendition of "High Hopes," a tune made popular by Frank Sinatra. As her father's fingers pressed the strings flawlessly, and as the simple silver band on his finger flashed in the overhead fluorescent light, the lyrics of the song ran through Kathleen's mind: *"But he's got high hopes, he's got high hopes . . ."*

So any time you're gettin' low, 'stead of lettin' go,
Just remember that ant.
Oops there goes another rubber tree plant.

There was more applause, this time from Eva and from a crowd of nurses, doctors, and visitors who had gathered at the door. Peter set the violin to his side, stood posture perfect, and took a deep bow in three directions. Among his audience were Dr. Segraves, Father Joe Ognibene, who had come to spend time with the kids, and Dr. Louis Dvonch. Before graduating from medical school at Loyola University, Dr. Dvonch had studied violin on scholarship at the Juilliard School of Music. The surgeon had put in agonizingly long hours performing skin grafts on his young patients; it was about time, Kathleen thought, that he enjoyed some music and a *kołaczki*.

Eva ran over to them, tin in hand, distributing the pastries.

In the months ahead, Dr. Dvonch would become a fan of Peter Adamski, inviting him to become a regular guest at Saint Anne's, playing music for the other children who needed cheering up.

To Kathleen's later delight, another fan of her father's would be thirteen-year-old Sal Martinelli, who would be treated to a private concert of his own the following month, the evening before being released from Saint Anne's.

22

At Saint Anne's, Sal Martinelli got to be known as the boy with a million questions. Driven by his innate curiosity, and now faced with pain that begged for distraction, Sal developed the habit of inquiring about every procedure the nurses performed, bending every doctor's ears, sponging up medical information whenever he had the opportunity.

Confined to the Stryker frame, which the hospital staff used to flip him over every two hours, he asked Dr. Dvonch about the origin of the contraption. "It was invented by an orthopedic surgeon named Homer Stryker," the doctor replied. "He wanted to create a hospital bed in which the patient could be turned with the least amount of discomfort. The idea came to him when he treated patients in the war in the '40s."

"Does every hospital have one?"

"Most do. We have several, but we had to borrow many more from other hospitals for all the kids burnt in the fire."

"Oh. How long will I be in this thing?"

"Until all your skin grafts are completed. You've had three of them already and there will be more."

More surgeries. I hope I'm strong enough to last that long.
"How many more?"

"We'll see how it goes." What Dr. Dvonch didn't tell Sal was that he anticipated as many as twenty skin grafts to repair the damage done to more than a third of his body.

"Do I have enough good skin to keep doing this?"

"I think you do. It is possible to use skin from other donors, and we are doing that with some other patients."

Sal could hardly imagine a healthy person actually volunteering to have his or her skin shaved off. "People do that?"

"Yes, people are very generous."

Sal learned from Dr. Dvonch, an attentive and encouraging doctor with a dimple in his chin, how remarkable the human body is at repairing and regenerating itself. "The outer layer of skin is made up of tough pieces of cells that are no longer alive. Underneath are layers of cells that are always multiplying and making new cells, which are pushed to the surface."

"So new skin will grow and I'll look normal again?"

"Yes pretty much, but healing isn't perfect. In full thickness burns, like the third-degree burns you received, you'll have scar tissue remaining on your face, neck, and arms. There are various ways to smooth it out, which we will address later, along with reconstructing your ears, Sal, and we'll bring in a plastic surgeon to do that." Sal admired Dr. Dvonch's honesty, even if it made his gut churn. Definitely there would be more surgeries and weeks of painful recovery that he wasn't looking forward to.

He also learned that he could assist his body in healing by eating a high-protein diet, with more carbohydrates and fat. "The body loses protein through burn wounds, which causes muscles to break down. You need glucose for energy, and fat for extra calories."

Although the hospital meals were nutritionally sound, Vince Martinelli, on Dr. Dvonch's advice, would occasionally stop at a local steak house and bring Sal a huge steak, grilled just the way he liked it—"rare, just like me," Sal told his dad. And if Sal was flipped upside down in the Stryker frame at the time, his face just inches from the floor, his mother—like so many other moms—would lie on the floor feeding him so that his food wouldn't get cold in the hours it would take before it was time to be flipped right side up.

So as the earth and the planets revolved around the sun, Sal revolved in his turning frame—facing the ceiling for two hours, then the floor, sometimes with stops in between. This restricted orbit gave him a lot of time to think.

One evening he confided in his mom, "You can't imagine the weird things I think about in passing my day."

"Nope, I can't imagine." She tried to laugh.

"Sometimes I think about what I'm going to do when I get out of here."

"And what's that?"

"I'm not going to be shy anymore. You know how afraid I was to raise my hand in class. I was embarrassed to be wrong. I'm not going to do that anymore. I'm going to ask anybody anything when I don't know an answer. Life's too short."

"My thirteen-year-old boy is talking like an old man," Anita said. "I never thought you were that shy."

"Well, I am," he said. "I was." *I shouldn't have held back. I should have pushed my way to the other window and got out a lot sooner. I shouldn't have wasted my time praying for help to come.* "I'm not anymore."

Just saying that reminded Sal of the many things he wasn't anymore. Handsome. A daydreamer. *But maybe I'm other things now. Smarter and more determined. I'm not going to give*

up. Let the doctors do what they want with me, then I'm going
to get out of here and get busy living. I'm going to learn lots of
stuff, have some kind of career . . . I don't know what . . . travel,
maybe even get married to someone who likes a guy with scars.

Sal thought he wanted to be like some of the people he
was reading about while traveling in his own little Stryker
circle. He wanted to be spunky like Holden Caulfield—even
though he thought Holden was a whiner and a rich kid who
didn't have a clue about the bad things that could happen to
kids. He was going to read every book in the library himself,
hold the books in his hands, turn the pages with new healthy
fingers, read whenever he wanted to without having to wait
until someone else had time to read to him.

He felt unlucky and lucky at the same time. Unlucky for
the obvious reasons, but lucky to have found Trudy, a cute
student nurse who would come by after her shift with books
in hand to read to him. That's how he discovered books he'd
never considered reading before, when he had the options of
riding his bike, playing pinball at the bowling alley, and just
hanging out with the guys, talking about the Bears, the Cubs,
the White Sox, the Blackhawks.

It was Trudy who introduced him to Holden Caulfield in
Catcher in the Rye. A spunky ginger-haired nurse of twenty-
one with Mamie Eisenhower bangs and a ponytail, she didn't
mind reading the swear words aloud one bit, which Sal appre-
ciated. His mother would have closed the book on the first
F-U-C-K. "Salvador, is this how we've raised you?" she'd say.
He could hear her chastising tone in his head.

Trudy was just the kind of girl he wanted—she also brought
hard candies for him to suck on—but she was taken. She wore
an engagement ring with a tiny diamond that flashed in the
fluorescent light whenever she turned her left hand a certain

way. Her fiancé, Mo, was a butcher-in-training at Kroger. Now that Sal was a regular meat-eater, he thought about asking Trudy to get information from Mo about the various cuts of steaks, the difference between porterhouse and T-bones, but, tactfully, he refrained. She was so kind in volunteering to read to him; he didn't want to put her to more trouble.

Whenever Sal would thank her—which he always did at the end of the evening—she'd say, "It's my pleasure, Sal." Then she'd add on an extra comment that always made him feel better about himself. "You're a smart kid, Sal," she'd say. "I think you're a lot like Santiago," which was the highest compliment she could give him.

It was also Trudy who introduced Sal to Santiago, in *The Old Man and the Sea* by Ernest Hemingway. Santiago was an old fisherman with sun-and-wind-wrinkled skin who was unlucky when it came to fishing: he had gone eighty-four days without so much as catching a fish, and he was the laughingstock of more successful fishermen, but he never gave up. One day, Santiago decided to go too far out to sea where it was dangerous, and that's where he landed a giant marlin, the catch of his life. He fought the humongous fish for three days and three nights until his hands bled, until he was beyond exhaustion, until he felt like he had nothing more to give. But "his eyes were undefeated," Hemingway wrote, and he kept fighting. Bringing in that marlin was the greatest challenge he'd ever faced in his life. As the waves pounded him and exhaustion weakened him, as he suffered in the blistering sun, froze in the cold, starved, and longed for a drink of fresh water, the fight continued; it was his will against the great marlin's.

Finally, Santiago outlasted the marlin, hooked it with his harpoon, and started dragging it back to shore. But just when he thought he had victory in his back pocket, there were more troubles: the dead marlin's trail of blood attracted sharks, who started following the boat and eventually began chomping on the marlin's flesh.

Still hearing Trudy's compliment in his mind, Sal spent much of the night contemplating how he might be—could be—like Santiago. He had fought fire; now he was fighting infection, pain, and the overwhelming temptation to give up, which overcame him in the dark. But then he'd be jarred by the cry of another kid down the hall, someone in even worse shape than he was in, and he'd say a prayer for that kid and say to himself, *Sal, this isn't going to last forever. Stick it out like Santiago.*

Or could he be like the marlin? No, the marlin was more like the fire that fought him and was still giving him the battle of his life. Every surgery was like another shark attack, making him afraid, making him hurt.

When Trudy wasn't available—Sal imagined her either studying or out eating steak with Mo, or maybe dancing, her red hair tied in a high ponytail jiggling as she jitterbugged to fast music—he'd ask his parents to read him the newspaper. Usually it was his father who complied. Vince, who had a tendency to get worked up over world events, became Sal's primary link with the outside world, faithfully reading him the front page of the *Chicago Tribune* every evening.

On January 3, Vince had said, his hazel eyes peeking out over the newspaper, "Hey, get a load of this. Today we have a new state, Alaska. Can you imagine that, son? Think of all the new flags they're going to have to make. It'll be good business for flag-makers." Then in another breath, he said, "What's Alaska going to contribute to the economy? Ice?" In an afterthought he added, "Think you can name the other forty-eight states, son?" He was mumbling then, barely audible through the protective mask covering his mouth.

Sal had had a rough day. He looked down at the graft sites on his arm, covered gently with protective gauze. "I'll name them for you in a few days, Dad. I think I need to sleep now."

Several days later, as two nurses were checking the results of those skin grafts, painfully picking fuzzy bits of gauze off his wounds with tweezers, Sal closed his eyes and mentally began with the letter *A* and ran through the alphabet: *Alaska, Arkansas, Alabama, God, let this be over.* He could only get to Mississippi before he screamed. "I'm sorry," he apologized, looking up at the startled nurse, because he knew every other kid on the floor had heard him cry out, and what hurt one of them seemed to hurt them all. A week later he did name all forty-nine states for his dad.

Later in the month, Vince Martinelli read a story aloud about Pope John XXIII proclaiming the Second Vatican Council. "It says here the pope is calling for a spiritual renewal for the Church, that he wants to modernize things." He set the paper on his lap and shook his head. "Not soon enough, in my book," Vince observed. Sal's dad was a churchgoing Catholic, but that never prevented him from grumbling about things he saw wrong with his church. "Maybe they'll allow priests to get married," he mused. "It's unnatural for a guy to be celibate."

Sal had no comment, but all he knew is that it was contrary to what the nuns taught him. *It's probably something I'll understand later*, he thought. All he knew was that he liked Pope John, because he had a chubby grandpa kind of face, and because after the fire he had sent the survivors a special blessing.

In March, relaxing in the straight-backed wooden chair he had come to think of as his own, Vince jabbed his finger into the inch-high headline of the front page and announced, "Here we go again, son. Would you believe it? It says here that Ike signed a bill making Hawaii our fiftieth state." He looked over at Anita, who was lying on the floor feeding Sal his evening meal, this time spaghetti and meatballs. "Just when I've come around to accepting Alaska because they're connected to us up there, I've got to get used to those islands floating out in the middle of nowhere . . . *Humph*. All they're good for is pineapples and hula girls."

Sal looked away from the meatball his mother was holding out for him on a fork. "I hope those flag-makers didn't make too many new flags yet, Dad, because they're going to have to redo them."

"Righto, son."

On April 5, the red-letter day when they were going to remove the bandages from his ears after plastic surgery, Trudy asked Sal whether she could put the mirror back up in his room. "I think you'll be pleased with what you see, Sal."

"If you think I'm ready."

"I do."

His friend lifted the mirror stored behind the dresser and hooked it onto the wall. From about ten feet away Sal saw a kid who slightly resembled him, except for some lighter patches of new skin on his face. A closer look later would reveal areas of scar tissue. All his dark hair had grown back in, and actually, he looked presentable—at least from afar. Mercifully, his ears were repaired and looked pink and right where they should be.

On April 22, now out of the Stryker frame, Sal sat in a stiff wooden chair watching a ball game on the portable TV his dad had brought in and set on the dresser. The Chicago White Sox scored eleven runs in the seventh inning against the Kansas City Athletics, with only one base hit. Along with Nurse Trudy and a few doctors, they cheered louder as each run came in. It was the happiest the Martinellis had been in four months.

"Yippee!" Sal cried.

"Did ya see that, son?" Vince cried, pumping a fist at the TV.

Their voices resonated with others from rooms down the hall full of patients listening to the game on radios or watching on their own portable TVs. The Sox won 20–6. A good omen, Sal thought.

Sal would never forget that day, because that was the day he was cleared to go home—after fourteen skin grafts and one plastic surgery. It was also the he day he got to know Kathleen Adamski.

———

As Sal rolled down the corridor with his dad pushing from behind, Vince continued the conversation he'd started thirty minutes ago when he finished signing Sal's discharge papers. "Are there any other kids from OLA still in the hospital, son?"

"The only one that I know of is a girl, Kathleen Adamski. She was a seventh grader."

"Let's go visit her, son." Vince checked his wristwatch. "It's still visiting hour."

Sal's first inclination was *No, we can't bother her*, but before he opened his mouth, he remembered the vow he'd made: He wasn't going to run away from opportunities. He was going to pretend he was confident, even if he wasn't. He wasn't going to let his taut, two-toned skin prevent him from meeting new people. And furthermore, Kathleen was burned herself, and probably wasn't much to look at. And furthermore, Sal didn't care how she looked if she could tolerate looking at him.

Yet he was as nervous as he'd been on his first day in kindergarten. He clutched his burnt, white fingers, functioning stiffly now with new skin from his backside, and said to himself, *What the heck!*

The nurse at the front desk at orthopedics directed Sal and his father to Kathleen's room, and Vince skillfully pushed his wheelchair through the wide-open door.

23

It would be romantic to say that the encounter between Kathleen and Sal was like a destined lovers' meeting on a Hollywood set. Boy and girl lock eyes and give each other knowing looks. Girl tilts her head shyly, flirtatiously; boy offers her a rose he just happened to have behind his back.

But that wasn't what happened between Kathleen and Sal. No flirtatious glances, no knowing looks, and no rose.

Kathleen was recovering from a second hip surgery and was napping. Her mouth was wide open and she was also snoring—delicately, but still, she was snoring.

Vince slowly rolled Sal's wheelchair up to Kathleen's bed and Sal watched her sleep. Kathleen's eyes were closed, but her new pink plastic-framed glasses were still balanced on her nose. Her golden hair was splayed across the pillow, not exactly like Sleeping Beauty's in the Disney film, but that's what he thought of when he saw Kathleen. The skin on her face was smooth and fair, not a blemish. But her arms resting at her sides bore the same patchwork of skin graft scars that his did, and her legs were masses of skin in various colorful stages of healing. She was in traction, suspended in a canvas sling, her hips slightly elevated off the mattress. He didn't want to wake her, because he knew how hard it must have been for her to fall asleep in that medieval-looking contraption in the first place.

"*Sshhh,*" a small voice said from foot of the bed. "She's sleeping. She had a rough morning."

A gentlemen dressed rather formally in a dark suit stood up and offered Sal his hand. "I'm Peter Adamski, Kathleen's father, and you, young man, look like you might be a classmate of my daughter's."

"I'm Sal Martinelli. Eighth grade. Pleased to meet you, sir." He looked over his shoulder and gestured up to his dad, "And this is my dad, Vince Martinelli. I just got released from upstairs today and my dad asked if anyone from Our Lady of the Angels was still here and the nurse said Kathleen was, so we stopped by to visit her." He took a deep breath.

The two men smiled and shook hands. Peter Adamski was tall and courtly in manner, Vince Martinelli, shorter, rounder, and uncourtly. But what bound them instantly were the thorns of emotion they felt watching their teenagers suffer, and their own helplessness in easing their pain.

Sal noticed a violin case leaning beside Peter's chair. "You're the musician," he said, loud enough to make Kathleen stir.

"Yes," Peter whispered. He looked over at Kathleen and smiled because her eyes were open. "You have a young visitor," he announced gently.

"Hi, I'm Sal," Sal said into her sleepy face. He waited for her to come to awareness, and then he added, "I was in 209, Sister Davidis's class." He remembered seeing Kathleen around school, always traveling with a group of girls. He thought of her as one of the popular kids, but he had never spoken to her until now.

"I was in 208, Sister Canice's class. She died, you know."

"I know. I had her last year. She was a good teacher."

"I've seen you around. You used to be an altar boy."

Sal nodded shyly.

Suddenly self-conscious, Kathleen smoothed her hair with the palms of her hands, which gave Sal a better look at the white scars on her arms.

"The itching is the worse part, isn't it?" he said.

"I know." She felt the undersides of her arm. "I wanted to rip my skin off! The grafts are pretty much over. Now I just have to get out of traction and learn to walk again." Her eyes widened prettily. "I might go home in June."

"That's really soon," Sal said, trying to be optimistic, but thinking how crappy it was that she had to be confined in that thing for another two months.

"What's this about you being the music guy?" Vince asked Peter.

"Yes, I play the violin."

"Professionally?"

"With the Chicago Symphony Orchestra. We're just concluding the season, but rehearsal was called off this afternoon, so I'm free to visit Kathleen. Her mother will be visiting later. Eva is busy now with our younger daughter, our little Camille."

"How old is Camille?" Sal asked Kathleen.

"Seven. She's too young to come. I miss her."

"I know. My sister Alice just turned eight. I guess kids can't visit because of germs." Sal turned to Kathleen's father and asked, "Do you practice every day?"

"Yes, I do."

Vince Martinelli chirped, "Are you going to play something for us before we leave? I hear you're pretty good."

"Dad!" Sal said.

"Go ahead, Papa, play something," Kathleen encouraged.

Peter lifted his violin case and set it on the table. "Take a front-row seat, Vince," he said, gesturing to a comfortable but worn brown visitor's chair beside Kathleen's bed, "and enjoy the brief concert."

"What would you like me to play, Kathleen?"

"How about 'Flight of the Bumblebee,' Dad?"

"Very suitable for the occasion," he laughed, "since you're leaving this esteemed establishment."

Kathleen rolled her eyes.

"Are you familiar with 'Flight of the Bumblebee'?" Peter asked Sal. "It's a piece written by Rimsky-Korsakov for an opera, *The Tale of Tsar Saltan*, around the turn of the century. Kathleen loves it," he said winking at his daughter.

"It's crazy," she said.

Sal remembered hearing "Flight of the Bumblebee" about four years ago in a film featuring Victor Borge, a comic and pianist who interrupted his piano playing with jokes. At the end of that particular comedy routine, Victor Borge played "Flight of the Bumblebee," his fingers moving across the keys faster than wild bees on a rampage. Father Joe Ognibene, whom the kids loved, had brought the film into Sister Seraphica's fourth-grade class to celebrate some saint's feast day. Sal remembered that they didn't have a screen in the classroom, so they took down the bulletin board and watched it on a white wall. He thought of telling this story to Kathleen, but decided not to, because Sister Seraphica had died in the fire and he didn't want to remind her.

With shining eyes, Peter slowly looked at each of the faces in his three-person audience and gracefully lifted his violin. In the silence, Kathleen raised an eyebrow at Sal and smiled. *She has a nice smile*, he thought. And then, all at once, the whole room seemed to come to life with the frenzied tones of bees. Peter ran the bow over the strings with such speed and precision that the simultaneous notes sounded like an angry, dancing, crazed swarm of buzzing insects. Then in no more than two minutes, and with four final pings, the music stopped.

Kathleen and Sal looked at each other and laughed. Vince shook his head in amazement. "Never thought I'd hear anything like that in a hospital. Bravo!"

"Holy cow!" Sal said. "That's crazy, Mr. Adamski! How do your fingers do that?"

"Practice," Peter said, smiling at the boy. "The piece has 810 notes that are semiquavers. Violinists compete over who can play it fastest. I'm still in the slow department."

Sal looked down at his healing hands, "I am too," he said.

Before Sal and Vince left, Kathleen invited Sal to visit her again if he could stand returning to Saint Anne's. "But if not, maybe we can talk on the phone, OK?"

"OK," Sal said, meaning it.

Vince patted Peter on the back as he rolled Sal out of the room.

24

My little red light burns day and night in Catholic churches. They call it a sanctuary lamp—a sturdy red candle set in a golden cage that hangs near the tabernacle where the consecrated Hosts are kept. It's there to remind people that God is ever present, always watching.

But what they forget is that I'm watching too. I'm alive and aflame and aware of everything that goes on in that church, day and night. The days are busy with Masses, funerals, and weddings—the rituals that anchor Catholics' lives. But the nights are a cold and shadowy bore. The place is as empty as Jesus's tomb on the third day. It's just me in the sanctuary light and in the scores of votive lights that are left everywhere, in white cups in the fancy racks before statues of saints. As darkness descends, one by one they flicker out, except for the sanctuary light, which always stays on. It can be spooky in there. Sometimes the place even gives me the trembles.

It was about six months after I demolished the school, sometime in June 1959, that I came to life in a place of secrets in that church: a confessional, of all places.

It was a late Saturday afternoon and the lines outside the confessionals had disappeared. Monsignor Cussen and Father

Ognibene, clad in their black cassocks and clerical collars, had heard the last of that day's confessions. They closed up shop and walked back to the sacristy, piously, wearily.

The place was cleaned out, except for a few old ladies in flowered babushkas who knelt in pews reciting penances for sins that couldn't have been *that* bad . . . but who am I to judge? Old ladies were once young ladies.

The kid was there too. The kid who loves me. He was kneeling in a pew in the front of the church, reciting his penance after confession.

His head was bowed and his hands were cupped over his face. After the babushka ladies left, he and I were alone in the vast church. He was kneeling on a padded kneeler, all alone, whimpering softly. With his head in his hands, he was the saddest little picture I've ever seen. I could feel his heartbeat, almost hear his tears.

Then, just as he did with his grandma that first evening I met him before the procession, he walked up to a metal rack of vigil lights close to the Communion rail. He counted out two silver dimes from his pocket and slid them into the money slot. *Ka-chink. Ka-clink.* His thin pink lips moved in prayer.

What was he praying for this time? A father? A fresh start? A clear conscience? He stood up and took a wick in hand, lit two little candles, and *poof*, reliable me, I came to life. I had a close-up look at him now. Behind his eyeglasses, his blue eyes were tearing up, and the pouches of skin beneath them were puffy and red. Did the priest make him cry in the confessional? I see a lot of this on Saturdays. Grown men with their heads hanging down, twisting their hats in their hands. Teenage hard guys in black leather looking humbled. Crabby old ladies who whack their husbands and holler at the kids cutting across their lawns, silenced. Some priests are known for giving people a hard time, whether they deserve it or not.

I wish I could have hugged the chubby little guy. He blew out the light on the wick and he kept praying, staring at me like he could see clear into the tiniest speck of red flame in my center.

It must have been some long penance he got, because he was there a while. Then in the silence of the vacant church, the kneeler rattled and the kid stood up to leave. He took a step backward, but on second thought stepped toward me again. With trembling hands he lifted one of the glass vigil cups that held me and removed me from the metal rack. I thought he might be taking me home to keep in his room as a reminder of his confession—like a souvenir—but instead he walked me in a slow and somber procession to the same confessional he had been in earlier.

I'd been inside a confessional a couple of times before, when some addicted priests just had to have a smoke. The confessional is a place of darkness and mystery and millions of secrets. Priests are bound by sacred oath never to divulge what they hear in that little room. No wonder they look weary when they leave, carrying the sins people dump on them.

If you've never been inside a confessional, I'll tell you how it is. Think of it as a fancy wooden room the size of a phone booth, and then add on two more matching rooms, only smaller, one on each side. They're not made of any ordinary wood. They're usually thick mahogany or oak, carved with fancy spindles and crosses on top, and shined up with lots of varnish. Although the three rooms are all connected, each has its own door. The priest sits on a cushioned bench in the middle, and the sinners kneel on hard kneelers on either side, alternately confessing their sin to the priest from behind screens. When one person leaves, the priest closes a door over that screen and turns to the person waiting on the other side.

What's a sin, you ask? Catholics believe it's an act a human being willfully commits that is wrong and hurtful to God. After a person confesses his sins, he recites the Act of Contrition: "*O, my God, I am heartily sorry for having offended you. I detest all my sins, because I dread the loss of heaven and the pains of hell . . .*" blah, blah, blah.

The priest gives absolution: "Go and sin no more." He also gives the sinner a penance—usually to say a couple of Hail Marys or maybe a rosary or even a novena if the sin's a real doozy, murder or something carnal. He also lectures the sinner on how to make things right.

So the kid's small hand opens the center door of the confessional, and I'm in my glass cup wiggling as he walks, and before I know it, the kid sets me on the floor beneath the priest's bench, and he tears off a piece of purple curtain from the door and sets it close enough so my tongue can leap out and touch it. He closes the door and walks away. What? I didn't expect that. But hungry for any snack—even a hunk of dusty purple velvet—I do what I was created to do. I lick and bite and swallow and smack. And I spread. It's party time and I'm excited and I set the curtain on the door ablaze.

This time, though, the party ended quickly. I need air to survive and there wasn't enough of it in that stuffy old confessional to keep me going. God knows I tried to make the good times last. I gasped and sputtered and choked and fought to keep myself going, but in the end I just couldn't hold on. My flame went out. And that's all I know about that.

The next morning, watching from the sanctuary light in my gilded cage near the altar, I saw three parish priests examining that confessional, hauling out debris, and cleaning up my mess. There was not a mention of it in the press.

Hmmm.

25

It got so that Belinda hated leaving her home on Springfield Avenue. Every sight along the way reminded her of the fire, and of her son whom she suspected had something to do with it. No new fires that she knew of had erupted in their neighborhood since the school burned down—things were unusually quiet in that department—but, like the stench of smoke that still seemed to hang in the air everywhere she went, she couldn't shake her suspicions that he was involved.

Memories were everywhere. It seemed she couldn't get to the A&P, the Laundromat, or the savings and loan without seeing someone who bore the scars of the fire—a patch of white skin on a boy's forehead, a young girl bravely struggling to balance her broken body on crutches, a parent pushing a boy in a wheelchair in the snow. To Belinda it seemed as if her neighborhood was a vast, grid-like stage on which victims of the fire were endlessly, mercilessly on parade.

It was the newspaper shack on the corner of Hamlin and Chicago Avenues that Belinda particularly avoided. In this five-by-five-foot ramshackle wooden structure, Géza, a whiskered and beaten-down Hungarian, had been hawking newspapers, magazines, and racing forms ever since she could remember. At one time she liked the guy, because beneath his whiskers and sad bravado he had a kind smile—a smile that told her, when she counted out nickels for her monthly issue of *True Romance*, that he understood she was young and sexy and he approved of her reading material. Now the very prospect of seeing Géza hawking a paper with a new fire-related story—"Janitor suspected, read all about it!"; "Our Lady of the Angels school to be torn down!"—sent her running the other way.

In November, in the midst of subzero temperatures, Belinda caught a miserable cold she couldn't shake. At Manny's insistence—"You're worn down and the kid doesn't help things"—she made an appointment with his doctor in the Medical Arts Center on Chicago Avenue and trudged five blocks into the wind to be there on time. She thought she'd be in by three o'clock, out by three fifteen with cough medicine in hand—but instead she was forced to wait her turn in an overheated waiting room crowded with a dozen other red-eyed cold and flu sufferers, some in worse shape than she.

Still, to Belinda's dismay, they weren't too sick to talk, in sentences punctuated with wheezes and sneezes, about the topic that still consumed them—the fire that had happened almost a year ago. As their voices argued and leapfrogged over one another, Belinda sat quietly, staring down at the *Better Homes and Gardens* magazine open in her lap, a wad of tissues pressed to her nose, not looking up to distinguish one speaker from another.

"I'm so glad they tore that place down."

"The school?"

"Yeah. No one wanted their kids to go back there after what happened. That place would have been haunted."

"Yeah, I couldn't imagine sending my kids back there, no matter what they did . . . even if I had kids, which I don't."

"Yeah, they'd fix it and tell you it was safe, but I wouldn't trust them. No sir, not after what happened. Makes Joe and me want to move to the suburbs."

The chair to her right shook and a man hacked out another offering: "Some fancy company from downtown is building a new school right next door." He coughed, cleared his phlegmy throat, and added, "A one-story building with all the safety stuff that Mayor Daley's blue ribbon panel said a school should have."

"Yeah, automatic sprinklers, fire doors, an alarm that's connected to the fire department. Enclosed stairways, no more transoms over doors."

"I hear they're going to use paint that won't burn."

"Flame retardant."

"And they're going to limit the number of kids in a classroom. Something like you gotta allow twenty square feet per student."

"They should have thought of that sooner."

"That old school was a firetrap."

"And overcrowded, to say the least."

"All our schools are overcrowded."

"That's that way it still is everywhere."

"I hate to bring it up again, but those damn nuns did nothing but pray with the kids while the place burned down."

"I beg to differ with you," a female voice across the room said.

Following the voice, Belinda glanced at the galoshes-bundled feet of a woman across the room.

The woman ceremoniously crossed her knees. "My daughter Joanie's teacher, Sister Andrienne, got her kids out quickly. There were seventy kids in her classroom, and she lined them up and made them crawl down the stairs. When they got out she realized some of 'em were missing, so she ran back into the black smoke and got them out by actually rolling them down the stairs to safety. I know because my daughter was one of 'em. That nun's a hero. She saved my Joanie's life." She uncrossed her knees.

"Yeah, you were lucky, but most of the nuns stayed there and prayed."

A brief silence.

Belinda felt the woman to her left shift in her seat. "My husband says for the sake of our kid's safety we should move to the suburbs. He's got a sister in Niles—maybe we'll move to Niles."

"A lot of folks are saying the same thing. Look around you. There are already a lot of FOR SALE signs and FOR RENT signs on the streets, and there'll be more of 'em this spring. Folks are going to move away in droves. Mark my word."

"Where's your kids going to school now?" the guy with the cough asked the woman to Belinda's left.

"A bus picks them up and takes them to Our Lady Help of Christians . . . temporary."

"How are they doing?"

"They're OK. Their new nuns don't talk about the fire, though. They say it's time to forget about it. My Joanie said something about Sister Andrienne and what she did, but her new nun, Sister Constance, shut her down. She told Joanie to keep her memories to herself, because it would upset the other kids."

"They're telling the parents not to talk about it at home either."

"I think the children need to talk about it, get it out."

"No, they say it's better if you just try and forget. Hashing over things again and again doesn't get you anywhere."

"Yeah, yeah, yeah. The whole thing makes me furious. If I had a kid who was hurt in that fire, I'd sue that goddamn church."

"My, my."

Opinions flew faster now. "What good's that gonna do? It wouldn't bring your child back again."

"I wouldn't have the guts to sue my church. It was an accident, an act of God, whatever you call it, and who am I to quibble with God?"

"A lot of people feel that way. Suing the church would be like suing God."

"Ya know, Catholic lawyers are forbidden from taking those cases."

"I heard the same thing."

"There'll be lawsuits, mark my word."

"Did you know that Jim Moran the Courtesy Man sent a check to each family that lost a child?"

"Yeah, that big-shot Ford dealer."

"It was *very* generous of him."

"I still think the janitor did it."

The room was getting stuffy. The words leaped and twisted into a threatening jumble. The walls and the people and the smell of wet wool and sweat were closing in on Belinda. She felt trapped, sure that everyone knew her secrets, her fears. She had to get out of there and breathe fresh air, or she would faint or break into tears, and then who knows what she might say?

A door opened and a nurse in white appeared, clipboard in hand, efficiency written on her face. "Mrs. Belinda . . ." She scanned the waiting room.

"Yes, yes. I'm here," Belinda said, rushing her words and springing from her chair.

———

It was in that doctor's office, on that miserable afternoon, after she somewhat regained her composure, that the thought of moving entered Belinda's mind. Heck, Manny, who just about lived with them now and always complained about the lack of space, might be ready for such a change. Although he still kept his own apartment a couple of miles away, he slowly had been moving his stuff in—his record player, his bowling ball, his recliner, which he positioned directly in front of the TV set, blocking the kid's view of it from the couch. It's time, she thought, to get a larger place, preferably somewhere farther away—maybe the South Side—where they could start all over again, maybe even have a rumpus room for TV watching, maybe a garage. They could be a legitimate couple, get married even. As for the kid, it wouldn't make any difference to him. He hardly complained about anything these days; in fact, he was unusually quiet and cooperative, so she knew she wouldn't be in for an argument there. He wasn't attached to his new, temporary school anyway. Heck, the kid didn't even have a friend he would miss.

Part IV
1960—1962

26

As with most disasters that capture worldwide attention, there comes a point at which there is little more to say and the conversation stops. That is what happened after the fire at Our Lady of the Angels.

There were sporadic human interest stories in the newspapers about the survivors and how they were recovering, and about the safety improvements to schools that were already sweeping the country, but those became relegated to the inside pages.

When the doors of the new Our Lady of the Angels school opened in September 1960, the children were welcomed into a $1 million single-level modern building constructed of steel, glass, and concrete.

———

The view wasn't perfect for me the day of the dedication of the new school. There were no candles—quite unusual for a Catholic ceremony, but understandable. Of course there was the regular hoopla, and bell ringing, prayers, and songs—enough to draw hundreds of neighbors who came dressed in their Sunday clothes for the goings-on. It was a jubilant crowd of smiling and tearful parishioners, proud of their new school building.

It was through a number of lit cigarettes and cigars that I captured the action.

I'll bet you every priest in Chicago was there. Rows and rows of them, dressed in their ecclesiastical best, parading slowly around the school building, smiling and unsmiling, holding their prayer books and crucifixes close to their bellies; followed by entourages of altar boys in their lacy surplices and festive yellow capes; flanked by members of the Knights of Columbus marching in precision in their dark uniforms and hats with wispy white plumes that looked like feather dusters; surrounded by men, women, and children and nuns crowding the sidewalks.

The star of the show was Archbishop Cardinal Albert Meyer, recently promoted to one of the highest positions in the Catholic Church. Looking princely in a white vestment, wearing his spiky golden miter on his head, and gripping his crosier, a tall golden staff with a carved hook, he sprinkled holy water in every corner of the new structure to protect it from evildoers like me. At the entrance to the school building, he removed his miter, revealing the little red zucchetto beneath. He read a blessing from a missal held by an altar boy and passed through the doorway, and then it was lights out for yours truly. I was not allowed inside.

I read later in the newspaper that the cardinal moved from classroom to classroom praying and sprinkling the rooms with holy water.

———

Despite the addition of this spanking new building into the Our Lady of the Angels neighborhood, the close-knit feeling of just a year ago had begun to fray, as families started moving away. It was too emotionally difficult for folks to stay in an area where reminders of the fire were everywhere.

Belinda and Manny were one of the many families from Our Lady of the Angels who had moved away from old memories, but their motives where enhanced by additional factors— a job change for Manny, a new car to replace Manny's clunker, and Belinda's incessant pleas to give the kid a new beginning.

"We need to start over," she pleaded with Manny.

———

I was there when the subject came up once, and I venture to say it wasn't the first time they talked about it.

They were sitting in a booth at the White Castle where Manny took her out for lunch one sunny Saturday afternoon in July when they had nothing better to do than take a spin in Manny's new Ford. Waxed paper wrappers with bits of wilted lettuce and tomatoes and balled-up napkins sat on the plastic table before them, and the place reeked of greasy sliders. I popped to life three feet from Belinda's pretty face when Manny lit a cigarette after their lunch. At twenty-six Belinda was still a looker.

Manny had just been offered a new job on the South Side, so Belinda had her opportunity.

"Manny, are ya going to take that job in Cicero?" she asked, sitting against the booth's hard white back. I watched her rub her teeth with her tongue.

"How can I turn it down? The pay's better."

"That's good," she smiled sweetly. "Are we going to have to move?"

"Nah, we got a reliable car now," he said, gesturing out the smudged window at the used two-tone red-and-white Ford Fairlane parked in a space directly outside, its two enormous front lights looking at them (and me) like giant glass eyes with chrome eyebrows. "It'll take me what, thirty-five, forty-five minutes to get home to your place or mine, and ya know how I love to drive." He sat back and did a full-bodied driving motion, squinting his eyes, gripping the imaginary wheel, shifting gears, and probably pressing his foot on the accelerator pedal under the table. "I feel like Elvis Presley at the wheel of that hot little number."

"Maybe it would be better if we moved, moved in together, sweetie pie," she cooed.

"What for?"

"Ya know."

"Ya know what?"

"To get a fresh start, Manny. My grandma's gone now. The boy's ready for a change. We're paying double rent. We're already running out of room in my place. We talked about having another kid, maybe getting married." She reached over and rubbed the top of his hairy hand with her own. "How about we start all over?"

"Wait a minute, Linny. I think you're getting a little ahead of yourself here . . ."

That's when Manny, the coward, pulled back and crushed me into the metal ashtray—ground me in, actually. He couldn't face it. Just when Belinda was finally asking for what she wanted, what she dreamed of . . . to have a husband, to give the kid a father, he snuffs me out.

That happens a lot in the life of Fire. Just when things are getting interesting.

———

But Belinda prevailed, and a month after eating sliders at White Castle, Belinda and Manny packed their Ford Fairlane solid to the rooftop with bedding, lamps, and glassware, loaded a rented pickup truck, and drove to their new home:

a second-floor, two-bedroom apartment on Fiftieth Avenue in Cicero, a community about seven miles west of downtown Chicago and five minutes from Manny's new job.

Cicero wasn't the sweetest of towns—it had its share of racial tensions and, replete with gangs, gambling, and strip joints, still bore the sordid reputation as headquarters for Al Capone and his crowd in the 1920s. But it also had its share of tree-lined neighborhoods established around Catholic churches and populated by hardworking European immigrants, like the one where Belinda and Manny settled. On a sweltering August morning in 1960, they were married amid minimal fanfare in a small ceremony at Saint Attracta, a red-brick church much like Our Lady of the Angels.

———

I was there for the service, held not in the main church but in the sacristy, because Manny wasn't much of a churchgoer and neither of them had enough friends to fill two church pews, and it was also less expensive. Which was fine for the kid, and even better for me.

The priest lit a stubby candle on a small table, which put me nearly three feet away from and at eye level with the kid who loved me. Throughout the service he and I played googly eyes together, and although things had been quiet for a while, we both knew our connection was much more than a game. We were a team. We had done serious business together. We had our secrets. *People will say we're in love.*

The poor kid could have been a squiggle on the flocked wallpaper for all the attention the adults paid him that day. There were two other people at that poor excuse for a wedding, the sponsors: a cutie-pie friend of Belinda's, and Manny's brother, who wore his hair in a pompadour and rode the nighttime train up from Dwight, Illinois to stand up for him. When it was over, the priest took everyone's picture with Manny's Kodak, at first leaving the kid out, then snapping another shot to include him—"for his scrapbook," the priest said, which made the kid wince. As they exited the sacristy, the kid followed five steps behind, lingering long enough to stare at me longingly and swipe a matchbook from a pizza joint the priest had left on the corner of the table.

Good work, kid.

———

That day did not go down in the annals of the kid's most favorite days to remember: Manny was now a daily presence in his life, and in a turnaround prompted by guilt and an uncommon rush of desire to please his new bride, Manny announced that he wanted to adopt him.

Holy shitballs. This is not going to be good, the kid thought. *But there's nothing I can do about it. Manny calls the shots. He pays the bills. He tells Mom and me what to do. He makes me call him "Dad." To keep the peace, I'll just have to call him that until I'm grown up. Then when I'm old enough I can get the heck out of here.*

Thus they started the new life Belinda always wanted—as a real family with fish on Friday, bingo with prizes in the church basement, a paper route for the kid to make him responsible—and perhaps even another child.

"We all deserve a fresh start," Belinda said.

"Let's hope it works out," Manny replied.

———

Then in 1961, a series of fires erupted in their Cicero neighborhood. On October 9, a fire was started under the staircase
of an apartment building on Cermak Road. On October 24,
flames threatened an apartment building on Twenty-First
Place after someone lit a pile of crumpled-up papers at the
base of a stairwell. On October 25, a similar fire was started
on the back porch of an apartment on Forty-Ninth Court.
The Cicero Fire Department quickly put out all three fires.

On October 26, an anonymous handwritten letter was
delivered by mail to the fire department naming the kid as the
perpetrator of the fire set two days earlier. Someone had seen
him roaming around the apartment building with newspapers
in his hands. Cicero fire chief William Zahrobsky decided to
question the boy, now thirteen, at Cicero Public Elementary,
where he was an eighth grader.

The kid, still chubby and bespectacled, was alone, waiting
in the principal's office, when Zahrobsky arrived.

"I'm Chief Zahrobsky," the officer introduced himself. He
was carrying a clipboard with notes he had hastily scribbled
before leaving the firehouse. His voice was gruff and his stat-
ure was imposing—a combination that would intimidate the
most brazen youngster, but his manner didn't seem to faze
the kid, who immediately jumped to his feet.

"I had a feeling you were going to come and see me," the
kid said, wiping his sweaty hand on his pants and extending
it to the officer.

"And why is that?" Zahrobsky asked, noting the kid's bold
show of respect. In his day, he would have been trembling in
his socks if a fire chief had come to question him. He shook
the kid's hand.

The kid straightened his spine and looked him in the eye.
"Because I was the one who saw that fire on Twenty-First

Place. I was the one who called it in. The fireman driving the pumper told me I did a good job, that I probably saved a lot of lives." The boy grinned as if he expected the fire chief to pin a medal on him.

Zahrobsky looked at him disbelievingly. "I'm here to question you about setting that fire and some other ones."

"Yeah?" the kid said without blinking. "I don't know nothin' about who started 'em."

Zahrobsky noticed that the boy was fidgeting with something in his pocket. "What you got in there?"

"Just stuff."

"Empty both your pockets and let me see."

Out fell two books of matches, one of them from the Playboy Club.

"Do you usually carry matches with you, son?"

"Sometimes."

"Do you smoke?"

"No."

"Then why do you carry them around?" he asked, his jaw hanging down, waiting for an answer.

"Some kids need me to light their cigarettes." The kid wasn't smiling now.

"Where did you get them?"

"Well . . ." he stammered, "I took them from my father's jacket pocket." The kid broke eye contact with Zahrobsky and stared at the floor.

"Look up at me, kid. You stole those matches from your dad? What does he do when you steal something from his pocket?"

The kid looked up. "He punishes me."

"And how's that?"

"He punches me," the kid mumbled, demonstrating with a quick jab of his fist the kind of punch his dad gave him.

"Has he ever punished you for playing with matches?"

"Well, yeah."

"What did he do?"

"Once he held my hand over the burner of the stove." The kid closed his eyes as if remembering.

"Look at me, son. Are you afraid to tell us about setting those fires because you're afraid your dad's gonna hurt you?"

He sucked in a deep breath. "Yeah."

"It's important that you tell the truth, son. You're a Catholic kid, aren't you?" Zahrobsky had learned that much from checking his school record before the meeting. The boy had a history of truancy and "deplorable" behavior. He had recently transferred to the public school from a local Catholic school, Saint Attracta's. What he didn't know is that the kid's parents had taken him out of Saint Attracta's before they got around to expelling him.

"Yeah."

"Well so am I. Catholic. We know that lying is a sin, don't we?"

"Yeah."

"And we know that lies stay on your conscience forever, don't we?"

"Yeah."

"So let me ask you again. Did you start that fire on Twenty-First Place?"

The kid fell back into the chair and folded forward. He grasped his hands between his thighs. "Yeah, I did, but I couldn't help it," he whispered. He reached up and wiped his cheek with the back of his hand. His fingernails were chewed down to the quick.

Zahrobsky checked his clipboard. "How about the other one the day after, on Forty-Ninth Court?

"Yeah, I started that one too."

The fire chief softened his tone. "Why do you start fires, young man?" He squatted down to the kid's level.

The kid looked at him with teary eyes. "I guess I just like the sound of fire sirens. Didn't you when you were a kid?"

The officer reached over and picked up the matchbooks from the floor. "We need to call you mother now, you know that? I'm going to tell her to meet us at the police station."

————

At the station, Zahrobsky led the kid past a row of desks piled high with papers and file folders into a drab cement-block interrogation room, where he sat him down at a wobbly metal table. A minute later they were joined by Lieutenant Victor Witt, and for the next half hour Witt plied the kid with more questions.

"I understand you've admitted to starting two fires in Cicero."

The kid nodded.

"Have you set any others?" The police officer's full face, marked by a strong jaw, was menacing in its lack of expression.

"No," the kid answered, lips quivering.

From across the table Witt looked the kid straight in the eye. "It is just as serious if you started one fire or a hundred fires, young man. Now, be honest with me, are you responsible for any other fires in Cicero?"

"Yes," the kid admitted. "I started the one on Cermak Road."

"The one in that three-story apartment building on October 9?" Chief Zahrobsky interjected, checking his notes.

"Yeah, I started that one too."

"Why do you start fires?" the police officer asked.

The kid thought awhile. "Aw, I could give you a lot of BS, but I won't. Ya want an honest answer?"

"I do."

"I love fire trucks," the kid explained matter-of-factly, as if it were the most reasonable explanation in the world. "I have since I was a kid. I have a siren on my bike and I ride around with it on half the time. I like to set fire to garbage cans. I like to light a stick and carry it around from can to can like a torch."

The police officer's eyes widened. "And then what do you do?"

"I stay in the neighborhood and goof around and when I hear the sirens and the fire department comes, I run back and watch."

"Look at me, son."

The kid felt his face redden. He bit his lower lip and looked like he was going to cry. He looked up as instructed. With four grown-up eyes staring at him, waiting to hear more, he did his best to stay tough. "I promise never to do it again. I've learned my lesson. Please give me another chance," he pleaded, matching the officers' unflinching gazes. He was telling them what he knew they wanted to hear.

Witt and Zahrobsky pushed themselves up from the table. "Stay here, young man," Witt said. The kid heard the door lock behind him. Except for the wobble of the table when he leaned a certain way, the room was as quiet as a vault.

———

When Belinda arrived, out of breath and disheveled, Lieutenant Witt got right to the point: "Madam, your son confessed to starting three fires," he said. Zahrobsky, who was beside him, showed her the matches he'd found.

"Oh my God," Belinda mumbled. "Those are my husband's. Our son must have taken them."

"That's what the boy said."

She looked up at the Lieutenant Witt, her wide brown eyes flooded with tears. "Sir, please give him another chance. Please let him go," she begged. "He's really a good kid. He's a Cub Scout and has a paper route. Give us both another chance. I know he has a problem, but he's just a boy and he's full of mischief, and I'm his mother and he'll listen to me, and I'll make sure he won't do it again."

With Belinda's assurance that the kid would get the counseling he needed, Witt released the boy into her custody.

————

The scene at home that night was anything but tranquil.

"Hell, what kind of delinquent are we raising?" Manny shouted after he heard Belinda's story.

"Simmer down, Manny, the neighbors will hear." She dashed to the kitchen window and drew the café curtains shut.

"Like that's gonna help!" he threw up his arms and mocked. "This kid is nothin' but trouble. I adopt him. We move to the South Side. I try to make a man out of him, give him responsibility, and this is what we get? Where is he?"

"In his room."

"I'm going to give him a piece of my mind," he said, yanking his leather belt from the loops of his trousers.

"No, Manny, no."

He lifted his hand above her face in warning. "And you, Linny, be quiet."

Belinda stood stunned. The heat of her husband's breath stung her face; his voice echoed in her ears. She ran into the living room, turned the television set on loud, and flopped onto the sofa. With her hands pressed against her ears she rocked back and forth and listened to the crack of Manny's belt and the sobs of her son.

———

From then on Belinda hardly allowed the kid to leave her sight. She drove him on his paper route, trying to keep an eye on his every move. But still the spate of fires continued. Next was a fire set on the porch of an apartment building on November 16. This time an elderly woman was hospitalized for smoke inhalation. Again hauled into the police station, the kid admitted setting it. This time a juvenile complaint was filed, but at a hearing in family court the boy recanted his admission of guilt. Again he was released to Belinda's custody.

On December 21, 1961, firefighters were called to the apartment building on Fiftieth Avenue where the kid lived. A fire broke out in their basement. A woman who also lived on the second floor identified the blond, bespectacled kid as a resident of the building and someone she saw leaving the basement after the fire started. "I've seen him down there before, sometimes with a lighted torch. I'm deathly afraid of him."

Then at 10 PM on the night of December 30, another fire destroyed the Town Hall bowling alley, a block and a half from the kid's home. Four men were killed in that blaze.

27

The kid dreamed he was running through a deserted alley littered with overturned trash cans, torched jalopies, mounds of debris, black fissures in the asphalt, and countless places for bad people to hide. It was an alley he'd run through many times before in his dreams, a place where he always felt danger. Any moment now someone could leap out, pounce on him, hurt him. He needed to get somewhere and he knew there was a shortcut somewhere, but he couldn't find it. The alley became a maze. He wasn't making time; he felt like he was running through ankle-sucking mud. It would take him forever to get where he needed to go.

When he woke up, he couldn't shake the dream: the loneliness, the desperation, the threat of something sinister ready to attack. But as most dreams do, details of this one slowly faded into reality—the budding light of day, the warm feeling of his wool blanket tucked around his neck, the trusty clock beside his bed telling him it was only 5:30, that dusky time, not night, not yet morning, when he had time to himself, when no one was telling him to do something . . .

"Eat something or you'll fall asleep at your desk."

"Did you do your homework?"

"You're thirteen, get off your lazy carcass and play a sport, show me you're a man."

This hazy, lazy, warm hour before his day began belonged to him. It was his thinking, planning, plotting time.

Early light brightened the brown shade on his window. The football Manny had given him years ago sat on his dresser, as clean and as unscarred as the day it was made. The calendar pinned to his wall where some of the dates were crossed out in black (the boring ones), a few circled in red (the exciting ones). It's how he kept track of things. Today was January 12, 1962, a Friday.

Before bed the previous evening, his mother told him that he wouldn't be going to school today, that she'd be taking him to "a laboratory" downtown in the afternoon for a lie detector test. She had been threatening to do this for some time—to get to the bottom of the business about the fires—and this time she'd made the appointment and it was for real.

"What do I need that for? I already told you about the fire on October 25 on the back porch on Forty-Ninth, and I told you about the one in our basement. And I told you about four others in apartment buildings. I confessed, Ma, I told you I did them."

He looked at her with weepy eyes. "I need you to give me another chance."

Belinda stared at her son. "And what about that fire in the bowling alley two weeks ago. I can't get a straight answer from you about that one. Four guys died in that fire!"

"I told you I didn't start *that* one," the kid said. "I was home with you watching TV. Don't ya remember?"

"I remember falling asleep on the couch that night, but the cops think you left the house and did it," Belinda said. "Did you?"

"No!"

"They keep questioning us about it, hounding us about you. I thought this move to Cicero would be for the good, but things have only gotten worse. I can't count how many times I've been at the police station with you. The only reason they don't lock you up is because you're a juvenile and they can't do it. They release you right back to us, and we don't know what to do with you anymore. Four guys died in that fire!"

"I know guys died. You said that already. But they don't know what they're talking about. So I set a few fires, but not that one. I promise you I didn't."

"I don't know what to believe," she said, knocking her hand against her forehead, a gesture that looked like a military salute to the kid. "It's time. Your dad and I talked about it. We're going to get to the bottom of this fire business once and for all. Guys died in that fire," she said for the third time. "The cops have been hounding us. They say you should take a lie detector test. Manny and I talked about it and we're paying for the test ourselves." She stomped her foot.

The kid wanted to laugh at how silly his mother looked saluting him and stomping around. Her hair was all frizzled up and her eyes were smudged from the eye goop she painted on them, and her big pregnant belly stuck out like a balloon—but he was smart enough to know that this wasn't the time to make fun of her. Furthermore, the hint of a snicker would only put him deeper into the doghouse with Manny, a guy he was supposed to respect because Manny had married his mother, adopted him, and paid his bills. He'd given him a fresh start away from Our Lady of the Angels in a new neighborhood. At last he had what he always wanted—or what his great-grandma had wanted for him—a real father.

But is this what a father was like? How could he respect a tough guy like Manny, who made him feel as worthless as a crunched-up piece of paper, who shouted a lot and had a short fuse and hit him with his hand, a metal spoon, whatever hard object that was within reach? He remembered the time when Manny had caught him playing with matches and grabbed him by the shoulder and dragged him into the kitchen. "What in the hell you doing, kid?" Then he turned on the stove and held his hand above the gas burner. "Feel this? This is what fire feels like, kid. You wanna end up in the electric chair? You wanna end up on death row?" It was as if marrying his mother, buying him stuff, gave him license to be the cop of the family, the warden in the family prison. *If I had a dollar for every time he threatened me with the electric chair,* he thought, *I'd be a millionaire by now and, what would I do then? I'd take off and buy a bus ticket and see Las Vegas and buy a leather jacket and skedaddle to California. Then I'd start all over being what I want to be: cool and rich and friends with everyone.*

As the sun brightened his room, the kid counted the hours out on his fingers. The lie detector test was eight hours away and he didn't have a plan, which gave him butterflies, but not too many. He didn't have any idea of how he'd answer the questions they'd ask. That depended on who asked the questions and whether he felt he could outsmart the guy who asked them.

If there's one thing he'd learned, it was to lie and to get people to believe his lies. It had become a game with him. He could tell the kids at school the most preposterous stories and they'd believe him. He could be charming if he wanted to. He could widen his eyes and look innocent. He could make grown-ups feel sorry for him. He could tear up and make promises to be better. It worked with the nuns and with his mother. "Give me another chance, one more chance . . . please," he would say to the lie detector guy, and it might work again.

He was frightened, but he also was curious about lie detector tests. He'd seen guys take them on *Dragnet*—bad guys with bands strapped to their chests and cuffs fastened around their arms, connected to a machine. He was curious about how it all worked and whether he'd be able to outsmart the equipment and the guy who was using it, a Mr. Reid, his mother told him. He never knew of anyone in real life who took such a test. He'd be the first, and that would make him important, taking it in a laboratory downtown on Michigan Avenue, on a high floor in a building with an elevator. He'd never been in a skyscraper or a laboratory. It would be something he could brag about to the other kids who made fun of him.

28

"**W**ait here," Belinda told the kid when they arrived for their appointment.

The kid waited in the reception room—a nice enough space with a sofa, flowered drapery swagged off to the side, potted plants, and framed pictures of Chicago cityscapes on the walls—while Belinda met in an office with a staff examiner, a guy about her age in a slick blue suit, who sat at a polished oak desk.

Without ceremony, the young man stood up and extended his hand to her. "I'm Robert Cormack," he said with a half-smile. "Make yourself comfortable," he said, politely gesturing to the chair across from him. He sat down and jauntily selected a fresh yellow pencil from a holder on his desk and opened a manila file with forms inside. From upside-down, Belinda watched him print her name in large capital letters on the top form. The only other object on the desk was a pack of Chesterfield cigarettes. He offered her one. Oh how she wanted one, but she shook her head. She didn't want him to see her chipped nail polish and trembling fingers.

Mr. Cormack asked what she suspected about her son, and she told him about the fires her son confessed to and the ones she wasn't sure of. Intentionally, she didn't mention Our Lady of the Angels. That wasn't what she was there for, and she was too afraid to even think about that fire, much less raise the topic herself, although it crossed her mind every day. And Manny's.

She thought about the morning she had made the appointment with Mr. Reid. She was so distraught after another run-in with the Cicero Police that she called an attorney for advice on how to get the cops off her back. Their attorney advised that their best weapon was the truth. He too suggested a lie detector test and gave Belinda Reid's name and number.

At 3 AM the night before, they had both been tossing and turning. Manny reached over and took her hand: "Do you think he did it?" Belinda didn't have to ask what he was referring to, because she knew they both had been thinking the same thing: *Did he have something to do with the big fire at Our Lady of the Angels?*

"Yeah, I think it all the time," she whispered in the kind of verbal shorthand they had come to know. "The kid was there, and fires happen when he's there," she said, her voice cracking. "I thought maybe he'd give it up when we moved . . . but no. Her deepest thoughts though remained hidden, unspoken: *Manny, do you think we're raising a monster?*

That night Manny had wrapped his arms around her and held her longer and tighter than usual. She remembered how he smelled of sweat and Colgate. "We're going to get through this, Linny," he whispered in her ear. Just how he said "Linny" made her feel protected, as if she were a little girl again. But she wasn't a little girl. She was a mother with huge problems she could no longer ignore.

"Tell me about the boy's background," Mr. Cormack said.

"He was born on October 3, 1948."

"An autumn baby," he said casually, shaking a cigarette out of the pack and tapping it on the glass covering his desk. He reached into his pocket for his Zippo lighter, flicked it open, and ignited a flame.

———

Instantly I came to life, and was staring at Cormack's smoothly shaven face. His hair was parted on the left side, straight as an Iowa highway. He looked pretty sure of himself sitting behind his fancy desk. Belinda was a different story. My dear Belinda looked defeated. Who wouldn't, with her baby boy sitting in the hot seat?

———

Belinda thought of her pregnancy in the autumn of 1948, when she was entering her sophomore year of high school. "The boy's illegitimate," Belinda confessed. "When I was fifteen, I was raped." She didn't tell him—it was none of his business—that she'd been raped by her stepfather. She hadn't even told this to Manny.

"And what happened to the boy's father?" the examiner asked, flicking ashes into a clean copper ashtray.

"He's out of the picture. Then my ma took off and left me with my grandmother, who pulled me out of school and sent me to a home for unwed mothers. A Catholic place. I wanted to have my baby adopted, 'cause what kind of life would the kid have with me? I didn't know anything about being a mother. But the adoption fell through and I didn't want to go through the paperwork, the arrangements all over again. And the nuns hated me . . . you know, 'cause I was a sinner.

So I kept the boy. My grandma had a house on Springfield Avenue, and we lived there and she helped take care of him while I took typing classes and worked at a pizza joint." She sighed, then sat up straighter in her chair. "But now the kid has a father, Manny."

———

I learn things about people, hanging out with them like I do. How could I not feel for Belinda, getting pregnant at fifteen by her own stepfather, and her parents hightailing it out of town and dumping him with his great-grandma? Holy Jesus, I'm fickle and cruel and creepy, but I'm still more loyal than that. I really feel for the girl. When she's telling her story, she leans closer to the examiner and sets her hand on the desk. Her wedding band—nothing special, just a dull silver band that could be a ring on a bathtub plunger—*clicks, click, clicks* on the glass desktop because she's nervous, and who wouldn't be? She pushes her back into her chair and braids her fingers together in her lap. She unbraids them and crosses her knees. She pulls her cardigan sweater tighter around her chest to stop shivering. If I could I'd carry her right out of there and keep her warm, I'd do it, but she wouldn't want that anyway, because I don't know when to stop and I wouldn't let her go and I'd smother her with my kind of love. Anyhow, no problem today, because I'm not getting any farther than the tip of Cormack's Chesterfield.

———

"What does Manny do?"

"He works on an assembly line in a plant."

"How do he and the boy get along?"

Belinda took a deep breath and her words flew out in exasperation. "So-so. We have our good days and our bad. God knows Manny tries. He keeps buying him sports equipment, but the kid's not interested. He's not interested in much."

"Does he get sexual gratification from it?"

"Manny?" she asked, her face flushing.

"I'm sorry. No, your son, from starting fires," Cormack clarified.

"Heck if I know." Belinda patted her rounded tummy self-consciously. Manny wants a boy he can start all over with. Teach him sports. Me? I'm hoping for a girl. They gotta be a lot easier than boys."

The examiner gave Belinda background on how the polygraph machine worked. The machine would record blood pressure, pulse, and respiration rate, and also muscular activity in the forearms, thighs, and feet. The muscular movements would be picked up by metal bellows in a band wrapped around the chest and under the arms, and in the seat of the polygraph chair. Sensing her apprehension, the examiner reassured her that John Reid was a nationally recognized expert in polygraphy, and that he would handle her son kindly. "There will be no intimidation. We won't give him the third degree," he assured her. He also assured her that since she initiated and paid for the test, the results would be kept confidential.

29

A half hour later, the chief examiner, a Mr. Lindberg, led the kid into the laboratory. It was an overheated room with tan walls, an opaque window, a table with the lie detector sitting on it, and four chairs. The kid felt like he was in a police station.

That's gotta be a two-way window, he thought. *Someone's gotta be watching on the other side.*

He stared at the lie detector machine, a gray and black box a little larger than a table radio, with knobs, dials, and a small screen with an arc of numbers behind it, sort of like an odometer in a car. There was another glass screen over a roll of paper, where the results would be recorded in spikes and valleys by a fan of needles.

Mr. Lindberg introduced him to still another guy, the head interrogator, Mr. John Reid, who welcomed him nicely enough but wasn't too friendly. The kid was hoping for a jovial sort of examiner like his pediatrician, Dr. Morissi, who had a chuckle in his voice and would say, "Relax, I'm just going to give you a quick exam and get you out of here in no time." But this guy was stuffy, a tall, formal kind of guy like the kid sometimes saw in movies, who wore a gray suit, drove a sedan, and rode an elevator to his office, the kind who couldn't laugh until he took his tie off. All business.

"You sit here," Mr. Reid said, gesturing to a chair behind the machine with belts and straps attached. The kid wondered who'd sat in that chair before him—Bugs Moran, Baby Face Nelson, maybe Al Capone himself.

"This is Miss Mildred McGuffie," Mr. Reid said, pointing to a middle-aged woman in a flower-patterned dress sitting, knees crossed, beside him. "She's our stenographer and she'll be writing down everything you say. And, of course, Mr. George Lindberg, my assistant." The two sat beside Mr. Reid.

The kid nodded. He wanted to get the whole thing over with after waiting forever in the stuffy waiting room, but to his chagrin, Mr. Reid didn't hook him up to the lie detector machine immediately. "I want you to talk to me and tell me the truth before we attach you to the polygraph," he explained.

"I will. I'm not going to lie," the kid said, shaking his head.

"Very good."

The room felt dry. The kid licked his lips. When he rubbed them with his tongue they felt like the scales on his goldfish that had died from overfeeding. His eyes burned from the fluorescent lights above and he imagined his hair standing on edge and catching fire from the static electricity in the room. *Would serve me right*, he thought.

Mr. Reid's cold brown eyes bore into him. "Were you responsible for these fires in Cicero . . . the one on the back porch to Kenneth's house on Forty-Ninth Court?"

"Yeah. I started that one." The kid remembered that evening very well. It was the night he was collecting for his paper route. Kenneth, a boy who pushed him around, lived there. He wanted to get even with him, so he sneaked into the rear porch of the building and set fire to some rags he found in a box. He had a book of matches in his pocket from a Chinese restaurant. The Chinese Fire, he called it in his mind.

"And the fire in the basement of your apartment building on Fiftieth Avenue?"

"I started that one too. And four other fires in apartment buildings." Instantly he knew he shouldn't have offered his interrogator that much information.

"When was the first time you set a fire?"

"When I was five. In a garage."

Mr. Reid sat back in his chair. "Why do you start fires, lad?"

"Can I have a drink of water?"

Mr. Lindberg shot up from his chair, and before the kid knew it there was a Dixie cup of water in front of him. He gulped it down in one swallow.

"Why do you start fires?"

The kid shifted in his seat. There were so many reasons. He liked the power, the excitement, the surge of electricity that ran through him at that split second when the fire came to life, that moment when a lapping tongue of gold awakened every cell in his brain, his heart, even down there. *Too much to tell Mr. Reid, and I don't think he'd get it anyway. So keep it simple.*

"I like fire trucks. I like to set fire to garbage cans. I like to strike a match and light a twig or a branch and carry it from can to can like a torch, and sometimes the cans will burn like rockets. When I set a fire, I'll stay in the neighborhood and find some kids to play around with. Then when I hear the sirens, we all run over and watch."

"Any other fires?"

"Yes, on Ridgeway Avenue in Chicago, where I used to live. I took lighter fluid, matches, and paper and spread it around and set fire to a hallway and the door to an apartment there." He looked at Mr. Reid sheepishly, "Do you have any others as bad as me on this test?" he asked.

"Many much worse. There were murderers that sat in that same chair you're sitting in," Mr. Reid answered.

The kid looked at Mr. Reid and then down at his hands clasped in a knot on his lap. He squinted to hold back tears. "I feel so bad after I set fires. I wish I was never born." He looked up at Mr. Reid to see his reaction, but there was none. *The guy's a stoneface*, the kid thought.

"Is it only boys who set fires?" he asked Mr. Reid.

"Usually boys or men."

"Why wasn't I born a girl?" the kid responded.

Mr. Reid changed the subject. "What school do you go to?"

"Cicero Public School."

"What grade are you in now?"

"Eighth," the kid answered quickly. *This is easy.*

Mr. Reid smiled.

The kid smiled back. *I think he likes me.*

"What religion are you?"

"Catholic."

"But you don't go to a Catholic school?"

"Nope," the kid replied. Then, feeling more comfortable with their conversation, he added, "I used to. I went to Saint Attracta in Cicero, and before that, when I lived in Chicago, I went to Our Lady of the Angels."

———

Reid was taken aback. "Our Lady of the Angels?" he said, trying not to show surprise at the kid's revelation. Up until this point no one had made the connection, because after Manny adopted him, the boy was given a different last name. "Were you there at the time of that fire?"

"I was. Fifth grade."

"Did you start that fire?"

"No." The kid shifted in his seat.

Mr. Reid adjusted his glasses and looked the kid in the eye. "Remember, young man, you promised to tell me the truth. Is this the truth?"

The kid adjusted his own eyeglasses and then rubbed his sweaty palms against his corduroy pants. "I didn't do it."

"You knew your way around that school pretty well, didn't you?" Mr. Reid asked.

"Better than some of the priests and nuns," he bragged.

"Will you draw me a picture of the layout of the school as you remember it, son? Just draw the basement of the school, will you?"

———

No problem, the kid thought. He picked up the pencil, bit down hard on the yellow shaft, then drew the basement from memory: the largest space for the chapel, which he marked with a CH; the boiler room, which he marked BR; and the boys' washroom down the hall, which he marked with a BW.

"Where did the fire start?"

"Here," he said, pointing to the exact spot in the stairwell where he started the fire. He marked it with an X.

"We're going to hook you up to the polygraph machine now and I'm going ask you a number of questions, and I am going to cover the fire at Our Lady of the Angels."

"OK."

Mr. Lindberg hooked him up, tightening a belt with sensors around his chest to pick up the beat of his heart, strapping a cuff to his arm to pick up the pressure changes in his blood flow. The kid felt like he was in an electric chair. He couldn't break out and run. He felt trapped. He needed to give himself a pep talk. OK, *so I like to set fires, but there's good in me. I'm a normal kid. I like to laugh and have fun too. I say my prayers like everybody else. I'm smart. I've gotten out of bigger stuff before. I can get out of this.*

"How do I know this machine is telling the truth?" he asked.

"It's superb at doing that," Mr. Reid answered. "Here, let's do a control test and I'll show you how that works."

"OK."

Mr. Reid reached into his desk drawer and pulled out seven cards, the size of playing cards. Each card had a large number on it, one to seven. He laid out the cards on the desk before him. "What I want you to do is to pick a card in your mind, but to answer "No" to every question I ask you.

"OK." In his mind the kid selected card number 5. *A high number but not too high. The number of bites in a Tootsie Roll. The number of fingers on his hand,* he thought. He took a deep breath and sat ramrod straight in the chair.

"Is it number seven?"

"No." The needles on the machine indicated little movement.

"Is it number two?"

"No." Again the needle marks remained steady.

"Is it number five?"

"No."

This time the needles went jaggedy, indicating that the kid had lied.

"See, that's how it works." Mr. Reid inserted an opaque plastic divider behind the machine, blocking the kid's view of the needles.

The kid squirmed. He felt heat build inside his chest and heard a pounding inside his head, like he was sealed inside a beating drum. He shifted in the chair. *There's no way out. Maybe some of the crooks on TV can get away with fooling this machine, but not me. Not with this Mr. Reid and his fancy equipment staring me in the face. I bet this contraption can even read my mind.*

"I'm going to ask you some questions now. Ready?"

The kid nodded.

"Where do you live?"

"Cicero, Illinois. 1836 South Fiftieth Avenue." He heard his voice get raspy, like it did when he was in a tough spot.

"How old are you?"

"I'm thirteen."

"What is your birth date?"

"October 3, 1948."

"What school do you attend now?"

"Cicero Public School."

"Before you went to Cicero Public School, where did you go to school?"

"Saint Attracta."

The kid noticed that after every question Mr. Reid paused and jotted a mark on a piece of paper. *So far, so good.*

"Before you went to that school, where did you go to school?"

"Our Lady of the Angels."

"Did you go to Our Lady of the Angels school at the time of the fire there?"

"Yes."

"Do you recall the date of that fire?

"It was on December 1, 1958."

"What grade were you in at that time?"

"Fifth."

"Do you recall your room number?"

"206."

"What was your teacher's name?"

"Miss Tristano. I don't know if I could spell it or not."

"When you went to Our Lady of the Angels, did you usually come home for lunch?"

"Well, yeah." *What's this guy asking me about lunch for?*

"Did you go home for lunch on the day of the fire?"

"Yeah."

"What time did you come back from lunch that day?"

"One o'clock."

"Did you come back from lunch with anyone?"

"Yeah, my buddy." *I can't tell Reid I walked alone, because he'll think I don't have any friends and that I'm some kind of weirdo. It's just a fib, but maybe this machine can handle it. It's just like tossing a couple of ants into a box of chocolate-covered raisins. Chances are no one will notice.*

"What was the boy's name?"

Holy shitballs, now I have to tell another lie. "I think it was Bob. He wasn't really my buddy. I hardly knew him. He was just a little kid who lived by me and tagged along. I think he looked up to me."

"I suppose you were talking to Bob when you were coming back with him."

"Yeah."

"Do you recall what you talked about?"

"Murders and horror pictures."

"Did you say anything about your school when you were coming back?"

"I told him I had matches in my pocket and I said I was going to burn down the school so we wouldn't have no more school for a couple of weeks or days and that we'd have a vacation."

"What did Bob say?"

"He thought I was kidding."

"Were you actually kidding?"

"Yeah."

"Did you think any more about burning the school down after that?"

"Yeah, that afternoon."

"What did you do?"

"I asked my teacher if I could be excused and went to the washroom. After coming back from the washroom I went to the chapel to see if anyone was in there. Then from the chapel I went back upstairs to my room."

"After you got to your classroom, what did you do?"

"I went back to my seat and was talking and goofing around, bothering kids, and then my teacher opened the door because someone said they smelled smoke and there was smoke coming in and she ran to the fire alarm upstairs and she turned it on so everybody could get out."

The kid looked at the lie detector machine. *OK, I don't think it's doing anything strange, it's just humming along. I already told some fibs, so I might as well tell some more.* "Then she got all us kids over to the window and had to wait until the firemen could get there with the net and she pushed us out the window and she jumped herself."

"What floor was that on?"

"Second."

"What street was that facing?"

"Avers."

"What time did the fire start?"

"About a quarter to three."

"What did you do then after you got down into the net and out?"

I can't tell him I watched the fire. I can't tell him about the pregnant lady with the extra jacket who put her arm around me, was nice to me, he thought, *but I can tell him exactly what happened next.*

"I ran to my den mother's house, because she was going to have a den meeting."

"Was your den mother at home?"

"Yeah, 'cause she was expecting us for a den meeting."

"Did you have your den meeting then?"

"No."

"Why not?"

"Because of all the confusion and excitement of the fire." He remembered, though, that the radio was on. It was a weird feeling to hear the fire engine sirens on the radio behind the announcer's voice, and also through the window on the city streets. The announcer was giving the number of dead kids— twenty, then thirty, then fifty. The rising numbers scared the hell out of him.

"What did you do then?"

I remember exactly what I was doing then. I was rubbing my arms and scratching my wrists and knocking my shoes on the floor, but I can't tell Mr. Reid that, because it sounds weird, like I was some kind of monkey in a circus. "She tried to calm me down and she asked me for my mother's telephone number at work. It took her a while to get it out of me, because I was nervous, and she kept dialing wrong numbers, and finally I got it right and she called my mother and she told her what happened so that my mom wouldn't hear it on the radio and faint or anything."

"What did you do then?"

"She told me to calm down and watch TV, or do something else to keep busy."

"Was anybody else there?"

"Just her kids."

"What did you do then?"

"I waited until Manny came and got me."

"Where did you go then?"

"Home."

The kid remembered the car ride home, Manny asking him bluntly, "Did you have anything to do with that fire?" "Of course not," he'd answered. He remembered glancing at Manny's stiff profile as he drove. The muscles in his jaw were tense. He knew that Manny knew. His mother hugged him when he walked in the door. She wiped soot off his face with a damp dishcloth that smelled like sour milk and made him take a bath before supper. Manny stayed over that evening; there wasn't much talking at the supper table, and the adults didn't watch TV until after he went to bed. Then he remembered smashing a pillow over his head to block out the sound of Fahey Flynn reporting the fire on the news.

The kid looked over at the pad on Miss McGuffie's lap. "What kind of foreign writing is that?"

"Shorthand," she answered.

"Did you set fire to Our Lady of the Angels school?" Mr. Reid asked.

"No," the kid answered. He heard the scratching of the needles on the lie detector machine. He couldn't see the screen, but this lie was a whopper, and he pictured the race of needles in dips and spikes on the paper behind the glass screen.

Mr. Reid looked up at him. "Son, just remember that your mother wants the truth, I want the truth, and you told me you're a Catholic boy. You know telling a lie is a sin. There are ninety-two children and three nuns looking down at us right now from heaven who want the truth. Now tell me, did you set the school on fire?"

The kid bowed his head. He thought of his great-grandma Filippa up in heaven looking down on him, wagging her pointer finger. *"Tell the truth, bambino, or shame on you."* He was too scared to answer. All he could think of doing was to pray. So he prayed—not one prayer but a mix of prayers he knew, and some he made up on the spot.

Our Father who art in heaven . . . Hail Mary full of grace . . . Oh my God, I am heartily sorry for having offended Thee, and I detest all my sins . . . Get me out of here, Jesus. He told himself to relax. *There's got to be a way out of here. I heard if a guy stays calm, he could outsmart a lie detector machine.* He took a deep breath and tried to look unconcerned but helpful. But he couldn't stop lying. "I didn't start the fire, but I'll let you know who did."

"Go on," Mr. Reid said.

"I told you about this kid I walked home with at lunch-time . . ." The kid paused. Mr. Reid didn't move, just sat there upright in his chair staring at him, waiting for him to say more. *This guy could be a statue, like those gray plaster statues in church, the ones with marble eyes, that you always think are going to come to life and leap out at you.*

The scratching of Miss McGuffie's pencil on her steno pad stopped, but the hissing of the radiator behind her didn't. *That radiator hisses like those nuns hissed at me to kneel straight up on the kneeler in chapel, when all I wanted to do was sit down because my back hurt from kneeling so long.* He remembered that one nun had a clicker that sounded like a frog that she clicked when she caught kids slouching or whispering in chapel. He hated that clicker, but he hated the hissing nun and he hated the hissing radiator even more. But now he hated Mr. Reid even more than that. *The guy doesn't even blink. I gotta stop the sound of that radiator. I gotta say anything. Talk my way out of it. Make something up.* He gave himself a pep talk. *You can do it. You've done it before. You're smarter than these guys.*

The kid took a deep breath and continued: "But on the afternoon it happened I was coming back to school from lunch with that buddy of mine who lived on Springfield Avenue . . ."

Mr. Reid looked him directly in the eye. "Son, I don't think there's any other kid at all in this case."

A flush of blood rushed to the kid's cheeks. "How do *you* know?"

"The lie detector shows that."

The kid slouched in his chair. Heat rose up into his head and he brushed his forehead with damp fingers. *Reid's on to me. It's all over. The machine won.*

"Well, I guess I better tell you the truth then."

"I guess you better. Just before we started, you drew a picture of the layout of the basement for Miss McGuffie, Mr. Lindberg, and myself. Is that right?"

"Yeah."

He set the drawing in front of him. "Will you point this drawing out to Mr. Lindberg and tell him again what you did after you left your room at Our Lady of the Angels school on the afternoon of December 1, 1958?"

"I went downstairs to the boys' washroom. Then . . . I went to the chapel to see if there was anybody in there and there wasn't anybody in there so I walked back to the rubbish can."

"What kind of can was that?"

"It was a round cardboard rubbish can for papers and it had metal rims on it at the top and the bottom. I looked around and I didn't see anybody. I threw three matches in the can and then ran up the stairs to my room."

"Did you light those matches?"

"Yeah."

"Did they catch fire?"

He looked down at his chewed cuticles. "Yes."

"Where was the can located?"

"In the middle of the stairwell near the stairs and the chapel."

Mr. Reid tapped his finger on the drawing. "In the drawing you have here it seems as though you have the can located under the stairs." He pointed to the X the kid had made on the drawing. "Is that where it was?"

"Yes."

"What was your reason for setting this fire?"

"What do you mean?"

"What did you do it for?"

"Well, I thought we'd get a couple days off from school because of the fire."

"Did you see the flames in the can before you left to go back to your classroom?

"Yes." He closed his eyes and felt hot wet tears behind his eyelids. *Don't cry. Tough guys don't cry.*

"Did you have any special feeling at the time you started this fire?

"Just that I didn't think I was going to hurt nobody. I just thought we'd get out of school early and the firemen would come and put it out."

"Did you tell anybody about starting the fire at Our Lady of the Angels before?"

"No."

"Why are you telling us about it now?"

He looked Mr. Reid directly in the eye. "I wanted to get it off my chest."

"Why didn't you tell it to anyone before?"

"I was afraid my dad was going to give me a beating and I'd get in trouble with the police and I'd get the electric chair or something."

"Why are you thinking about the electric chair?"

"On account of what my dad told me. He said there was this guy who shot his parents and a couple of kids and he got the chair for it. My dad said, 'You wouldn't do anything that might kill somebody, would you?'"

"Was he referring to anything in particular?"

"I don't know."

"How did your father start talking to you about the electric chair?"

"He always talked about the electric chair. A couple of days ago we were watching a movie on TV . . . a movie about a guy who got the chair for nothing. He didn't do it, and my dad kept telling me things about it and about the gas chamber."

"Who played in that movie?"

"Edward G. Robinson."

"He never said anything to you about that before that time?"

"No, except for when I set that fire in the apartment building on Forty-Ninth Court in Cicero." *The Chinese Fire.*

"Did your father learn that you set that fire?"

"Yeah."

"What did he say to you then?"

"He said the next time I set any place on fire and if I kill somebody and if the police don't get me, he'll come after me himself personally and kill me."

"Did you believe your father would do this?"

"Yeah." The kid's thoughts reeled back to the beatings Manny gave him, even before he and his mom got married.

"What was the reason why you didn't tell anyone about the Our Lady of the Angels fire?"

"I was scared. I was scared of my dad, not my mom . . . I could talk her into believing me, giving me another chance, but that my dad would give me a beating."

"Do you know where you are now, son?"

The kid shook his head. "The building, no. I know we're downtown in Chicago at some place near the lake."

"You are in our laboratories, John E. Reid & Associates laboratories at 600 South Michigan Avenue in Chicago. How did you get down here today?"

"A bus and the subway."

"Your mother is sitting out in the next room waiting."

"She better be. I can't find my way home alone."

———

Mr. Reid unstrapped him from the machine and told him to wait alone in the room while he and Mr. Lindberg spoke with his mother and Miss McGuffie transcribed the interview.

The kid stretched his plump arms, relieved to be free of the bands, sensors, and the blood pressure cuff. He studied his drab surroundings. "Sounds like I'll be here awhile. Do you have any magazines I can read?"

Miss McGuffie came back with a *Look* magazine in her hand. It was the January 2 issue. On the cover was a color photograph of President John Kennedy riding in a golf cart with his daughter Caroline on his lap and a bunch of chestnut-haired, grinning Kennedy cousins piled around them. The kid could almost hear their summer laughter rising off the page. *I never had fun like that.*

He flipped through the pages with sweaty fingers that stuck to the slick magazine paper. His thoughts were unfocused. His head was buzzing like bees had been set loose inside. *What are they talking about out there? Are they calling the cops? Is someone going to come back with handcuffs and take me away?* The waiting was harder than answering the questions. He closed the magazine, then opened it again.

His eyes landed on a photo of the Kennedy family posing in front of an enormous sparkling Christmas tree in the White House. *Some kids have all the luck. Me? I just got problems.* He thought of Manny and the trouble he'd be in when he got home, if he ever got there. *Now my mom's going to hate me too.*

He stared at the door. *What's taking so long? Is she that slow a typist? She probably makes a lot of mistakes. What are they talking about? Are they waiting for the cops?*

Still no one was coming. He flipped through the magazine one more time. His head started to hurt. He looked at his wristwatch. Eight o'clock. He'd been there all afternoon and evening, mostly waiting. The lie detector part couldn't have taken an hour. *Oh yeah, in between they gave me a dry half of an egg salad sandwich—something Miss McGuffie probably had left over from her own dumb lunch, and a chocolate soda, but don't they know I'm a growing boy and that ain't enough. Don't they know I need to go home and eat supper? Maybe I'll never go home. Maybe my next meal will be in jail and it'll be bread and water there.*

He felt jittery. He scratched his legs, rubbed his arms, tried to sit still, but couldn't. He turned around and looked at the opaque glass window in the middle of the wall. *Yeah, it's probably a two-way kind of thing like on* Dragnet, *and they're watching me so I don't escape.* He smiled at the glass, the toothy, wide-eyed, innocent way he smiled every year when he had his school photo taken—photos the other kids would trade with each other, but never with him. He pictured Mr. Reid, Mr. Lindberg, and his mother standing behind that window frowning at him.

30

I have a ringside seat to what happens next. John Reid lights up a cigarette and meets with Belinda, who this time also lights up and inhales in shallow, uptight breaths.

Reid doesn't waste time. He tells her the kid confessed to setting a number of fires, including the one at OLA. Although Belinda isn't the sexpot she was nine years ago, I still have feelings for her. Who wouldn't, given the hot water the poor girl's in? Her hands tremble as she smokes, which means I tremble in her hand. Her head's twitching as well. Even the tips of her short hair are trembling. She reminds me of a candle sputtering in the wind.

"We promised confidentially, ma'am, but given your son's confession and the loss of so many lives, we need to readdress this," Reid says.

She shakes her head no. "I paid for the test and I should own it. That's what we agreed on, didn't we?"

I have to admire her spunk.

"Yes," he nods. "But your boy is dangerous and in need of psychiatric treatment. What's to say he's not going to go out and set fires that kill more people? You and your husband have a moral responsibility to do what's right and bring the authorities into this and get him treatment while he's still a child. Under Illinois law, your son can't be prosecuted for a crime he committed under the age of thirteen, so he's not going to end up in jail. But if he goes on and sets more fires as an adult, you can be assured he'll spend time in prison."

"You promised confidentiality," she says, looking up at him with grief-stricken eyes. She sets me in an ashtray and drops her head into her hands and sobs. I want to comfort her. She needs someone to hold on to her. "I gotta call Manny to tell him to come over."

———

An hour later, Manny storms into the office. "Parking around here's a bitch" is the first thing he says. His hair is windblown; his work jacket is spotted from coffee he spilled on it while driving, and the soles of his work boots hold a rim of slush from the snow outdoors. In contrast to Reid, who's calmly standing near a potted plant in his perfectly pressed suit and shiny shoes, Manny's one hotheaded mess. Reid tries to settle him down by thanking him for coming. Then he starts telling him about the lie detector test. All the while, Manny's giving him the evil eye, like he wants to leap out of his boots and strangle him for the inconvenience of having to drive downtown to discuss the kid and me.

"Mind if I smoke?" he interrupts Reid's explanation. Music to *my* ear.

"No sir, be my guest."

Manny lights up a Camel and paces the room in a small, angry circle, jiggling me around, allowing the ashes to build to an inch before flicking them, sometimes missing, into the ashtray on Reid's desk.

Reid tells him that his boy admitted to setting the school fire and that he, in the company of Belinda and with witnesses, read, corrected, and signed the eight-page testimony that included the boy's confession. Manny shouts, "He did what? He signed what? Why that little *sonofabitch*! Where is he?"

"Calm down, sir," Reid says.

Manny glares knives at his wife. "Did you talk to him?"

"No."

"Lemme see him. Where is he?"

Reid points down the hall to the closed door of the examining room where the kid is waiting.

"Lemme see him." He storms into the room and leaps toward the kid with a velocity that reminds me of myself at my peak performance. "Goddammit. Did you set that goddamn fire? You tell me now!" He points down at him with his cigarette.

The guy makes *me* shiver.

The kid looks up and there's fear behind his thick glasses.

"No!" he answers immediately. The muscles in the kid's face are as taut as a stretched rubber band.

"Then why did you say so?" Manny screams at him.

The kid points to Reid, who is right behind Manny. "Because he told me to," he shouts back.

Manny turns and steps so close to Reid that I think he's going to slug him. But all he does is what he does best: shout. He shouts with so much force that white spittle collects in the corners of his mouth. "You coerced him. You forced a confession out of my kid. You made him sign it. I knew this was going to happen. Linny said you were a cop before you started this lie detector racket. Is that some kind of cop tactic? Coercing little kids?"

"Let's talk in another room," Reid says to Manny.

"Don't tell me I have to leave the room. I can stay where I want and I can talk to my kid if I want to."

"First you're going to talk to me, sir. Let's go down the hall."
Reid says forcefully.

I admire this guy, Reid. I always have. He is like a UN dip-
lomat or something. Cool as the frost in his grandma's icebox.
I can almost feel his blood boiling, but he doesn't show it.
Probably a technique he learned at the police academy, or from
reading all those psychology books on his bookshelf.

Reid grips Manny's elbow firm-like and walks him out of the
room with Belinda trailing behind.

Now in his own office, behind closed doors, he lets him have
it. "That's no way to talk to a young boy, and attacking him or
me is no way to solve a problem. Sit down and calm down," he
says, gesturing to a wooden chair facing his desk.

Manny drops into the chair and shifts around uncomfortably
in the space, the way he does when he can't settle down in
bed at night and makes a big production of it and blames it on
Belinda, their crummy mattress, the kid. Belinda takes a seat
beside Manny. He taps his jacket pocket to feel for another
cigarette, shakes out two from the pack, and offers her one. She
nervously accepts it. He helps himself to a book of matches on
Reid's desk, a matchbook that says JOHN E. REID & ASSOCIATES
in truthful blue letters.

Reid leans against the corner of his desk facing them. He
can't be more than a foot away from Manny, almost on top of
him. Intimidating, if you ask me. He lights his own cigarette
from a fancy silver table lighter and eyes Manny from above
my flame.

Everyone's puffing and it's becoming a real smoke fest, like
in a pool hall or the mayor's office or a wingding in the church
basement. I'm in my element.

Reid stands tall. "Let's get a few things straight. For the
record, your son was not coerced by me or anyone else to say
what he did. He made his confession voluntarily. His confession

was witnessed by two other professionals, Mr. Lindquist and Miss McGuffie. A transcript of every word uttered in that room was prepared and then signed by the boy. You will receive a copy so you will know verbatim the questions I asked and the answers he gave."

"But the kid makes things up," Manny interrupts.

"That may be so," Reid says. "That's why we also have the polygraph tapes, which will support whether or not your boy was lying, but my experience in reading them on the spot tells me he was telling the truth about the fires."

"But . . ."

"Let me finish, sir. One copy of the transcript is for you. I suggest you and your wife read it very carefully and consult with your own attorney. The other copies are for the authorities and for our files."

"No!" Belinda butts in. "You said it would be confidential and now you want to turn the results over to the cops. That's not fair," she whines.

Manny lurches to the edge of his chair. "They're going to put the kid in the electric chair if these transcripts get out, and how am I supposed to believe that machine of yours? The kid's probably lying," he shouts. Belinda pulls on the hem of his jacket, urging him to control himself.

"Now, let's look at the facts," Reid says, setting his cigarette into the ashtray. He straightens his tall body and looks Manny directly in the eye.

"As I explained to your wife, sir, the Illinois criminal code of 1961 states that a child under the age of thirteen cannot be held liable for a crime, thus he cannot be prosecuted for it. So he will not end up in the electric chair. What will probably happen is that this case will go to the family court and the judge will put him in a juvenile home where he will get help, or he will be returned to your care. But, let me make this very clear: if your son is not given help right now, there is no doubt he will set more fires that result in more deaths. Do you want to have that on your consciences?" He glares at both of them.

Belinda shakes her head.

Manny looks away at a darkened window decorated with flowered drapery drawn back with fancy brass clips. Lights are still on in some of the offices in the skyscraper across the street. Through the frames of windows, cleaning people are moving around with their carts and mops.

"No," he says. "But we're going to call our attorney."

"I suggest you do, sir. Then either you provide the transcript to the authorities, or I will. I don't want this on my conscience either."

Mr. Reid extends his hand to Manny, then to Belinda.

———

After they leave, Reid sits at his desk for a long time, chain-smoking and thinking. He keeps me close to him for the rest of the night, puffing as he walks down the street to his apartment, carelessly flicking ashes onto the sidewalk. At home he is so distracted that he almost takes me into the shower with him. Last thing he does is light up. Lucky for him, he remembers to put out my flame in the ashtray beside his bed.

31

The moment the kid mentioned he had been a student at Our Lady of the Angels was the moment John Reid knew he had one hot potato on his hands.

The next morning he got to the office early, picked up the phone, and called Alfred J. Cilella, the judge of family court. He knew Cilella was an early riser as well. He wanted to tell him about the boy's confession, and perhaps even gain his support over his decision to violate the confidentiality agreement he had with the parents. After a few pleasantries, Reid began to explain the purpose of his call, but the judge immediately cut him off.

"Stop right there, John. You know I can't go further, because if I listen to you, I'll have to disqualify myself from this case. This is going to have to come to me from a delinquency petition filed by any citizen or law enforcement agency, and then I'll deal with it."

"You're right, Al, but I just wanted to alert you what was coming down." They hung up.

Through the windows of his Michigan Avenue office, Reid watched a weak lemon sun ascend over the frosty lake. How placid things were this time of day, that one hour before his associates reported for work, the time when, high above the din of rush hour traffic, he could organize his thoughts, prepare for meetings, analyze data, and get ready for a new parade of suspects who would pass through. The pace was going to increase hour by hour, reaching a crescendo by late afternoon, and then dip again into silence as winter darkness descended over his building.

He walked over to the corner window overlooking the city he loved. Raised on the South Side, Reid had attended Leo Catholic High School, Loyola University, and DePaul University, where he was a guard on the DePaul football team in 1933. A few years later he joined the Chicago Police Department and, while working as an officer, took his bar examination and was admitted to the Illinois bar. Never comfortable carrying a gun, he put in for an administrative job and was assigned to the police crime lab, where he was responsible for lie tests.

Reid was also a scientist and an inventor. Becoming increasingly interested in pairing electronic lie detection technology with interrogation methods that involved gaining the subject's confidence, Reid eventually set up his own firm and received a patent on the lie detector machine he invented and used. Now he administered about twenty-four hundred lie detector tests a year, with 60 percent of them being for corporations testing the honesty of their employees, and 40 percent being for criminal cases.

Reid was never more convinced of the truth of a confession than he was now of the kid's, yet the results of lie detector tests were not always admissible in court. There was a new state criminal code that stated that the court may not suggest, require, or accept evidence provided by a lie detector test.

Like all Chicagoans, Reid had kept abreast of the proceedings following the school fire, the details of the coroner's

inquest in particular. Given his background, he had a wide
network of friends in the police force, the legal system, and
the Catholic Church. In the end, his experience told him
that not only was the kid guilty of starting the fire but officials influenced by the Catholic Church must have deliberately withheld information to save the Church from liability.
After Reid learned that the kid had attended Our Lady of
the Angels he'd made a few discreet phone calls to his police
officer and lawyer friends. He learned that the kid himself
had been questioned after the fire. Hundreds of other kids had
been questioned and some pointed their fingers at the kid as
a suspect. Yet nothing was done. Now, even though he had
a confession that was made voluntarily, his instincts told him
the whole thing might fall apart.

His instincts served him well.

Three days later, the *Chicago Tribune*, without revealing
the kid's name, ran a story about his confession. It turned out
that this information had been leaked to a *Tribune* reporter
who was following the story. The reporter contacted Reid
for a statement. Under pressure, Reid confirmed that the kid
had visited his office, but he gave no details. He said that if
any information was forthcoming, it would come to family
court from the attorneys for the boy's family. According to
the newspaper account, Judge Cilella, who only reluctantly
agreed to comment to the reporter, said that "if the confession
is found to be accurate, the boy should be taken into custody."

The following day, after reading the kid's confession in the
transcript, Judge Cilella turned the kid over to Cook County
juvenile authorities at the Audy Juvenile Home, where he would
undergo psychological tests to see if he was mentally fit for a
hearing. Reid knew the boy would plead not guilty. He was also
afraid that Judge Cilella would discredit the lie detector test.

32

The Audy Home, a four-story gray brick facility with bars on the windows, was attached to the much smaller three-story juvenile courthouse. It was added on to the courthouse in 1923 to temporarily house about three hundred boys ages ten to seventeen as they awaited adjudication. Then they'd be released either to the custody of their parents or to a long-term detention center where they'd serve their sentences.

When this Cilella guy sentences me, I'll be off to God knows where, the kid thought. *Maybe Manny's right—maybe I'll be heading to death row and the electric chair, if not now, pretty soon.*

They said he was going there to get help at Audy, but if this was help, the kid would have preferred hell. He was locked in confinement—by a guard with a key as thick as the crucifix on a nun's rosary that, when turned in the lock, *ka-clink*, shut him off from contact with the world. He was in a jail inside of a jail.

It was better to be alone, he rationalized. From the looks of the place, the kids at Audy were the kind of kids he wanted to stay away from anyway. Most of the other boys were physical giants compared to him, some with tattoos and rippling muscles like Manny's, most of them Negro or Puerto Rican. He had never seen such a range of skin shades—from toffee to Tootsie Roll brown to coal black—and he'd never heard the kind of shit that came out of their mouths, like "*Yo' mama,*" and "*I'll shove my dick up yo' ass.*" They scared the hell out of him. They were there for rape, stealing cars, robbery, possessing guns. Even though his crime was far worse than theirs, the kid felt like a baby in their midst. *Good thing there's a lock on my door. If they let me out there with them, I'd probably be dead in a week.*

Confinement meant a cell with beige twelve-by-twelve-inch tile floors (there were forty-eight floor tiles in his cell; he knew because he counted them), beige walls, a lime green mattress on the floor, a barred window too high to see out of, a toilet, a Bible, and nothing else—not even a clock. He didn't bother with the Bible, because he knew most of the New Testament stories anyway, and reading the Old Testament with its *begets* and *begots* was a bore. A stone-faced warden brought him three meals a day that he ate with forks and spoons—no knives. He couldn't even wear shoes in his cell; he had to leave them heel to wall outside the metal door. *What do they think I'm going to do? Hang myself with my shoelaces?*

Every three days the same burly warden (or another; they all looked alike to the kid, like robots, he thought) would walk him down the hall for a shower, where another warden stood and watched. *As if I'm going to try to escape buck naked. And then where would I go? This neighborhood's the shits.*

His walks to the shower room at the end of the hall and across the building for psychological testing were the only times he was allowed to leave his cell and observe the other inmates, the only times he got a chance to see what time it was on the round clocks mounted high on dingy beige walls. After a while the days ran into one another, and he only knew it was Friday because of the fish sticks that appeared on his metal dinner plate.

Every other day or so he got tested by a psychologist, Dr. Horowitz, who he thought of as Dr. Horror-Wiz. When he least expected it, a key would *ka-clink* in his lock and some warden would say, "Put your shoes on and come with me." The guy would walk him through several locked metal doors and through another long cell block, where he got a good dose of the stale air saturated with sweat and bad breath because there was hardly any ventilation in the place. On the way he'd pass cells and sights that scared the hell out of him. Faces suctioned to glass, mostly black, staring out of smudged cell windows the size of a medium-sized pizza box, smirking at him; angry hands pounding on the glass, taunting, shouting unintelligible words to get his attention. Everywhere robot wardens were leading boys in lines, ordering them around, doling out punishments for laughing, talking, cursing, shoving, anything. "Up against the wall," they'd bellow, lining the boys against a brick wall a foot apart so they couldn't touch each other. "Count the bricks." When the kid would finish his testing an hour or two later, the same kids would still be there, standing like statues, counting the bricks. *You can't do anything here without permission—you can't talk, walk, even fart.*

After weeks in isolation with nothing to do but think, he came to look forward to the tests, because they kept him from going crazy. Most of them were stupid tests, he thought, especially the inkblot test with the funny name, Rorschach, which was more like playing a game than taking a test.

"How do you spell it?" the kid asked. "R-O-R-S-H-O-C-K?"
"No. It's spelled R-O-R-S-C-H-A-C-H."

"I was never good at spelling."

Dr. Horowitz would hold up cards with gray and black images that looked the same on both sides and ask him what he saw in the design. "Say the first thing that comes into your mind, son."

The kid adjusted his eyeglasses.

"A bear hide."

"Two men wearing funny caps."

"A Tootsie Roll,"

"A butterfly."

"Two nuns in cahoots with each another."

"A drawing I saw in a sex book."

"A flame."

"Guys fighting."

Figuring out the designs was the most fun he had at Audy. *And to think, some German guy with a ton of ink made a living inventing this game.*

Then when it was over, Dr. Horowitz would put away the cards and tell him he did very well. Another warden would come and walk him back to his cell. On the way back he'd wonder what the test said about him. That he liked Tootsie Rolls? That he wanted to fly out of there like a butterfly? That he was a sexy kid? All of the above, he thought.

Once Dr. Horowitz offered him a Life Saver from a foil roll on his desk. *What does he think, this one little peppermint's going to save my life?*

Some days Dr. Horowitz tested his knowledge of arithmetic and reading comprehension. Those tests were pretty easy, and he knew he could thank the nuns for preparing him to shine. He knew he passed tests that most of the other kids at Audy would fail. So if nothing else, this made him feel superior. *Take a bow, Miss Tristano.*

Other days Dr. Horowitz would just want to sit back and talk. He'd roll his chair away from his desk, the wheels would squeak on the tile floor, he'd link his fingers together across his fat belly, and he'd ask him questions: about his mother, biological father, adoptive father, schools, teachers, friends, fires, even his dreams.

"I don't dream," he told the psychologist. *Look at what happened when I opened up to Mr. Reid. There's no way I'm going to tell this guy I dream about burning this place down.* In his dreams he'd be wandering the halls looking for matches that he knew were hidden somewhere, but he never could find them.

Mostly, the kid just shook his head, looked into his lap and gave short answers. That's what he learned at Audy: to keep to himself, to say as little as possible, to let the robots lead him around, and to figure out how to burn the place down. *I'd be doing Chicago a big favor,* he thought.

33

When the transcript of the lie detector test reached Judge Alfred Cilella's desk, it became his hot potato to deal with. A conscientious judge, Cilella felt the burden of his cases throughout their duration, and often afterward. This particular case posed a moral dilemma that traveled with him throughout his workday and into his home life, and occupied his sleepless nights.

Now that the case had been sent to family court under his jurisdiction, the fate of the kid had become a frequent topic of conversation when he and his wife, Mabel, lingered at the dining room table after dinner. They had a close marriage in which they shared most everything, offering each other honest advice even when it hurt. Three years ago, Mabel, like mothers across the country, had watched the horrors of the fire at Our Lady of the Angels on TV and read about the aftermath in the newspaper tossed on her doorstep. By now her opinions had crystallized into solid beliefs.

One evening, while she was spooning caramelized apples onto a slice of pound cake for dessert, Al was musing over the lifelong burden the kid might carry were he to be found responsible for the school fire. Mabel looked at him sideways and set her spoon on a china plate with a *ping* forceful enough to stop her husband midsentence. She threw her hands up in the air. "Al," she said, stretching out his two-letter name the way she did when she was angry at him, "he killed ninety-two kids and three nuns. Fifty-six little girls and thirty-six little boys. How would you feel if one of those kids were Al Jr. or Linda?"

He looked at her with troubled eyes. "Want to know honestly, Mabel? I'd want to kill the kid. But that's the problem. There are a lot of other people out there who'd want to kill him. You know the hot-blooded Italians in that neighborhood. If I find him guilty, his days would be numbered. You know it as well as I do."

"You have sympathy for a killer?"

"Mabel, the kid was only ten when he did it. His mother was raped by her stepfather. He was unwanted. His adoptive father beat him. He didn't have a chance from the start, God Almighty."

"He's a bad seed," Mabel stated emphatically.

"He's a troubled boy, Mabel."

"You believe he's guilty and so do I," she said. "He should be held responsible."

Al closed his eyes. The truth stung. This wasn't the first time he and his wife had this argument, and he was sure it wouldn't be the last.

Ever since he first heard the results of the polygraph test at John E. Reid & Associates, he believed in his heart of hearts that the kid had started the school fire, and he shared his thoughts with Mabel, whose commonsense opinions he respected. But at times—especially now—he was sorry he had, and he wished she'd just keep her thoughts to herself.

Judge Cilella was in a tough spot. It was shortly before the fire at Our Lady of the Angels that he'd been appointed to his dream job of circuit judge of the family court. It was a position he had sought and felt perfectly suited for, because of his genuine interest in children. A solidly built man with gentle eyes and an infectious smile, Cilella was one of those people whom kids gravitated toward. He loved baseball; he'd been lucky enough to try out for the New York Giants while he was in high school, but he'd passed up a career as a professional athlete to attend Northwestern Law School, because he was a kid who also had brains, his father told him. He had never looked back. Now, tossing sports statistics and a baseball back and forth with his teenage son was satisfying enough for him.

Cilella had been involved with the Boy Scouts of America for years and even received the Boy Scout Silver Beaver Award for distinguished service. Although he had a reputation as a tough judge who wouldn't let a juvenile offender get away with much, he also took the code of the children's court very seriously: "To serve the moral, emotional, mental, and physical welfare of the minor and the best interests of the community." He believed Chicago needed more foster homes and more qualified child psychologists on staff to treat kids and advise him, and since his appointment to juvenile court he had been willing to stick his neck out to make those changes.

Now his dream job had become his personal nightmare. It would be up to him to decide the fate of this kid whom he believed set fire to Our Lady of the Angels. He had studied the transcripts of the inquest and the results of the polygraph test administered to the kid. He had talked to psychologists, experts in juvenile arson, his own colleagues, even his confessor. The kid was of average intelligence and not psychotic.

One particular piece of information from a social worker stuck in his mind: early victimization can train children to become violent. If a kid is taunted and bullied and beaten, he grows up to do the same.

As for the polygraph information, Cilella respected John Reid as a professional. He thought Reid was a guy who knew his business, whom the police went to with their major crime suspects, and who was as responsible for many high-profile convictions as he was for setting a lot of innocent people free. He remembered the headline of an article published some years back in the *Chicago Tribune*: KILLERS FIND THEY CAN'T LIE TO JOHN E. REID. So true, he thought. But now he had misgivings about several statements in the boy's testimony— not that the boy was coerced by Reid, because he believed John was an ethical man and wouldn't do that, but that the kid was given to fantasy, since he told the lie about jumping out of the window. Maybe his confession was also a fantasy, a story he made up for attention. Possible? Yes. Probable? Unlikely. In the end, the judge believed the kid did it.

During another one of their after-dinner discussions on the matter, Mabel threw him another curveball that would haunt him forever. That particular evening they were lingering over coffee after Al Jr. had headed out to shovel snow and Linda had dashed into the rumpus room to watch *To Tell the Truth*. Linda's choice of TV programs had triggered Mabel's question: "Al, tell me the truth, how much pressure is the Church putting on you to keep the kid out of this?"

For five long seconds, Al didn't answer. The look of sadness mixed with irritation that crossed his face made Mabel regret raising the topic again, especially after a delicious meal of beef stroganoff and a glass of sauvignon blanc enjoyed amid the lob of laugh-inducing stories told by the kids.

The Cilellas were lifelong Catholics, deeply involved with their church and their kids' parochial school educations. Al was an active member of the Knights of Columbus and tried to uphold the principles of that organization as well: to do good works and always be loyal to the Catholic Church.

He stirred his coffee, watched the cream he had poured into it swirl in his cup. Then he looked up at his wife, whose unblinking eyes were waiting for an answer.

"Mabel, of course I'm concerned with the Church's reputation. They've taken a lot of hits over this already—the gossip that the Church knows something they're not telling, that the inquest was a whitewash . . . that the Church would rather keep the cause of the fire 'undetermined' than find the perpetrator. True or not, they've suffered too, and I don't want to dump any more problems on their laps. If it were ever proven that this kid or any other one in their school was responsible for so many deaths, there'd be liability issues: the Church could be held negligent for providing an unsafe environment, for failing to effectively supervise a troubled kid who roamed the halls when he should have been in the classroom, who had the freedom to sneak off and start a fire that killed so many. What's to be gained from that?"

Mabel could have backed off, but she didn't. "I know you talk to Cardinal Meyer. Have you discussed this?"

By now the judge's coffee was too cool to drink, and he pushed the delicate china cup away. *I wish she'd use mugs*, he thought. *Easier to hold on to*. Oh, if all problems could be as simple as ceramic vs. china. But they weren't.

"We can't go back. We can't bring back these kids. Cardinal Meyer is a good man. You heard that he went to Saint Anne's the evening of the fire and stayed with the families, blessing them and the kids. And Monsignor Cussen has suffered enough and is not in the best of health, I hear. I know they'd give their own lives to bring those kids back, but we can't bring them back."

"Is it always Church first, Al?" She was pushing it now.

"That's not fair, Mabel. You don't know how much I think about those ninety-two little ones and the nuns, how heavily it weighs on my mind. You don't know how many times I've looked at that picture in the *Chicago American* of each of them dressed in their school uniforms or First Communion clothes. Innocent kids whose faces stare back at me. But now I've got to consider the future of another kid, who messed up and probably didn't intend for it to go that far."

"When he lit those matches and tossed them in the trash can, what did he think was going to happen?" Mabel asked. "It was a school with thousands of kids upstairs. You say he was of average intelligence. It must have occurred to him that someone could get hurt!"

Al ignored her question. "The boy's sitting in a cell in Audy now waiting for a hearing. I want to do what's right, and I'm considering all the people involved—the parents who lost their children, the kid in question, the safety of the community, and yes, the Church."

"But, Al . . ." She could tell he was nearing his limit.

"Mabel!" He raised his voice. "I'd appreciate you backing off."

She knew he was agonizing over the case. She waited to hear her husband out.

"The boy's a troubled kid, severely troubled," Al said. "Maybe he'll always be mixed up, but I can't leave him to rot in some institution without giving him a chance. God, he was only ten years old at the time."

His wife leaned into the upholstered back of her armchair. She licked her index finger, stretched her arm, picked up some crumbs from the apple cobbler they had for dessert, and carried them to her mouth. "Al, I'm going to make one more point and then I'm going to shut up. Honey, I know you're going through hell over this one, but this kid went on to set more fires in Cicero which probably resulted in the deaths of four more innocent people, and maybe those deaths could have been prevented if someone did something sooner."

He stared at her without blinking.

Mabel continued: "Didn't you tell me that before the inquest, the arson and police investigators interviewed hundreds of kids at Our Lady of the Angels, asking them who was in the basement that afternoon and who could have been responsible, and that this kid's name came up again and again, yet they kept it quiet, so as not to embarrass the Church?"

"I know," Al said. He lifted his body off the chair. He was a tall man, stocky. But the former athlete looked more fragile to his wife now. Haggard and vulnerable. He threw his napkin on his plate and walked off.

His office door slammed, and amid the canned laughter from *To Tell the Truth*, Mabel remained at the table surrounded by plates caked with beef stroganoff gravy and dried noodles, and her own thoughts.

34

Judge Alfred J. Cilella was so distracted hooking the fasteners on his judicial robe that he skipped a hook and had to start over.

"Humph," he muttered as he made his adjustments. "Pay attention, Al."

Actually, the judge had been paying attention. On this overcast February morning in his chamber adjacent to the courtroom, the trivia of daily life seemed irrelevant to him. He was now, in the last moments before stepping into the courtroom, focusing all his attention on reviewing the salient points of the case he was about to hear.

A month ago, Cook County state's attorney Daniel P. Ward had filed a delinquency petition in family court charging the kid with the three fires set in Cicero in three apartment buildings, including one in the basement of the building in which the boy lived. The fires in the bowling alley and several others were not included in this petition for lack of evidence. Later an amended petition was filed charging him with arson in the school fire.

Today it would be Judge Cilella's duty to decide whether the thirteen-year-old, who was still being held in the Audy

Home adjacent to the courthouse, was guilty under the petitions. If so, it would be up to him to sentence the boy, either to return him to his parents or to send him away for rehabilitation.

Judge Cilella glanced at the oak-framed clock above the door leading into his courtroom. It was 9:59. Cilella was a stickler for punctuality—you could ask any of the attorneys who worked with him. As he reached for the doorknob, Judge Cilella caught a look at himself in a small rectangular mirror that hung at eye level beside the door. Offering not only a final check on his grooming, that unobtrusive mirror, placed there by a conscientious clerk, also provided him an insight into his level of confidence or uncertainty. What he saw today was a stocky, pale-faced judge with a receding hairline who looked dangerously sleep deprived—and, yes, uncertain.

The judge knew what to expect on the other side of the door. It would be a closed-door hearing with only the defendant, attorneys, witnesses, and members of the press in attendance. Within the four walls of the stately oak- and mahogany-paneled courtroom, the youth would already be seated beside his attorney, John Cogan. An eager upstart attorney representing the state, Martin Gillespie, would be studying his notes at the prosecutor's table. Witnesses would be seated in the front pew-like benches of the gallery. A gaggle of reporters, steno pads on their laps and pencils in their shirt pockets, would be clustered in the rear, where there was ready access to the bank of telephones outside the heavy double exit doors.

Cilella opened the door and stepped into the courtroom. At the clerk's call of "Please rise," everyone stood.

Judge Cilella stepped up to his bench and adjusted the knot in his dark tie, visible above the V of his black judicial robe. Not only was he cognizant of the many players in the impending drama, but he was also aware of the painting that hung behind his back, slightly above his head. Framed within the thick mahogany paneling on the wall, it was a picture he had commissioned several years ago of a blindfolded goddess of justice holding a sword in one hand and scales in the other. The painting was meant to be a reminder to litigants, lawyers, and always to himself that justice is blind and should offer no favoritism based upon gender, race, or social standing.

"You may be seated," the clerk announced.

Judge Cilella made himself comfortable in his high-backed leather chair and looked out into the courtroom. What caught his eye first was the young boy seated next to his attorney. The kid was frightened, pale, and visibly trembling. He was unlike so many of the cocksure delinquents he faced on a daily basis. *How could someone so innocent-looking be responsible for nearly a hundred deaths?* But then he remembered the painting of the blindfolded goddess behind him: his job was to be unbiased, and bias runs both ways. His task now was to examine the facts.

Sitting behind the boy were his parents. The father was fidgeting with the brim of his cap, looking like he'd rather be anywhere else. And who could blame him? The mother's face was hidden in the shadows of her narrow-brimmed cloche, the kind of hat Mabel sometimes wore. From what he could see, the woman looked as terrified as her son. And who could blame her?

The judge began. "The purpose of today's hearing is to determine whether the defendant is guilty of delinquency under petitions filed by the state's attorney. The petitions state that the defendant is charged with setting three fires in Cicero, Illinois, on October 24, October 26, and December 21, 1961, and setting the fire at Our Lady of the Angels school on December 1, 1958." His voice was rough as gravel, and he reached for a glass of water. "Will the defendant please rise," Cilella said.

John Cogan signaled the kid with a tap on the arm, and they stood.

"How do you plead?" the judge asked.

"My client pleads not guilty on each petition filed, Your Honor." The judge tried to hold eye contact with the boy, but the kid couldn't sustain it. Cilella watched the boy's bespectacled eyes jump to the racing fingers of the court reporter who, at the foot of his bench, was entering every word into her steno machine.

After several more formalities, Judge Cilella addressed the prosecution. "Mr. Gillespie, will you please call your first witness."

Martin Gillespie sprung from his chair with notes in hand. "I call John E. Reid to the stand."

A model of preparation and self-assurance, John Reid stepped forward and climbed into the witness stand. The clerk swore him in.

"Mr. Reid, you are a professional polygraph operator?" Gillespie began.

"I am."

"What is your position?"

"I am the head of John E. Reid & Associates. We are nationally known experts in the field of lie detection."

"How long have you been in business?

"Fifteen years. Since 1947."

"Is it correct that you administered a lie detector test to the juvenile defendant on January 12, 1962?

"That is correct."

"And what were your findings?"

John Reid, comfortable in the witness stand because he had previously testified in many cases, spoke to the court in a firm, self-assured manner.

"The lie detector evidence we obtained indicates that the boy set each of the three fires in Cicero. The defendant also confessed to starting the fire at Our Lady of the Angels school."

John Cogan raised his hand to object, then withdrew it.

"Please proceed," Gillespie instructed Reid.

"As for the school fire, the defendant drew a sketch of the layout of the basement of the school and indicated exactly where he started the fire. After my secretary, Miss Mildred McGuffie, transcribed the lie detector interview, the boy read the eight-page document, corrected and initialed a few changes, and willfully signed the document. I sincerely believe the defendant set fire to Our Lady of the Angels school."

"Objection!" John Cogan, shouted. "Your Honor, we ask that the court strike from the record the testimony Mr. Reid has just given pertaining to the youth's alleged confession, on the grounds that the defense believes his alleged confession was obtained by Mr. Reid involuntarily and under color of coercion. Mr. Reid's opinion regarding what he 'believes sincerely' is not fact and should not be construed as such."

Gillespie adamantly shook his head.

The kid, equally adamant, nodded, then smiled sweetly at the judge.

Cilella studied the boy's demeanor. *He's a manipulator,* he thought. Then he locked eyes with John Reid and after only a split second's hesitation made his decision. "I order the witnesses' remarks stricken from the record."

An audible groan came from the depths of the courtroom where the reporters sat.

"Order!" demanded the clerk.

"Your Honor, may I continue to examine Mr. Reid?" Gillespie asked.

"You may."

Marty Gillespie slid a paper from a loose stack of material in his hand and handed it to Judge Cilella. "I have a copy of that drawing mentioned earlier. I wish to enter this as evidence, Your Honor."

"Mr. Cogan, do you have an objection?"

"I have no objection," the boy's attorney said.

"When was this sketch created?" Martin Gillespie asked Reid.

"The boy drew it right before the polygraph test began."

"Please describe what he drew."

Reid turned slightly in his chair and spoke directly to the judge. "As you can see in the sketch, he drew the layout of the basement. He drew the path he walked to the stairwell, indicating exactly where he started the fire. He drew an X on that spot."

"I accept the drawing as evidence," Cilella said.

Next, John Cogan cross-examined the witness.

"Mr. Reid, remember that you are still under oath."

Reid nodded. "Yes."

After a number of general questions, Cogan got to the key point he intended to make. "Mr. Reid, can you tell me about the agreement that you had made with the defendant's parents"—he gestured toward them—"before administering the lie detector test to their son?"

"Our agreement was that the results be kept confidential, but as we know, by the nature of his confession, I was obligated to come forward with what I knew."

This had been a sticking point for the judge. Did Reid mislead the parents, all the while knowing that the process of law could demand the examination's disclosure?

After a short recess, Gillespie called Pearl Tristano to the stand. On her way up the steps Miss Tristano primly adjusted the skirt of her black-and-red plaid suit.

"You were the boy's fifth grade teacher at the time of the fire?"

"Yes, I was."

The kid stared at her, unblinking.

"Tell us about him."

"He was a problem boy. Any kind of mischief possible, he was in." Firmly, with a schoolmarm's surety, Pearl Tristano refuted the story the kid told Reid about jumping into a fireman's net to escape. "After smelling smoke, I led my class to safety down a stairway. No one in my class jumped into fire nets. That did not happen. You can ask any of the other children who were in my class, if you haven't already." An authoritative nod of her head punctuated her statement like an exclamation mark at the end of an oath.

The kid's prone to fantasy, Cilella thought.

Next, the state called officials from the city fire and police departments to the stand. Under questioning, Chief James Kehoe of the Chicago Fire Department's arson squad testified that the fire started in the exact spot where the kid made the X on the sketch for John Reid. Police sergeant Drew Brown took the stand and agreed with Kehoe. He introduced as evidence a photo showing the floor in the stairwell, with a round mark indicating the location of the charred trash barrel. That photo had never been released to the press; it was something that, aside from the police and fire officials, only private fire investigator John Kennedy, the Catholic Church, and the perpetrator would know. To the rest of the world, the spot where the fire had started had been identified in general terms: in the stairwell.

Cilella adjusted his eyeglasses, studied the photo, nodded, and set it aside.

Finally, John Cogan called his young client to the witness stand. The kid approached slowly, as if he were trudging to the gallows. He stepped into the stand and sat on the edge of the broad wooden chair.

"Son, did you set the school fire?" Cogan asked.

"No, I did not," the kid answered, twisting his fingers in his lap. His chin was trembling.

He's lying, Cilella thought.

"Then why did you sign the confession?" his attorney asked.

The kid looked over at his parents, whose eyes bore into him.

"Because Mr. Reid said if I did I could go home. I'd been there all day . . . and I was scared . . . and exhausted. I was there from one o'clock until almost nine. It was dark out when we left."

"Let me direct your attention to the pencil sketch that has been presented into evidence. Did you draw this sketch?"

"Yes, I did."

"What were the circumstances when you drew it?

"I just drew what Mr. Reid told me to draw," he said quietly.

In his cross-examination, Martin Gillespie tried to get the kid to recant, but the kid held firm to his position that John Reid had coerced him.

At the end of the day, after both attorneys made their closing remarks, Judge Cilella reiterated that it was now his duty to determine whether the boy was guilty of delinquency under the petitions. "I promise a decision by March," he said, sighing deeply.

The attorneys packed up their briefcases. Cogan delivered the kid into the hands of an attendant from Audy, who would lead him through the side door, past scanning eyes, back to his cell. The young suspect briefly glanced over his shoulder at his parents. No smiles or nods of support were exchanged.

————

Judge Cilella had never experienced such a moral quandary, nor lost so much sleep over a single legal decision. He had presided over high-profile cases before and was used to being hounded by the press, but nothing like this where he was pressured by so many groups to serve their particular interests.

John Reid was adamant that the boy was telling the truth when he confessed to starting the fire. He believed in the accuracy of his polygraph machine when coupled with skillful interrogation. He felt he had acted ethically in breaking confidentiality, and seemed professionally affronted by the accusations of coercion. He believed the families of the victims were entitled to know the cause of the fire.

News reporters were digging for truth, and they weren't going away.

The Archdiocese of Chicago, backed by Mayor Daley's office, wanted to minimize liability.

Parents who lost children wanted answers. They wanted a name. Some wanted revenge. To many others, declaring the cause of the fire "undetermined" seemed like a whitewash, trivializing the loss and devastation that had been inflicted upon them.

Judge Cilella's wife, Mabel, wanted the kid to be held responsible.

The kid was terrified and wanted it all to go away.

Although he had tried to maintain a composed demeanor on the bench, Judge Alfred J. Cilella felt like a bale of straw torn apart by many hands in every direction.

———

The kid probably did it, Cilella believed. He acted impulsively and had never intended it to go so far. The fact that the boy was only ten years old when it happened should partially inform his decision. But the kid had probably been responsible for additional deaths in subsequent years, and he would likely continue on this path were he returned to his parents, whom Cilella believed had given up on him. Cilella was also aware of the exploding national attention being given by doctors and psychologists to parental child abuse. There was no doubt that this was a sick adolescent who was a danger to the community and to his own family.

Although Judge Cilella felt conflicted, in the end he knew he had to abide by the charter of his position as family court judge: do what he believed was right for the parents who lost children, the safety of the community, and the young boy.

———

On March 13, an unsmiling Judge Cilella again took his place on his bench in family court. The session was kept closed to reporters as well as to the public. Dressed in his judicial robe, he took a sip of water, unfolded his eyeglasses, perched them on the bridge of his nose, and looked into the courtroom.

"Will the defendant rise," he instructed.

The kid, in a white shirt tucked into navy wash pants, his hands trembling at his sides, rose along with John Cogan. This time his parents, Belinda and Manny, chose not to be present.

Judge Cilella read from his twenty-one-page document: "The child's denials of the Our Lady of the Angels fire, when considered in light of all the other evidence, were quite convincing. His similar denials with respect to the setting of the Cicero fires were not convincing."

He pointed out two discrepancies in the kid's lie detector testimony: First, at one point the boy stated that the trash barrel was under the staircase, but Chief Kehoe and Sergeant Brown testified it was near the foot of the staircase. A minor discrepancy, Cilella knew, yet he pointed this out anyway.

Second, the boy said he jumped from the second-floor window into the fireman's net, a falsehood that was refuted under oath by Pearl Tristano. "The boy is given to fantasy," Cilella concluded. "Thus, under the circumstances, the court cannot speculate as to which portions of the statement are true and which are false," he said. With this pronouncement Cilella discounted the validity of the lie detector test in regard to the school fire.

Then he ruled that the kid and his parents were misled by John Reid, who had assured them that the testimony would be kept confidential knowing full well that the process of law could demand its disclosure. He redressed Reid for the manner in which he obtained the information. Reid, from his place in the gallery, sighed and shook his head.

Then Judge Cilella did an about face and accepted the kid's lie detector confession about starting the fires in Cicero. He had decided to find the kid delinquent of the three lesser crimes that resulted in no deaths.

In conclusion, he declared, "Upon the evidence before it, the court does not have an abiding conviction that this child set the Our Lady of the Angels fire. Such being the case, the court will not burden this child with the judicial determination that he is responsible for this tragedy."

Back in his chamber, Judge Cilella slipped out of his robe and sank into a worn leather chair in the corner. He wiped beads of perspiration off his forehead. He should have felt immense relief, as he so often had felt at the end of rendering a judgment, but now he did not. He knew his decision was full of contradictions.

———

An Associated Press story filed on March 13, 1962 read:

> A 13-year-old boy was cleared in family court today of any connection with the Our Lady of the Angels school fire in which 92 children and 3 nuns perished in 1958.
>
> He was, however, adjudged delinquent in connection with three of seven fires set in suburban Cicero.
>
> The boy had been a pupil at the Roman Catholic parochial school at the time of the fire. A lie detector operator, John Reid, testified in family court that the boy, under questioning, told of setting the school fire. The boy declared in court that he had made the statement involuntarily.
>
> Judge Alfred J. Cilella of family court dismissed the delinquency petition based on the school fire. The boy's name was withheld because he is a minor under protection of the family court.

Part V
1962–1967

35

The fat-faced kid eventually got over me. All well and good, since there are so many other kids in this world that adore me and want to play. Like estranged lovers, we had run our course.

The long and short of it was that the judge removed the kid from the custody of his parents and made him a ward of the court. Judging by the masklike looks they'd worn on their faces at the delinquency hearing, I doubt Manny and Belinda were disappointed. If I were to venture to read their own troubled minds, I'd say they were relieved that the kid was now the state's problem and not theirs.

After a two-month confinement at the Audy Juvenile Home, Judge Cilella arranged for the kid to be sent out of state to Starr Commonwealth, a school for troubled boys in Albion, Michigan. In the past the judge had sent other problem boys who needed a fresh start to Starr. The place was founded in 1913 by a do-gooder named Floyd Starr, who believed that there was no such thing as a bad boy. (All of you probably attribute those words to Father Flanagan, who started Boys Town in 1917, but let me clear up that slight misconception: it was actually Floyd Starr who said them first.)

Starr Commonwealth was quite a place. I got my first look from the driver's seat of the Cook County paddy wagon that sped the kid up there one spring morning. The cop in charge lit up a smelly stogie the minute we crossed over into Michigan. Holy cow! I felt I was driving into a fancy family resort or something. No golf courses, no swimming pool, but lots of rolling lawn on a pastoral stretch of land on Montcalm Lake—I saw the WELCOME TO MONTCALM LAKE sign as we whizzed past.

There were no drab cells or mesh bars on the windows there. Instead, the school consisted of three tidy buildings on a sprawling green campus. The kid was assigned to a neat-as-a-pin cottage with a dozen other boys, some of them who snuck smokes. As the days unfolded, I caught glimpses of the kid through the tips of cigarettes and the flame of the gas stove in the kitchen. He was doing his homework, washing dishes, serving meals.

His houseparents were Mr. and Mrs. Fred Knickerman. Once Mrs. Knickerman, Gladys, was teaching the kid how to scramble eggs. In the kindest of voices she suggested the kid call her Mom. "You guys ain't my parents!" the kid mumbled.

But soon he was calling them that too, and before long it was like being in Hollywood on the set of *Father Knows Best*, and he was Bud. There in the kitchen I saw a lot of what was going on in the house. The Knickermans gave the kid hugs, discipline, and direction. They had rules and structure. Fred and Gladys called him on his lies, wouldn't let him get away with stuff like halfhearted attempts at cleaning the bathrooms and washing dishes. Although he didn't like physical work—he'd much rather be spread-eagle on the couch eating Tootsie Rolls and numbing himself with TV—the kid saw the other boys pitching in, so he did too. After homework and chores were done, I watch the kid leave for bed exhausted.

And to the kid's liking, no one forced him to play sports. He was required to play a musical instrument though, and he picked the drums. What the kid lacked in rhythm he made up for in volume. The Knickermans always attended their concerts, sitting on a sofa against the back wall of the assembly room, smoking cigarettes. Mr. Knickerman always wore earplugs.

Judge Cilella took another big risk. Somehow he was able to keep it a secret why the kid was there: his fixation on me. In the smoke-filled staff meetings where this kind of confidential stuff was discussed, there were no references to arson or pyromania. Cilella must've omitted those details from the records the court sent to Starr; maybe he thought they wouldn't accept the kid if they knew the truth—that he'd be a risk to their own safety.

Like Floyd Starr, the judge believed that the kid's love of me was a substitute for the love he never received from his father, friends, teachers—even his mother, who worried a lot but never made him face the music. It's beyond me to know whether the judge was right or wrong, because I'm no kiddy shrink. But needless to say, I had my own abandonment issues over the kid's withdrawal. They were short lived, though, because I'm fickle and I'm Fire and I just move on. As I say, there are lots of kids in this world who want to play.

———

Let me tell you about my last major encounter with the kid. It happened, believe it or not, at Starr Commonwealth.

It was a situation stoked with irony.

Every year before Christmas it was a school tradition to have a ceremony called the Little Builder of Christmas Fires. Founder Floyd Starr, a tall and angular white-haired grandpa of a gentleman, who always dressed in a suit, crisp white shirt, and tie, would sit in the parlor in his rocking chair beside a massive fireplace, with his boys gathered on the floor around him while he read a story about a little boy who brought gifts of firewood to homes where love was absent.

The story took about a half hour to read. You'd think the boys would get all fidgety during that time, start elbowing and side-eyeing each other because it was a corny, Hallmark Hall of Fame kind of story, but they didn't. They listened. Then, when Uncle Floyd, as the kids called him, closed his storybook and set it on his bony lap, he'd call the youngest boy in the room up to the fireplace. This lad would have the privilege of striking a single match—only one—and tossing it into the pyramid of firewood. According to tradition, if that lone match ignited a fire, it meant there was enough love in the Commonwealth to sustain them for another year. If it didn't, well, then they had problems within their own family. What Floyd Starr didn't tell the kids is that he had his staff presoak the wood in kerosene to ensure an instant and magnificent blaze.

When the littlest kid flicked the lit match into the hearth it was my time to shine. I exploded onto the scene, *POOF,* with all the drama I could muster. I flamed my little heart out, burned hot and hotter with a few dozen awestruck eyes pinned on me. The performer I am, year after year I'd give the lads a razzle-dazzle, magical Christmas extravaganza to remember. I'd dance and prance and blaze tongues of magenta, orange, and gold at this roomful of boys who'd relish every minute of it, feeling the love.

On each Christmas from 1962 to 1965, the kid was there, sitting cross-legged on the floor among the other boys. That first year he seemed terrified of the power I still had over him. He couldn't look me in the eye. I tried to get his attention by flashing a rare fuchsia tongue or two just for him, by crackling seductively in invitation, but he looked away and focused on anything but me—on the plaid flannel shirt of the boy in front of him, on a grouping of framed photos on the wall of Uncle

Floyd with some other boys, Starr's long arms wrapped protectively around two or three of them. Frustrated, the kid lowered his head and picked at his acne.

The second year, it was much the same thing, although this time as he sat cross-legged on the floor, he stayed closer to his buddies, the sleeves of their sweaters touching. He seemed anchored there, with no sign of wanting to get up and run. He had friends now who accepted him. This time, when our eyes finally met, I saw his pain and knew exactly what he was remembering. I also understood his guilt, but there was nothing I could do about it, because it was my job to put on a show—a spectacular Christmas show of crimson illumination—and frankly, by that time I was sensing him pulling away from me, and it didn't feel good. It never feels good to know you're being dumped.

The third year, he appeared relaxed. At one point he smiled, showing off a mouthful of crooked teeth. He was surrounded by people who cared, and although he might have been remembering the old times when he and I made hell together (who could forget those infamous times?), I could tell he didn't need me anymore.

The fourth year brought another change. That year his eyes hardly left me for a minute. But he was a different kid now, somber and more mature. His face had slimmed. He'd grown out of his acne. He still wore glasses, but no longer was there worship in those watery blue eyes beneath the thick lenses. It was sadness I saw now, and within the sadness a different kind of bond that he and I were forging: the indissoluble bond of shared memory. After being silent for three years, the kid had finally opened up and told our story to a patient, cigar-smoking chaplain (Episcopalian, this time) who was helping him deal with his guilty conscience. That was when I knew I had lost him.

That evening, the parlor smelled like oak and cherry. The air was hazy with woodsy, fruity smoke, and the boys' faces were youthful shadows within it. But in a clearing I caught a glimpse of the kid. I saw his conscience in his eyes.

Sometimes I imagine things, and sometimes I exaggerate. But this time I'm telling God's holy truth about what I saw. Just as I was leaping and snapping—reaching the climax of the evening's show—I saw an invisible tear roll down the kid's cheek, a smoky gray pearl of a tear that only I could see. And etched in the mirror of that tear were the faces of the ninety-two children and three nuns whose lives he and I had taken that overcast afternoon on December 1, 1958.

———

There'd be thousands of small moments after Starr Commonwealth when the kid and I would get together, but they'd happen in unexciting ways. Our paths still continued to cross—in the blaze of a campfire, against a star-pocked sky, during his months in Vietnam, where through two tours of duty in the marines there was every chance of us making mischief together but he refrained, and in the wreath of flame on the cigarette lighter of the truck he eventually drove out to California, near Los Angeles, where he settled. We'd meet in the flick of a match to light his smokes (he was partial to Old Gold); in supper clubs at dusk when a perky waitress with cleavage leaned across the table to light a candle for ambience; and when he was squatting in his basement to fix the pilot light on his gas heater. Yes, he did become a family man.

As I said, I followed the kid around for a long time, but in September 2004 I lost track of him forever.

———

Poor Judge Cilella never did find out how his gamble worked out. A couple years after he sent the kid to Starr Commonwealth, he died.

Of course I was in church for the judge's funeral service along with thousands of people, many of them lawyers and politicians wearing custom-made black suits and side-parted slicked-back haircuts. His fellow members of the Knights of Columbus were there en masse to pay tribute to him, dressed in their regalia with their swords and scabbards, red capes, and white-plumed chapeaux. I had a fondness for Judge Cilella, because now and then he liked his stogies and he could be quite a raconteur, so at his funeral I listened carefully to what his friends had to say about him.

"The poor guy's heart couldn't bear the burden of what he had to deal with . . ."

"He never got over the beating he took from the parents . . ."

"He was never the same after that fire . . ."

"I loved the guy, but that thing with the kid was a whitewash all around. He gave in to pressure and let the kid get away with murder."

Goes to show, it's not easy to give someone a second chance.

———

How do I feel when I run into people I've harmed? Holy smoke, that's a news reporter's kind of question! How do you feel after your house explodes? Your mother dies? You find out you have a month to live? How do you think I feel? Not great! When I'm contained and in my right mind and I see someone I've hurt, I long for someone to snuff me out.

Let me take you back to one of those times . . . It was Saturday, May 6, 1967, the day Kathleen Adamski and Sal Martinelli got married.

You'd think because of all the memories, they'd have wanted to get hitched somewhere else, but no, they decided to wed at Our Lady of the Angels. Everybody had been talking about the big wedding for months.

It's minutes before the service and the altar boys—all decked out in their cassocks and lacy surplices—light the candles on the altar, and *pffft*, I come to life. I'm on edge, and to make matters worse, from my places atop tapers in six golden candlesticks I'm surrounded by too many bouquets of stinky Oriental lilies that had been carefully arranged in vases earlier by a pair of overachieving nuns. I flicker nervously. I just want to have it be over, to get snuffed out, to escape those cloying lilies that smell like cheap perfume, and I want to be spared the humiliation of seeing Kathleen and Sal.

Music is playing softly, a flute, a piano. From my exalted spot on high, I anxiously watch as hundreds and hundreds of guests politely pour into the church through the arched front door and are guided to their pews by two dapper groomsmen.

Once they're seated, a single note from the pipe organ jabs the air with such force that I can almost feel the walls tremble. Then the bride and her father—Kathleen and Peter—begin their walk down the aisle.

There's a shuffle of satin and the brush of wool as everyone rises. As Kathleen and Peter step forward—Kathleen with the slightest of limps, Peter holding his daughter's elbow supportively—their guests smile, nod, sniffle, and wipe tears in clean white handkerchiefs.

I get a better look as Kathleen moves closer to the altar. Her blonde hair is partially covered with a swath of lace. From behind the fragile veil, her eyes, along with her shy smile, bounce from face to face. As she advances down the aisle, her attention shifts to the sandy-haired man, Sal, who is waiting for her, thoroughly smitten, at the foot of the altar.

Her gown is classically simple. Subtle ivory, not the garish shade of white that makes your eyes squint like high noon on a sandy beach. You can tell she's not much for the frills and flashiness so many young brides crave. I'm talking about the ones who opt for rhinestone tiaras that nearly touch the tips of the chandeliers; who encase themselves in bales of sequined netting so they end up looking like giant Easter eggs on display in Marshall Field's windows; who select flowing satin trains that make them look like they're pulling sleds across the snowy Russian tundra. And then you have those babes who insist on wearing four-inch heels that wobble like sticks in the wind and make you hold your breath for their safety. In my day I've seen many a slip and fall among those brides and it's never pretty. *Is there a lawyer in the house?*

Kathleen isn't like them at all. She is practical. She is cautious. She is classy. In spite of my humiliation, I must confess that I try anyway, because it's my dogged nature, to put on a show for her with my flickering and winking, snapping and sparkling. But it's impossible to capture her attention. She's not the kind of woman who messes with hotheads like me.

She's at the foot of the altar now, as close to me now as she's going to get, and I can see she is a beauty. Behind the veil, her blonde hair is sprayed into an elegant French twist, her high cheekbones blush with just the right amount of pink, her eyebrows arch perfectly above her sky bluest eyes. She's left her glasses at home.

And Sal? He's a smidge taller than his bride, and his hair is combed bashfully over his forehead. He has white scars on his cheeks and neck that make me remember and, yes, feel remorse. His smile has reached his eyes. His eyes, the richest of brown, melt like chocolate as he gazes at his darling. He's a strong fellow now, solid and reliable, I can tell. I know he's going to take care of this woman.

I look deeper into their faces and my guilty memories flash before me the way it is when you hit rewind on a reel-to-reel tape recorder and the tape spins wildly in reverse. I see more frightened faces than I care to remember: Kathleen at the age of twelve—in her classroom, room 208, when, unleashed, all I wanted to do was to chase her.

Then I see her at thirteen, in the flash of a candle on her birthday cake. "Get that out of here!" she cries. Again I am rebuffed. And so many times afterward. She has no use for me. Serves me right. She has every reason to treat me like a dirty old uncle with bad breath. I'm surprised she is tolerating my presence now, but as I've said many times, a wedding's not a wedding without me, romance is not romance without my glow, and Catholic ritual is lackluster without my pizzazz.

And Sal? I remember him at the age of thirteen, a sandy-haired kid, a docile kid, his hands in front of his face, running away from me in horror. Then I see him at the age of sixteen, when, with his high school buddies at a softball picnic in the forest preserves, he tries to blow smoke rings along with the guys. But smoking is a short-lived vice for him. A couple puffs and he looks me straight in the eye and stomps me out in a patch of gravel with the toe of his shoe, never to light up again. Over the years he's become more tolerant of my presence than Kathleen. From time to time he'll light a match, but always with the greatest care and respect for the monster he knows I can become.

OK, so the Mass begins. And inside the Mass is the wedding ceremony itself.

Joe Ognibene is saying the words that precede the vows:

"Love is patient. . . . It is not proud. . . . It keeps no record of wrongs . . ."

"Do you, Kathleen Adamski, take . . . "

And my attention wanders. I scan the pews. There's a lot of up and down in Catholic churches—stand, sit, kneel, sit, kneel again. Now, after the vows are said, everyone's seated. There's music flowing into the air from the choir loft high above, from the strings of a violin. Quiet as a church mouse, Peter must have made his way up the steps at the back of the church, because he is playing Franz Schubert's "Ave Maria." From a distance, all I see is his salt-and-pepper hair and the bow of his arm gliding the bow of his instrument lovingly across the strings. His head is tilted; his eyes are closed; it's as if he's feeling the transcendent melody. There is a children's choir behind him, a couple dozen beatific little boys and girls in white choir gowns singing the words:

Ave Maria, gratia plena,
Maria, gratia plena,
Maria, gratia plena,
Ave, ave Dominus.

Whenever I hear this song—I mostly hear it at weddings—I get the chills. For a moment I rise up from my flame into a nameless place that is grander and holier and loftier than any creature on earth or element in existence. If there is a heaven, I wish to soar there on the wings of this glorious melody, but I don't think they want me in heaven. I think my place has been predetermined.

Anyway, I feel elevated, and I see the same reaction on the faces of many of the people in the pews. Some are wiping their eyes with their handkerchiefs or with the edges of their index fingers. Some are squeezing the hands of their loved ones. Some are biting their lower lip to keep from crying. There is no fidgeting. No coughing. Not a whisper. I'm too far away to see their skin, but I know there are as many goose bumps on their arms as there are stars in the sky.

But wait, something else is happening. You know how it is when someone's staring at you. You feel it and eventually your eyes find them. That's how it is now, and I know I must locate that person. I scan the rows of pews. No.

Nope.

No.

And then I find him. There in the twelfth row is a skinny, freckled little kid dressed in his Marshall Field's wedding finery—a navy blue suit jacket with gold buttons, and a white shirt topped off with a red bow tie. He's seated on the edge of his pew, a noticeable distance between his father and mother, as if his parents have had enough of him already. There is worship in the boy's greenish gaze. I flicker and he follows my motion. I blink and he smiles. I can see he wants to play.

Eyes of expectation now are on the bride and groom, the newly proclaimed Mr. and Mrs. Salvador Martinelli. Father Joe smiles and nods. The couple kisses modestly, shyly, because they know hundreds of people are watching.

Things are as they should be.

Kathleen and Sal are husband and wife. With lightness in their steps, they turn toward each other and sweep gleefully out of the church into their future.

Peter slips his treasured Czech violin back into its leather case, wipes a tear from his eye, and makes his way down the curved mahogany staircase to join the bridal party.

The choir kids slip off their robes and wait for dismissal by their director, a newly installed nun at Our Lady of the Angels, Sister Redempta.

Row by row, people—inspired, elevated, renewed—leave the church: couples holding hands, older folks holding canes, nuns holding rosaries, and keepers of history holding Kodak cameras.

The ushers pass out little mesh bags of rice, each tied with a golden ribbon.

Flashbulbs pop.
Smokers light up.

———

There's a little stone angel with downcast eyes that stands at attention above the door of Our Lady of the Angels. Carved by the hands of an Italian immigrant, she's been there since 1939, when the new church was dedicated and Monsignor Joseph Cussen became pastor.

Over the years this little angel has kept watch over the thousands of parishioners who've passed beneath. She knows them by their voices—the romantic and guttural intonations of English, Italian, Polish, and German. She also knows them by their heads: braids, bangs, bonnets, babushkas, military caps, pillboxes, toupees and wedding veils. Now she witnesses the thunderous shouts of joy for Kathleen and Sal.

The boy in the jaunty red bow tie, looking forlorn and forgotten in the hubbub, skitters away from his parents and skips back up the steps into the nearly deserted church. He walks halfway down the aisle and smiles at me. I do a saucy little dance in my candelabrum to let him know I'm interested, because isn't it love that makes the world go round?

He blinks and steps forward.

I shimmy on my wick in invitation and say it's OK to come even closer.

There's a skip in his step now. A bold little fellow, he opens the gilded gate of the Communion rail and bounces up the pinkish marble altar steps. With his hands clasped behind his back, he gazes up at me in adoration. It gives me the shivers, it does.

Two altar boys eagerly dash out from the sacristy with their long bell-shaped snuffer poles, ready to put me out.

"Don't you know you shouldn't be there, kid!" one of them bosses. "It's a sin to be up here if you're not supposed to be."

The boy smiles at them innocently, turns and skips back into the sunshine.

I'm going to keep my eye on that kid. I'm a patient flame, and I can wait.

AUTHOR'S NOTES

As a child growing up in Chicago, I heard from our third-floor apartment the urgent and ceaseless blare of fire engines racing from all parts of the city to Our Lady of the Angels, a school three and a half miles from my home. From our living room we watched the blackening sky. The tragic story of the fire, which took so many children my age, was the first news story I ever followed from beginning to end. I read whatever I could about it in Chicago's four major newspapers—all of which my family received—and in *Time* and *Life* and the *Saturday Evening Post*. And of course, I followed the story on radio and TV. It's a disaster one never forgets.

Many years later, it was David Cowan and John Kuenster's incredible journalistic account of the fire, *To Sleep with the Angels*, that brought this devastating story full circle for me—from the first spark tossed into the trash container to the fate of the alleged arsonist; from the firetrap schools of the mid-twentieth century to how we build our schools today.

When I was exploring the idea of writing a historical fiction account of the fire, I contacted John Kuenster for advice. He told me he was surprised that no one had taken the approach I presented to him, and he encouraged me to pursue my ideas, offering the caveat that many writers had contacted him with intentions of writing such a novel but none had followed through. This doubled my determination to dig deeply into this piece of Chicago's history and to write my version of the story, using Fire as a character. But sadly, this dear man who so influenced my work passed away in 2012 at the age of eighty-seven before he could read a page of this book.

———

Most of the characters in *Fire Angels* are real. The handful of exceptions include Belinda and Manny, who are fictitious, as are Antonia Fiorello, Nurse Trudy, and Martin Gillispie. Sal Martinelli and Kathleen Adamski, as well as their families, are loosely based upon the experiences of Gerry Andreoli and Irene Mordarski, who after much consideration chose not to be interviewed for this book. As young survivors of the fire they met in Saint Anne's Hospital; as adults they married at Our Lady of the Angels Church. They now live in Arlington Heights, Illinois, where Dr. Gerry Andreoli is a chiropractor. Irene, a mother of grown children also involved in the medical profession, still suffers some incapacitation from her injuries.

Why did I give fire a voice? Why did I assign emotions to an entity that in this story symbolizes nothing but destruction? I chose to use the voice of fire to help readers feel the range of emotions fire conveys. Fire is an element essential to civilization and we couldn't live without it, but when uncontrolled, it can be deadly. I personified fire as lustful, insatiable, unforgiving, cruel, duplicitous, caustic, derisive, haughty, evil, secretive, cocky, and yes, friendless, except for those pathologically addicted to such friendships. I assigned fire a snarky sense of humor that erupts at times as it observes the world, and I also gave it a sense of remorse when, after the damage is done and fire is contained, it can look back on its feral actions in disgust. Fire has no self-control. In the end, man and nature are ultimately responsible for what fire does.

Why did I not name the alleged pyromaniac? Two reasons: First, the boy was never convicted of the OLA crime, although there was certainly enough evidence to do so. I remember John Kuenster telling me that he was 99.9 percent sure the kid was responsible for the school fire, and that many years later he had interviewed him, but even then "the kid," by then a grown man, wouldn't discuss those days, saying he wanted to keep the past in the past, and any confidences he shared were to be kept secret between him and his confessor. The suspect died in 2004 at the age of fifty-six, and although you can't libel a dead man, I wondered what good it would do to reveal his name—other than satisfy curiosity.

Second, were I writing a piece of investigative journalism, I might have been convinced to name the perpetrator in defense of the truth, but this is a novel, so I also chose to use his anonymity as a literary device that gave him a sense of "otherness" and set him apart from the innocent children he harmed.

———

As the story points out, this tragic fire left enormous scars and repercussions. Many residents of the OLA community harbored a deep-seated animosity toward the church for creating an environment in which such a disaster could happen. Yet many were too timid to even think of suing their church for negligence or wrongful death.

One exception was a joint lawsuit filed by five families against the Archdiocese and the City of Chicago in June 1959. The lawsuit claimed negligence in operating and maintaining the school, as well as lifelong physical and psychological injuries to their children. Each plaintiff asked for $350,000.

A month later, the first wrongful death suit was filed, seeking $30,000 in damages, the maximum under Illinois law at the time. By 1965, fifty-nine lawsuits had been filed against the archdiocese. Of these, forty were for wrongful death; nineteen were for personal injury.

It took seven years before all the lawsuits were finally settled. The settlements for the first suit filed in June 1959 resulted in each of the five families receiving substantially less than $350,000, the largest payment being $31,000. According to the wishes of Archbishop Meyer, each family who lost a child, even if they didn't file a lawsuit, received a payout of $7,500.

In total the archdiocese paid $690,000 to parents who lost their children, and $2.3 million for personal injury claims. In addition, the church—through payments made through Catholic Charities and a special fund set up by Mayor Richard J. Daley—spent about $1 million on funeral and medical expenses, and continued paying for the special needs of victims until the funds were exhausted.

Many families, however, were too timid to sue. They were eager to take what was given to them and move on.

Most of the survivors received no counseling and were blatantly told by the priests and nuns to forget what happened. Nobody talked about the fire in the temporary schools the kids attended, or in the new Our Lady of the Angels building. Nobody mentioned it in church. Parents, isolated in their misery, tried to take to heart what the church did tell them after the fire: that the children who perished were God's chosen ones, that He took them to be His angels, that the parents who lost children now had their own personal angels in heaven to pray to, that there was a heavenly purpose for what happened and it was their role not to question the mind of God but to accept it. In the dedication of the new school in October 1960, Archbishop Meyer reminded parents to "accept whatever befalls you . . . be patient, for in fire, gold is tested." He cited the Lord's words: "Suffer the little ones to come unto me . . . for such is the kingdom of heaven." Those who could not accept their fate felt guilty and sinful for their lingering depression.

Behind closed doors and under pressure from the priests to remain silent, the nuns survived in a hell of their own. Although Sister Helaine, Sister Davidis, and Sister Geraldita had done all they could to protect their children, and recovered from their injuries, they would never find peace.

Sister Geraldita struggled for the rest of her life to maintain emotional equilibrium, relying on her Irish wit but from time to time falling into depression and losing control. Several years after the fire she suffered a mental breakdown, weeping uncontrollably in front of her class. As a result she spent time in Loretto Hospital, the only Catholic hospital in Chicago with a psychiatric unit.

Sister Davidis fared the best, relying on daily prayer, especially for the two students she lost in her classroom. As for returning to teach at OLA, "I prayed I'd never have to go back there." Her prayers were answered. She took some comfort in knowing she may have prevented many more deaths by stuffing thin textbooks under the doors.

As the story points out, Jim Raymond's life was wrecked because of the false accusations that he bore responsibility for the fire. The same could be said about Judge Alfred Cilella. He believed the boy was guilty of the OLA fire and second-guessed his decision not to find him responsible for it until the end. Two years after the hearing, he collapsed and died playing golf with his son, Al Jr., at the Butterfield Country Club in Oak Brook, Illinois. He was fifty-four.

If anything good came from the fire, it was the new public clamor for safer schools worldwide. The rebuilt Our Lady of the Angels became the model for all new construction of schools across the nation. By the following year, some 16,500 older schools in the country were brought up to code. Since then most of the newly constructed elementary schools in the nation have been one-story structures equipped with all the safety features that Our Lady of the Angels lacked.

ACKNOWLEDGMENTS

My deepest gratitude goes to the team at Chicago Review Press: To Jordan and Anita Miller of Academy Chicago, who initially believed in my work. To Cynthia Sherry, publisher of Chicago Review Press, who rounded out the jagged edges of my first draft, and especially to developmental editor Devon Freeny, who guided the project to the end. Devon is an editor an author can only dream of. He edited this manuscript with meticulous attention to the smallest detail, and through his wise suggestions often saved me from myself. Thank you, Devon. My admiration also to proofreader Kristi Gibson, publicist Meaghan Miller, and marketing manager Mary Kravenas for helping to make my publishing experience at CRP the best.

My sincere appreciation goes to David Cowan and John Kuenster for their well-researched and insightful book *To Sleep with the Angels*. Their text gave me the foundation of information I needed to begin writing *Fire Angels*. Gratitude also goes to Eric Morgan, the webmaster of www.olafire.com, and to the many survivors and family and friends of the victims who have posted some of their most personal and heartfelt memories on its pages. The website, an archive of information and remembrances, serves as a living tribute to the brave survivors of the fire and the families of the victims who lived through those dark days and still carry painful losses in their hearts. It is also a repository of many of the important documents and newspaper reports that I have used in my novel.

I am also indebted to David Cowan for his book *Great Chicago Fires*, which helped me tell the story of Fire's deadly romance with the Windy City, and to a survivor of the fire, Michele McBride, who in her book *The Fire That Will Not Die* recorded her courageous lifelong struggle to overcome the disfigurement and depression she suffered as a result of leaping from her second-story classroom window with her body on fire.

Thanks to the friends, scholars, and family who have read all or parts of *Fire Angels*, who have generously offered their suggestions, and who have helped me avoid embarrassing errors. Any remaining errors are my own. My gratitude goes to Barbara Arendt, Susan Bono, Christine Dublin, Allen Jackson, Joan Jareo, Chuck Kensler, Margit Liesche, Halina Marcinkowski, Richard Markuszewski, Diane Mazur, Drew Meadors, Eric Morgan, Ed Rau, Dr. Mark Sloan, Janet Snyder, Terry Stark, Pat Tyler, Amy Meadors Warda, and Jeri Winkels, and to my dear friend and partner in several other literary projects, Sandra Sanoski, who offered her sage advice throughout the process.

Finally, let me also express my deepest gratitude to my husband, Lee, my encourager, critic, advisor, friend, and love. He and I met in California at Apple in Silicon Valley. One of the many things that drew us together was that we both grew up in Chicago and shared similar values and memories. I think of him as the Chicago boy to whom I owe my happy life.

BIBLIOGRAPHY

Albright, Joe. "Smoldering School Ruins like a Cavern of Death." *Chicago Tribune*, December 2, 1958.

Auck, Dale K. "Death in the Corridors of a Chicago School." Presentation made at the Federation of Mutual Fire Insurance Companies 31st Annual Fire Department Instructors Conference, Memphis, Tennessee, February 24–27, 1959.

Brendtro, Larry K. "The Worst School Violence." *Reclaiming Children and Youth*, Summer 2005, 73–79.

Brendtro, Larry K., PhD, Arlin Ness, MSQ, LLD, and Martin Mithell, EdD. *No Disposable Kids*. Longmont, CO: Sopris West, 2001.

Bruno, Hal. "Fire! Fire! Anatomy of Terror." *Argosy Magazine*, November 1974.

Callahan, Neal. "How Fire Was Fought." *International Fire Fighter Magazine*, January 1959.

Chiappetta, Robert. *The Immaculate Deception*. New York: Page, 2015.

Cook County Coroner. *Jury Findings and Recommendations, Our Lady of the Angels School Fire, Chicago Illinois*. Reproduced through the courtesy of Iowa State College Firemanship Training Engineering Extension, Ames, IA, 1959.

Cowan, David. *Great Chicago Fires: Historic Blazes That Shaped a City*. Chicago: Lake Claremont, 2001.

Cowan, David, and John Kuenster. *To Sleep with the Angels: The Story of a Fire*. Chicago: Ivan R. Dee, 1996.

Dostert, Mark. *Up in Here: Jailing Kids on Chicago's Other Side*. Iowa City: University of Iowa Press, 2014.

Dvonch, Dr. Louis. "St. Anne's Hospital Fire Remembrance." OLA fire memorial website, March 25, 2013. www.olafire.com/Dr.%20Louis%20 Dvonch%20Remembrances.asp.

Egelhof, Joseph. "Killers Find They Can't Lie to John E. Reid." *Chicago Tribune*, November 19, 1958.

Grove, Adam. "Our Lady of the Angels School Fire: 50 Years Later." *Fire Engineering Magazine*, December 1, 2008.

Hoy, Suellen. "Stunned with Sorrow." *Chicago History Magazine*, Summer 2004.

Kuenster, John. *Remembrances of the Angels*. Chicago: Ivan R. Dee, 2008.

Lake, Alice. "How the Doctors Saved Chicago's Burned Children." *Saturday Evening Post*, June 10, 1961.

Life. "Chicago School Fire Takes 91 Lives, Anguish the Nation Shares." Vol. 45, no. 25 (December 15, 1958).

McBride, Michele. *The Fire That Will Not Die*. Palm Springs, CA: ETC, 2004.

Mitchell, Martin L., and Larry K. Brendtro. "Victories over Violence: The Quest for Safe Schools and Communities." *Reclaiming Children and Youth* 22, no. 3 (Fall 2013).

Quinn, Robert J. "Tragedy in Chicago: An Official Analysis of Our Lady of the Angels School Catastrophe." *Fire Engineering Magazine*, December 1, 1959.

Reid, John E. "Report on Suspect Confession." January 12, 1962. Available at OLA fire memorial website. www.olafire.com/confession.asp.

United Press International. "10,000 Mourners at Funeral of Three Nuns Killed in Fire." December 4, 1958.

Warren, James, Maurice Possley, and Joseph Tybor. "Finding Answers Amid the Ashes." *Chicago Tribune*, February 10, 1987.